THE
IMMEASURABLE
HEAVEN

THE IMMEASURABLE HEAVEN

CASPAR GEON

SOLARIS

First published 2025 by Solaris
an imprint of Rebellion Publishing Ltd,
Riverside House, Osney Mead,
Oxford, OX2 0ES, UK

www.solarisbooks.com

ISBN: 978-1-83786-473-7

10 9 8 7 6 5 4 3 2 1

A CIP catalogue record for this book is available from the
British Library.

Designed & typeset by Rebellion Publishing

Printed in Denmark

For Bean, with all my love

AUTHOR'S NOTE

This is a story of another era, of a generation of stars long gone. Everything I heard and saw has been translated into context, and standardised measurements, minutes, hours, days and years are here broadly similar to those of your time. Lastly, the term *humanoid* is used to depict any bipedal, symmetrical being, regardless of size.

They had sent me to hell.

I licked the slime that grew on north-facing stones, drank the sour rain that swept in every second or third day. Fury fuelled me; a gnawing, gut-churning rage that flash-burned whatever energy I tried to store, so that my body was nothing but a bundle of sharp bones.

I was alone for many months, at least, before I found what I needed.

My first ship was built from nothing but twisted, dented scrap; pieces of something I'd discovered obliterated on the rocks of a mountain pass. No motor, no fuel, just a chassis of junk and the first bright thoughts of escape.

They'd sent me down to a place where nothing had lasted, where instant death had glowered over the lands and swept the place clean. A mistake, perhaps, or the product of some tension amongst the realms finally bursting its banks. It seemed they'd imprisoned me here—of all planes— deliberately, to a tragedy that might even have been of my own making, a place where I could sit and reflect, probably to starve or rave myself to madness. And so I did, for a while, squatting in the wilds, my dangling new arms folded in my lap, contemplating, observing the odd, rainbowed properties of the dawn with a detached delight.

Seeing that I could use this place to my advantage.

I remembered. I remembered where the cities had been. Out into the wastelands I limped, dragging my wreck behind me; a lone set of footprints scrubbed out by the trail of a hauled hulk, the great pale expanse stretching pristine to either side for mile upon mile upon mile.

They had sent me to hell, down and down through the incorruptible membranes of ten thousand realities, thinking there was no way I could return.

Mounds in the soft, whitish clay indicated that something had once stood there. I didn't sit, didn't rest, just knelt on my odd new knees and dug my fingers into the ground, gently at first, then picking up speed. The sun drifted across the sky, producing a faint, eerie ululation as it rose. It had taken me some time to understand where the noise was coming from, that what I was hearing was the star itself: where there had once been vacuum there was now atmosphere, enough to conduct a sound that I had never in my previous life thought it was possible to hear.

Night fell, a blizzard of stars and orbital detritus glowing so brightly overhead that it might as well have been an overcast day. I didn't stop. I kept digging, clawing my way down into the clay, patting wet chunks into steps along one steep side of my tunnel. I imagined it all caving in, collapsing on top of me and burying my strange stickman form alive, and then it really would all have been for nothing.

No time to waste. Back to work.

I dug until the ghost glow of the night brightened again to grey, my hands and arms and face white with clay, opening dark chambers in the ground. It didn't matter for now that I had no idea how it could be done: to climb to an older reality was supposed to be impossible, but I'd get to that in due course.

Deeper still and I was reduced to feeling my way as I scooped, knowing I'd slice my hands open on the first sharp tip of the buried city, hardly caring. One layer up and I'd get new hands anyway. None of it mattered, not for the moment.

Objects, indistinguishable in the slop, began to emerge. Days I spent toiling in the dark mines, moving stooped through propped-up tunnels, the ash-clay wet and malleable to my fingers. A gas filled the air, leaking in hissing belches from the mud as I scraped and dug, and the ideas began to form.

Seasons passed. I had no idea how many. I sat often at the mine's edge, gazing out across the featureless plain to a smudge of distant, creamy hills. Sometimes my old friend Fe'Tril sat with me, keeping me company. His presence unnerved me, but I always remembered, sooner or later: there was no way he could be here. I had killed him long ago.

It was a rare fine day, a break in the sweeping, ashen storms, and I remembered the mountains back on the Surface, their slopes carved into labyrinthine chalk cities. My Surface. A place of black, scent-drenched nights, the trillion sounds of the woods. My old face, studied so often in the mirror, was now a memory so blurred that it had lost all edges and features entirely. I had forgotten what I looked like, during my life.

I blinked my strange, deep-set eyes, focussing on the heap of detritus I'd brought up that day. I didn't know what it was—I'd pick through it all as evening fell and a gas fire

11

burned on the stove. I had found bones down there, yawning skulls with long, yellowed teeth, their throats clogged with clay. Things like me, as I was now.

I had never seen a species quite like the one I now inhabited. There were plenty like them, back on my Surface, but none precisely the same. Two long limbs for walking upright, a slim thorax and willowy arms, a rounded head set atop a slender neck, two spherical eyeballs and a trio of nostrils cut vertically, high up on the dark, wrinkled forehead. I'd caught my reflection again when the rains swept in hard one day, drenching my tunnel opening and filling its potholes with shimmering puddles. The body I inhabited possessed eight fingers on each hand and a set of pharyngeal jaws that could expand to swallow things much larger than its head—quite useless out here, where nothing lived but me.

Quite why I now appeared this way was a question never fully answered, at least not in my time. The Well had existed long before my species had come into existence— they'd found it by accident, a great invisible fissure drilled into the realities, like the scar from some kind of bomb, made by forebears nobody remembered—but I had been the one to reinstate it, to venerate it, hurling my enemies in at the slightest provocation. Contrary to popular belief it was not a lust for power that had guided me, then—it was the things I had come to learn, a knowledge that many assumed had driven me utterly, irretrievably mad. I alone knew that I was the quite the opposite. I knew the truth.

Nobody ever clawed their way back from that hole in the realities. Nobody. But *I* would.

The season must have changed again. The days were growing shorter. I could see no evidence in the sky of the buttresses around the world as the sun rose over the hills.

They must have crumbled too, filling the void with even more rubbish.

I went back to my work, beating an incandescent length of iron into shape. Hammer, flip, hammer, flip. Sparks spitting, hissing and fizzling into the mud. Metal glowing, enraged. Molten sludge and acrid stinks. Gas, piped from the ruins beneath the mine, pumped into soldered drums and stacked on racks by the tunnel entrance. Crystal salvaged from the tip of an unearthed spire. Heatproof padding dug from the walls of a submerged home and cut into strips. A makeshift, airtight suit lay like a cadaver on the ground, its outer layer sewn from scales of beaten skinsteel with eyepieces of glass, flash-heated from powdered clay, its lining spooled from melted plastics and stuffed with the wiry hair I snipped from my own beard.

Hammer, flip. A scorching drumbeat pounding pain into my ears. Pain that split a crack through my head, deeper with every blow; a crack from which fresh fury surged, rising like a tide.

SIGNAL

In the silt-suspended gloom something huge uncoiled. It scratched itself with a few lazy sweeps of its fins, scraping a peel of dead skin into the depths, before extending a tongue shaped like a fabulously intricate key and latching into the receiver. The apparatus glowed into life, startling a flitting ecosystem into the shadows and revealing the full, serpentine bulk of its user in a ghostly wash of light. The interior of the water-filled space lit up with every flicker and flash to reveal a cavern of gnarled, artificial stalactites and equipment that poked like instruments of torture into the creature's lair.

The Translator, hundreds of meters from snout to tail, had never seen the galaxy with its own eyes, for it possessed none. It was likewise completely deaf, as most other species understood the term, relying instead on the single most sensitive organ for light-years around: a tongue equipped with twenty million pressure receptors per cubic centimetre, a tongue it had never seen.

The receiver pulsed with flowing light as the Translator cycled through a wealth of options, sorting the signal vaults. Trillions of rising transmissions had been collected from the fissure in the realities as if with a giant net and left to stew, their caches of interference filtered and stored in separate branches of Obaneo station for further analysis. Today it was moving downwards through the datastores, so to speak, into a vault that had been left unopened for millennia.

The Translator clenched and relaxed one of the hundreds of muscles in its tongue in rapid succession, exploring a chronological sensochart and discovering that the signals in today's vault were pre-Throlken, over five hundred million years old, the deepest it had ever gone. It made itself comfortable, suckling a jet of Jatsotl milk from the reservoir below the receiver while a population of Tickler species went to work massaging its ancient, scaly body, and dialled the pressure volume to *medium*, looking forward to the stimulating glut of undiscovered languages it was about to sense for the very first time.

The Translator opened the vault, recoiling a moment later as the waters of its nest clouded with dark, sulphuric blood.

It shut the receiver off, yanking its tongue free and nursing it inside its mouth, every nerve howling in pain.

It could only think of one sufficient word for what it had sensed: it was a *scream*, a scream of such intensity that five hundred million years of signal decay had barely dampened it, a scream of a strength never recorded before. The older transmissions were always diluted and weak; nothing even a tenth that antiquated had ever come through so potent, so painful. Converted into sound it would surely deafen— perhaps even *kill*—anything unlucky enough to be born with ears.

The Translator gingerly reinserted, probing carefully through the data to check the signal strengths—something it really ought to have done beforehand. There. Nine thousand one hundred on the scale. No wonder its poor tongue had almost split in half.

It labelled the vault as unsafe and coiled into a knot

on the floor of its cavern, thinking, the nest's filtration systems already dispersing the blood. Such a signal would take colossal amounts of power to produce, whole star systems' worth, the output of a widespread and successful interstellar civilisation. All that power, channelled straight into its mouth.

Sweeping out into the passageway between the nests and down to the larger bauble beneath, the Translator touched tongues with its sleepy colleague. They opened the vault again together, the pressure volume dialled down to scale one.

A few days later every nest in the branching, tree-shaped form of Obaneo Well Station had been put to work interpreting the mysterious signal, and the Scream was sent out into the great lens of the galaxy for further analysis, liberally encrypted to protect delicate ears.

The Translator, freshly ensconced in more harmless data and well recovered after a month-long rest, was happy to be rid of it.

Yokkun's Depth was a galaxy named after a long dead emperor. Someone so ancient that nobody even remembered when the titular being had lived, what family tree, Sovereign line or even species he, she, it or they had ever belonged to, whether the galaxy had been owned outright from the very beginning or claimed piecemeal, and whether Yokkun (whatever Yokkun was) had been just, or cruel. Nor was the place particularly *deep* in any way: as galaxies went it was rather thinly spread, extending its star-drenched tendrils into the darkness like a diaphanous, glowing inhabitant of a black sea, both enclosed and connected to its seven neighbours by the branching, turreted coronet that bound the cluster together, known as the Olas. But lyrics from the Gigaverses had shown that the place did 'belong to Yokkun' for the last three hundred million years at least, possibly predating the Throlken's rule, before postbiological minds had remade the local tree of life. To claim an entire galaxy for yourself—a near infinity of individual kingdoms, states and rotting empires multiplying and dividing in a frenetic surge of violence and noise—was something that had seldom been heard of in all the histories, making this peculiar, glittering swirl of four hundred and forty billion stars quite famous.

The signal, sent out by the Translators at Obaneo as a multilayered stream capable of being interpreted by almost every known sensory organ and plastered with warnings and opening instructions, was intercepted by the augmented eyes of a dozen installations across the galaxy.

On the redolent world of Mizirri, the synthesiser Lirrelang dangled from the pastel canopy, inhaling the introductory notes of the Translator's message. Lirrelang's body consisted of a wide fungoid parasol equipped with two articulated tails; her species liked to hang from the branches of the pheromone forests, communicating with nothing but the spectacularly elaborate language of smell. An encrustation of equipment, growing from the muscle of her parasol rim, relayed the bulk of the signal through a squirt of blended, delayed-activation scents.

Lirrelang shuddered, shrivelling. This was not a good smell. It was the stink of danger, a stench the likes of which her species had forgotten.

She hung for a while in sensory silence, contemplating what she'd inhaled, before composing her own smelly addendum of notes and passing it on.

* * *

Gangohl of Horrikis received the transmission in his mountain observatory, examining the various tacked-on addenda and postscripts with prismatic eyes attuned to the vagaries of the magnetic fields. The warnings were now in triplicate: *To be played at your lowest signal strength. The sender(s) take no responsibility for damage incurred.* Scents could be transmitted across the void, too, and a revolting sensory envelope from Mizirri—which to the sender might have smelled delicious, but stank to high heaven as it met the humanoid Gangohl's nostrils—informed him that the ancient signal was considered high priority, and that his expertise would be greatly appreciated.

He dialled everything down, sitting cross-legged beneath a chamber open to the stars, and looked at what they'd sent him.

His hairless skin flushed, his heart thrashing as the sweat beaded on his brow, and he tapped his bracelet with fumbling fingers to pause the incoming data. What in all the worlds had they found, in the dark? Terror. Agony. A cry of such panic that his body still resounded from it, like a bell struck hard. And it seemed it had been made this way, for a reason.

He rubbed his sensitive eyes, breathing deeply for a few moments, and sent the message on.

In the dimness of a giant hollow Zutanga weed a Tortureling shuddered, extending a barb. Theirs was a society that spoke in the language of touch: specifically with carefully modulated levels of pain, a profoundly expressive dialect of the Pattern that only the most daring of alien naturalists attempted to speak.

The Tortureling Qushibba, feeling its way in the dark across a thorny braille of spined surfaces, came to its sentient prickler device and pulled it close. The machine latched on, growing a weeping bundle of stinging tendrils that coated Qushibba's bristling brown body, and the buzzing injections of information began.

The transmission was by now so plastered with forewords and preamble that Qushibba could barely make head or tail of it. It skipped the multiple warnings, uninterested in what the frail species of the galaxy perceived as dangerous, and opened the signal at full strength.

For an intoxicating moment it knew the secret of the ancients, heard the warning of a people long turned to dust, a warning sent into the future.

Then Qushibba spasmed once, and died.

ШHIRAZOMAR
THE SURFACE PHASLAIR

Over the near countless worlds of Yokkun's Depth ruled the sixty-seven Alms, emperors each commanding volumes thousands of light-years deep, billions of stars strong. Though they squabbled and spied and schemed, actual war—even violence itself—was unknown, outlawed by the Throlken, the machine gods who dwelt inside each star. In this age of plenty, however, there were other diversions to be found. The Alms and their subjects possessed a power that was more than technological, more than martial: the ability to visit parallel layers of reality.

These other realities, known as Phaslairs, were each the result of a rapidly and infinitely dividing universe, like a seething cluster of bacteria replicating exponentially and forevermore inside the boundless Ur-sphere of existence. It was estimated that a million or so new realities were born every half-second, and it was in this dense, honeycombed proliferation of near-infinite versions of Yokkun's Depth that the Alms played, tinkering with ideas and gaming strategies, staging colossal, meaningless conflicts and ruining the lower realities beneath them on a whim.

This ability was made possible with the use of a synthetic element: Iliquin. It had first been forged in the great Who Knows When (then rediscovered many times since), and was generally used to electroplate the hulls of craft and the skins of suits. Pass a current through it, and Iliquin's mass would suddenly swell to a hundred thousand times that of the densest neutron star, dumping whatever it contained through the burst skin of one reality and down into the next, and so on until the charge was shut off. Some explorers were still falling, the Phaslairs blipping past, tearing from one younger level of reality to the next until all their surroundings completely changed, the flashed refractions in a hall of quantum mirrors, their weak transmissions documenting what they saw until they grew too faint to make out.

And therein lay the catch: one could travel *downwards*, visiting as many younger universes as you liked—the realities becoming stranger and more disparate the farther you went—but the laws of existence barred you from ever retracing your steps. To those you had once known on your old, Surface Phaslair, you were lost forever.

They left Salqar without ceremony, departing the system slowly, one of trillions of colourful ship trails amongst the crowded crush of stars, hoping against hope that they wouldn't be noticed.

The ship was neither a vessel nor an organism, precisely; it was a spore, one of countless sentient bulbs of pollen that crossed Yokkun's Depth in the service of the cousin Alms Phrail and Thelgald, ferrying freight and passengers inside their inflatable bellies.

The spore fell, accelerating as gently as possible into what would become the first stage of a curving course through, beneath, and ultimately back up into the galaxy, drifting as a speck through a shoal of giant Ormwherls beyond the milky green periphery of Salqar and out into the luminescent, interstellar green.

Whira had first met the ship—that was not a ship—on the sunny concourse of the Customs House at Salqar. It was perching in the dappled bough of a tree, hunched over a spoolbook: a tubby, auburn blob of luxuriant, wildly uncombed fluff. Two pairs of gangly limbs gripped the branches above, while another set held the book, unrolling the thing as it read. She'd expected something very different.

She pointed, and her floating case and crozier descended to the flagstones beside her, her horned shadow long at her feet. 'I don't understand.'

The creature—she had been told its name was Gnumph—finished what it was reading and tucked the book into a cavity somewhere in its unkempt body, turning a scattering of coal grey eyes on her. 'Just a moment.'

She was about to speak when it held up a hand and took a vast, shuddering breath.

Whira stepped back.

The creature Gnumph expanded like a balloon, its eyes sliding apart as every inch of its fluffy skin swelled into a ball, tipping it out of the tree. The spore rolled, still expanding, one arm scrabbling for a grip on the concourse, the limb tiny now beneath the shadow of the ballooning shape.

It had grown to the size of a modest Salqar home when it vented a quick puff of gas and flattened slightly into a fluffy arrowhead shape patterned with a profusion of white-tipped tufts that looked like small, furred wings. An eye, now situated up near the thing's dorsal crest, peered at her.

Done, said a rumbling voice from somewhere inside the ginger-pelted shape. Great coiled hairs unrolled from beneath what might have once been its chin and unfurled across the concourse: antennae, she'd heard, feelers that dangled for miles as it navigated the galactic ocean. Whira noticed that it used its pale limbs for landing struts, grasping the scratched crystal surface of the landing strip with cruel, translucent claws that certainly hadn't been there before.

A flange in Gnumph's belly yawned open, the toothless flesh ungluing with a horrible sucking sound, revealing a softly glowing cave that seemed to stretch far too deep inside. *Welcome*, said that distant voice, like the sound of surf carried on the wind.

Whira hesitated, not picking up her bags. 'No. This wasn't what I agreed to. I need a real ship, a Sovereign vessel—do you even have a drive?'

Of course, replied the open mouth through some expert ventriloquism. *A Mode-Eleven, from the Zurmis workshop. I was refitted yesterday.*

'Mode-Eleven?' asked Whira, narrowing her pale gold eyes. The Zurmis engines only went up to nine, as far as she knew. 'And you're definitely expecting me? Whirazomar Swulis Zelt Ghenge of Thilean, within Lihreat?'

Yes.

She laced her fourteen ringed fingers together, glancing around the concourse. This didn't smell right. Cooperation between the smattering of humanoid Alms—including the elaborately antlered, three-pupilled Lazziar, the species to which she belonged—was common, each considering the other the lesser of all evils in the galaxy, but a mission of this duration and importance only came along every so often, and Whira didn't like to imagine just how many eyes might be watching her progress.

'Do you have your orders?'

Yes. We will be there in eighty-one days, give or take, depending on the you-know-whats in the you-know-wheres.

Whira felt a fluttering in her stomachs that she wasn't used to at this veiled mention of the Throlken, aware that anywhere sunlight fell, she could be watched. She nodded sharply, holding up a hand in case the spore said anything compromising. 'Alright. Fine. Let's get this over with.'

Beyond the Almoll's outer borders Gnumph began to accelerate harder, encountering a light turbulence the moment it joined the galactic medium, which curled like sea water into a river's delta. Over a hundred different galactic currents swirled around Yokkun's Depth, following the rotation of the galaxy. They were composed of an infinitude of specks of rubbish, discarded over billions of years by uncountable generations of life to be ground down like ocean silt and flung by momentum into great squalls that relentlessly battered the sentinel-protected star systems of the sixty-seven Almolls. Gnumph entered the current side-on, watching the great green rollers churning themselves as if in slow motion into breakers a few hundred miles beneath. The fabric of the storm flowed like emerald ink into the darker blend of the gulf below, feeding into tributaries that bled and drifted with the motion of the galaxy, sinking for millions of miles into the milky green haze.

Days and nights passed while Gnumph battled the current, the spore's tufted outer ears trained for any hint that they had been observed. It was only when the outlying stars of neighbouring Lihreat—Salqar's cousin Almoll—had brightened observably through the churn of colour that Gnumph felt safe activating its drive and dropping beneath the busiest shipping lanes.

Before leaving the Customs House, Gnumph's collection of eyes had been fitted with exotic lenses so that they could peer further and deeper into the vastness of the galaxy, dragging light into their pupils faster than might be considered natural, and a glorious pale green suit and helm of Iliquin armour that made the spore look more like a *spaceship* of Olden Tales. Gripped tightly in one of its gauntleted fists was a powerful Iliquin rifle capable of snapping potential antagonists out of existence and into a different Phaslair entirely; the bare minimum, Whira knew, for a mission like this, but an escort would attract undue attention. If they encountered a problem out here, they were on their own.

Dropping beneath the borders of Lihreat, their passage grew swifter still, stirring up a neon trail of bioluminescence as they arrived in the upper reaches of Orzil—a dense volume of a hundred and sixty million stars—the traces of a billion signals crackling into Whira's cabin. A billion languages, all subtly related, blathering into her ears. But no sound from any star, for that was where the Throlken, crouched and waiting inside the flaming hearts of each and every sun, were watching. Whira fancied she could feel their eyes searching the heavens for her, a blaze of peering stars. The galaxy of Yokkun's Depth had become one vast and paranoid brain, thrumming with energy and thought and able to glimpse every inch of its own interior. She was a rogue pathogen in its midst, dashing to find safe lodging, always at risk of being extinguished in a moment.

A handful of other Alms knew their plans, too, and were almost certainly sending ships of equivalent speed across the galaxy. Whira's only comfort lay in the knowledge that she was surely in the lead, hurtling faster and faster across the interstellar currents, striking livid bioluminescence in their wake.

Fifty days and nights passed: days spent watching, listening, travelling so fast now that the light had faded to an inky gloom all around them, a blackness that concealed the thickened waist of the galaxy from view. The Throlken had, in all likelihood, predicted they would come this way, and would be paying the lowest reaches special attention, watching out for any drives kicking in. The spore Gnumph maintained its speed until it had officially passed the border, finally revving its Zurmis to crackle like a falling star beneath the galaxy and into the gloaming below.

Down here, beneath the cauldron of Yokkun's Depth and its carcanet of glowing star nurseries, the temperature dropped. People claimed they saw ghosts in the blackness of the Without, tap-tap-tapping on their hulls. Of the ubiquitous Myriad, the microscopic third cousins of the Throlken who swarmed the galaxy in concentrations so vast that one could usually count three trillion or so in every litre of air, whispering strange things into people's ears and mischievously updating everything from hand-drawn maps to whole encyclopaedias, there was no trace either, besides a tame population of Microscopia still living inside the belly of the spore. They were now as alone as it was possible to be in this life-infested place, travelling far beneath the galaxy's centre, a void once home to a black hole, evaporated long since, now filled by the Throlken with a web of mysterious apparatus that all others were forbidden from approaching.

Whira dragged her gaze from the surrounding darkness and stared down into the gnarled crystalline branches of the Olas, the monumental structure that connected the eight galaxies: something she had never actually seen with her own eyes until that morning. It was a wonder of existence, a sight of such enormity that no mortal creature could comprehend it in a glance, and the entire experience made her nauseous, her stomachs lurching. She pulled her eye from the magnoscope (all that served as a window in the shabby interior of the spore) and clutched her arms with a phantom shiver. They were plunging deeper than most had ever been, days away from beginning the curve that would lift them back to the light and life of the galaxy and up into the far Almoll of Plitipek, location of the fabled Well. The

Alm of that place did not know they were coming. With any luck, they'd never find out at all.

Whira ran a finger along a branch of the painted antlers that coiled upwards from the back of her skull, gazing at the tatty, low-G environment beneath her. The state of the place had struck her like a horrible stench when she'd first walked in through Gnumph's gaping, dribbling mouth, and hadn't improved much with time. Its hollow body contained an amphitheatre with a fire pit at its centre, ringed with balconies that opened onto a warren of cavities, tunnels, floors and mezzanines, all knocked through and fitted with wooden doors, shelves, bunks and even a ramshackle allotment by the spore's previous passengers during its long stint as an interstellar transportation service. Due to the abruptness with which it had been repurposed for the mission, some of Gnumph's inhabitants remained onboard, waiting for their stop, returning home, hibernating or simply hanging on until their money ran out, all living inside this natural subdimension inside Gnumph's inflatable belly. Whira had tried her best to clear them out, poking her crosier into the nooks and crannies and causing so much uproar that she eventually gave up entirely, silently fuming until it was time to set off. Why in all the worlds His Majesty Phrail had hired this parasite-riddled thing and given it such a wonderful engine was beyond her. Any class of crystal Sovereignty vessel could cross the galaxy in a matter of weeks—Gnumph had clearly been chosen without regard for Whira's comfort at all.

Those passengers she had managed to turf out before she left had been sent on their way into Salqar with promise of recompense, but Whira had the distinct impression that they were only the tip of the iceberg, the few that were awake or lively enough or sufficiently cowed by a figure of authority to get dressed and come out of their rooms, and when she interrogated Gnumph about the true number of passengers it had remained infuriatingly circumspect. The spore didn't really know precisely *what* inhabited its belly now, let alone the numbers; it had been travelling too long, its ticket inspection growing sloppy. Travelling magicians, work crews, visitors of distant relatives and even a Yokkun-renowned writer of travelogues still lived aboard, Gnumph said, awaiting their various stops but unwilling to surrender their tickets to Whira for fear of a dreaded Replacement Service. The whole thing made her blood boil.

Once they were underway, of course, Whira had found she couldn't pay them to stay in their rooms, and only the prospect of the Throlken's wrath seemed to bother anyone much. Doors squeaked open and closed all day and night, music blared, and the single pan-species toilet seemed always to be occupied. Whira, who had begun using a bucket in her room, suspected someone actually lived in there.

Though she hated it, and it was quite against the rules, she suspected she was going to have to tell them *why* she had commandeered the spore, why they must travel under such a cloak of secrecy, and what they were letting themselves in for by staying aboard.

DRAEBOL
PHASLAIR 17,018

Darkness, unlit by any moon. In the depths of the walking woods a breeze stirred. Something with lambent, unblinking eyes craned its neck to peer down through the branch-fingers, its ears twitching.

A sound filtered through the valley, almost imperceptible in the darkness. A growing sigh of wind. And the first glimpse of light, flickering through drifting snow.

The creatures in their high nests squinted, watching the passing speckle of light and the great, darkly turreted silhouette as it whispered by, sliding on beneath the black ridge of mountains, darkness sinking back into its wake.

The giant knife-prowed sledship moved on, sliding deeper into the foothills through a softening blizzard, faint starlight finally lighting the way.

From an open window Draebol watched the dark land passing by, his borrowed face numbed by the cold, ears open to the silence of the mountains and the dim roar of the huge sledge's ivory runner far below as it cut a passage through the snow. Sleet wetted his new face, and he tasted it on a tongue that had only been his for a day.

The planet—on this, his seventeen thousand and

eighteenth Phaslair—was called *Ip*, and this reality was really rather odd in general.

Draebol looked out at the darkly moving woods, their grasping claws mimicking branches, contemplating all the fabulous and undocumented life that must live within. He had dropped in two nights before to find himself inhabiting the form of a creature the size of his real-self's finger, on a Phaslair in which progress within the greater galaxy had slowed, for some reason, to a crawl. His new body, when he'd found their equivalent of mirrors to peer into, was not the strangest he'd ever inhabited, but it came close: atop four stilt-like crimson limbs (carpeted with over forty wriggling fingers of differing lengths) his entirely white eyes gazed from a bluish, boneless thorax. A veined sack grew from the top of his head like a ripe fruit, emitting little whistling squeaks from a sphincter at its tip: the beings' method of speech. Draebol had named it the *tootle sack* in his notes, for want of a better word, wrestling with his multitude of fingers to scrawl out something he probably wouldn't be able to read when he left this place.

He glanced back inside the sledship, his colourful woven snood dripping with melted snow, and pulled the shutter closed. His real, Surface self would have crushed the vessel had he arrived here unchanged, and yet here he was, shrunk to the size of a toy, in a world without motors or computers of any kind. The worlds he travelled became stranger and stranger with each Drop, as unusual as anything he might have visited back on the Surface.

He folded his limbs awkwardly to sit on the heap of hairy pelts he'd claimed for himself. The air was a coiling haze of emissions lit only by the cold, white fires in the grates, the ever-present wailing of some poor utility creature—skewered every now and then with a poker—doing its best to warm the chamber with sound in place of heat. Something passed him, stumbling and whistling a wheezing song through the murk. It wasn't just the rocking of the sledship that made them unsteady on their feet; a local delicacy served on board—a kind of flesh, as far as Draebol understood—seemed to get them drunk. He'd bought and tried some of the bitter stuff already, and was only now beginning to feel the effects: a fabulous warming of his extremities while he contemplated the ultimate freedom of his life. It was good, whatever it was, and he wanted more for the journey down.

Draebol scratched the bites on his skin—all from the few minutes he'd spent on his pile of dirty furs—and watched the comings and goings of the sleeper deck. Each passenger here had spent a little money on a pile, and most were bundled and snoozing or whispering flatulently to one another in the dimness. He counted a few possibly off-world, fabulously coloured species—perhaps travellers, like himself—but they kept to themselves. Draebol watched them with interest as the poisonous meat did its work, chemicals coursing through him. A quirk of this place was that none of the cheap electronics he'd brought with him seemed to work. The physical laws of this Phaslair were off somehow, not quite as finely tuned as all the others. Fire still burned—though at a much lower temperature, producing little heat—and water still boiled, but all other bets were off.

He spotted an attractive member of his borrowed species scampering through from the next compartment, and felt the familiar surge of interest that never changed much across any reality he had ever visited, emboldened by whatever was in his system. The old, original him would probably have regarded these creatures as vermin, perhaps dinner; but here he was, to all intents and purposes *one* of them, right down to the wiring of his tiny new brain.

As far as anyone in Yokkun's Depth knew, it was physically impossible to return from a younger Phaslair to an older one. The membrane that separated them seemed to allow only one direction of travel—once you dipped a toe into the fresher reality beneath, you could never return.

This apparently inviolable law had encouraged the Alms over the ages to start dumping vast tonnages of waste into the lower Phaslairs at every opportunity, testing theories and tactics against versions of their fellows that they did not consider to be, in the strictest sense, *real*, to see how they could one-up each other on the Surface, and even firing their enemies down there on such a regular basis that whole genocides could be concealed in the blink of an eye. Entire pan-galactic experiments had been conducted on lower Phaslairs, their effects studied and data returned through the odd phenomenon of backwards-capable transmissions rising weakly through the membranes of the realities, the layer then marked as defunct and never visited again. It hardly mattered to the Alms, who possessed trillions of Phaslairs to play around inside, the furious younger realities quite powerless to retaliate. The Throlken, ensconced in their own mysterious, fiery business, seemed to turn a blind eye to whatever happened on other Phaslairs beneath the Surface reality, and even their counterparts below gave no sign of noticing the damage being done with reality-shredding Iliquin devices (use a projectile as simple as an arrow against any other living being, however, and you were magically struck dead before the shaft was loosed, all your synapses turned to mush). And so the interference continued.

Of course, after a long spell of fiddling with the realities beneath, it at last occurred to the Alms of Yokkun's Depth that it wasn't totally impossible that the same fate could befall *them*—that an older reality, situated in the unknowable darkness above, would descend suddenly upon them and cause whatever havoc it pleased. It would be the equivalent (as the Alms well knew, from their own tinkering) of a rival, technologically superior galaxy turning up on their doorstep unannounced, and doing as it liked without fear of retribution. As far as most of them knew this had not yet happened—the seams directly above were apparently lifeless, perhaps explaining the freedom their Surface had so far enjoyed—and their reality had not yet been visited by any other, but one day all that might change, and a fear of their sins repaid kept the uneasy entente of the Alms allied with one another, preparing for the day they were visited by an uncaring, older intelligence. They watched, and they waited, their agents roaming Yokkun's Depth on the lookout for any sign.

But moment by moment the number and variation of Phaslairs expanded around them: a widening pool of stars, habitats, species, cultures, inventions and physical quirks too colossally vast even for the Throlken to grasp. Any ruler hoping to maintain an advantage needed a legion of scouts willing to travel into the unknown and report back, eyes peeled for anything that might assist their masters during the unending spell of cold restraint forced upon them by the Throlken. It so happened that Draebol Naeglis Zelt Thurn of Eldra within Lihreat, Licensed Surveyor in the name of Thelgald the Only, had been commissioned to find that very thing, whatever, whoever and wherever it might be.

Draebol climbed unsteadily down from his pile of furs, disturbing a profusion of wriggling beasts in the lower layers, and pushed his way out into the aisle. Out here the less affluent travellers had heaped their own bedding and possessions everywhere, and a hundred pairs of white eyes stared balefully at him as he tried to negotiate his way across their patches of turf in pursuit of the female (or male—he couldn't quite tell), pops and squeaks and bursts of wind grumbling as his clumsy feet squashed their food, possessions, and various scampering young. His quarry strode quickly ahead on longer legs, disappearing through a particularly dense patch of fog. As Draebol got closer he heard a singsong in progress: a tooting, hooting orchestra of inebriated creatures. As he advanced, the song spread into the dim, carved ivory floors that rose around him.

A judder of the sledship caused him to stumble, perhaps a rock submerged in the snow, and the tune faltered. He squeezed his way through their mist. Perhaps to any other form he'd occupied the stink would be foul, maybe downright toxic, but here, in this body, it tasted pleasantly familiar—a phantom stench his borrowed brain remembered without ever having experienced it.

The beauty reappeared again through the haze, but he gave up. It was impossible to say hello in the sputtering windspeak that he'd never learned a word of, and something else was beginning to dawn on Draebol at last, after two days spent communicating in awkward sign language or through the imperfect telepathy of his plastic computer: this place really was different. There was little technology, the laws of thermodynamics being slightly off, and the *Pattern*—the ancient, Throlken-devised synthetic roots that nearly every language in Yokkun's Depth had evolved from—did not seem to exist here.

It was starting to look like this really was a Throlken-free reality, known as a Lawless Phaslair, where Artificial Intellects had never arisen. The first he'd ever found. Draebol had been beginning to doubt, after over seventeen thousand Drops, that they existed at all.

He swayed in the aisle, putting out one arm to steady himself and accidentally squashing someone's tootle sack. The young male grunted a wet burp of complaint and he moved swiftly on.

He'd come across more than a few mutated Phaslairs in his time—realities that had developed oddly, or not at all, either so full of matter that you could barely move or almost entirely vacuum—but this was unprecedented. No

Throlken at large inside the hearts of the stars. And if there were no Throlken here, unable to function in this version of the universe—perhaps never even born, back in the Great Long Ago—then the location of this Phaslair might be worth a substantial amount, to the right people. He'd heard of other surveyors being handsomely rewarded for less. Just thinking about it brought him out in the strange little creature's approximation of a shiver: nobody to see the Phaslair being used for tactical simulations, weapons testing, experimental wars or catastrophic dummy runs of Surface business. Zero consequences.

Here the Alms could try other things. They could use *real* weaponry.

Draebol had no idea who was receiving his transmissions and sending his Surveyor's wage, but they were going to want to know about this place. Phaslair seventeen thousand and eighteen. He'd have to get off-world somehow and take a proper look at the closest star before he reported his findings. It might well contain an Irraith or two—the indigenous helium folk that shared the stars with the Throlken back on the Surface—and maybe he could ask them directly.

But how to get up there, without conductors? There were plenty of modes of transport in the old Yokkun's Depth that didn't use electrics: Sovereignty ships, spores, swellcraft, tubes and homemades, but Draebol hadn't a clue if he'd find any around here. Only his cheap full-plastic computer would get him anywhere in speaking with the locals (communicating, at best, by reading his delta waves and mimicking things it had already heard), and that was locked up in the baggage train that dragged along behind the Sledship.

Draebol stopped again, leaning as the sled rode another bump. No sense going after her if he couldn't show off, tell stories, intimate what a generally excellent, fascinating and worldly fellow he was. On every other Phaslair he'd done his best to woo the opposite, same or even vaguely compatible sex with tales of all his derring-do: decapitating the fearsome Viddar, winning the Gugowesh games by accident, even speaking with an actual Throlken in its fiery lair on Ormo-Wapiir. Without all that he was reduced to a mute, handwaving lunatic or a wandering simpleton capable of yelling only 'Where Is The Toilet' or 'I Require To Buy A Ticket.'

Suppose I'm lucky not to have turned up as a microbe or something, he thought as he pushed his way back to the rear of the sledship. It was possible, he supposed—at which point he'd be trapped forever, unable even to take his own measly life—but the transition between the Phaslairs generally resulted in the closest approximation of the form he'd held before, as if the laws of Phaslair physics, so flummoxed by the arrival of something that should not even *be* there, sought to sweep Draebol's every incursion under the rug. Of course it wasn't as simple as that (the statistical mathematics of his fall between the realities was more akin to the passage of a bolt of lightning branching between charged clouds) but Draebol preferred to believe that he was *noticed* in some way by the universe, and given deferential treatment. This was anyway certainly the smallest he had ever been, and he could feel the sluggishness of the thoughts in his little brain, lodged somewhere at the root of the tootle sack, even as the excitement of finding such a rare Phaslair burned bright.

Draebol was musing on all this when he came to the entrance of the baggage train. He showed his token to the sleepy guard and was let through, hearing sounds up ahead.

He paused.

There were people investigating his things.

Oi! he thought, and the plastic computer in his luggage caught his words as he drew closer, relaying a very rough approximation of them around the carriage in a series of squeaky parps. *Get away from that!*

Four glowing eyes met his through the haze.

The old, malfunctioning computer coughed a rasping, slobbering question at him, and their gaze flicked back to the pile of Draebol's language.

He didn't know how to fight—not here, not anywhere. It was too easy to Drop at the first sign of danger. But he'd got lazy at last, putting too much distance between himself and his luggage, sitting on the middle shelf. *This is going to hurt*, Draebol thought, and the computer burped it out loud into the carriage.

The four creatures were advancing on him, the pattering of feet growing louder. If he wanted to Drop he'd have to get up to his Iliquin suit—currently lying in a state of rigor mortis on the shelf—and climb inside. Draebol feinted in one direction and then made a dash for it, scrabbling up the lowest shelves, his hearts racing as someone grabbed him by the ankle.

He kicked with all his might, feeling a strange *pop*, and when he glanced back he was missing a foot. *Hell*. The word, translated as best as the computer could manage, boomed and burped into the luggage compartment.

One last stretch and the suit, with his baggage sitting on top, was nearly in his grasp, the shelves groaning, cracking. *Got you.* His fingers found the clasp on the Iliquin-coated breastplate, unlocking it, as more hands closed around his legs.

With a great rumbling snap the shelves caved in beneath him and his pursuers, and Draebol felt his balance shift even as he tightened his grip. *Whoops!* screamed the computer, and everything came tumbling down with him, the suit landing with a thump on top of him.

After a few moments' stunned silence everyone groaned, beginning to stir beneath the ruins of the shelving.

Draebol shoved some snapped chunks of ivory to one side and opened his suit with trembling fingers, grabbing the luggage and stuffing it in before he climbed inside, snicking the helmet shut. His breath rasped, loud in the confines of the suit, some lingering after-effect of the fermented meat making his head spin. He pushed his hand inside the gauntlet, thumbing the charge.

At once he was plummeting through multicoloured foliage, squinting at the blaze of new daylight.

Draebol slammed into a branch, scrabbled for a grip and dangled, watching a few giant, patterned leaves fall languidly through the canopies to the rainforest floor.

He glanced down at his own elongated body, flicking his golden tail—visible beneath the now transparent sheath of armour—to study the cerulean feathers at its tip, the din of the forest ringing through the speakers in his suit.

That was close.

MINE

Years passed. Decades, perhaps. In the deeper reaches of my mine I'd discovered mummified bodies in their thousands, sustaining myself on leathery, tasteless flesh that caught between my rotting teeth and pulled them loose in their sockets. Fe'Tril looked on with dead eyes, a slumped figure in the corner of my vision. Sometimes I slapped and punched myself to be rid of him, or knocked my head against the wall. Sometimes he went away on his own.

By then the craft was almost done, sheltered in a wind-battered hangar, and it had been a small matter of igniting a primitive whizzer motor very similar to the kind I remembered building in my youth: burn chamber encased in a cooling sleeve, a smattering of regular holes drilled around the diffuser blades, all of it capped off with a compressor head and simple, quickly-welded intake cowling. It was not fast or efficient or particularly advanced in any way—indeed its basic principles harked back to the air-funnelling jets of prehistory—but it would do, for now.

It would work because I could hear the sun, and that meant there was atmosphere out there. Air, or something like it. Dense enough to fly through.

I stepped around the machine, my heart thumping, fingers kneading the hem of my grubby rags. The craft, a sooty bundle of coiled pipes and machinery made streamlined with a conical nose and hand-me-down wings, thrummed and whirred into sputtering life. My smile spread, exposing the tartar-caked needles of my remaining teeth. The motor was still turning, spinning a glinting whirl of light and heat.

The wind picked up outside, wailing across the flats, the flimsy hangar's metal sheets vibrating. I clambered into the cockpit to tinker with the basic instruments I'd installed and switched the motor off, the engine puffing out. I swung myself down again with a surge of joyous energy, and pushed open the hangar doors. The wind struck me full force, thrusting my bare feet backwards through the clay, and I hauled the doors closed again, moving instead to the rollable sheeting on the far wall. A stretch of carefully polished runway extended beyond the hangar and into the distance, its surface gleaming with wind-ruffled puddles. I gathered up what I needed and stuffed it into a corpse-leather bag, which I tossed onboard the ship, then I donned my baggy suit, connecting up the tubing to my oxygen system, and hoisted the ship on its chain pulley so that I could swing it to face the open section of wall.

Yes, my feverish mind whispered as I lowered the ship, bumping its patched wheels down on the dry clay floor, only the rumble of the wind penetrating my helmet. *Yes. Got to be careful. Got to be careful now.* The glass eye bulbs were already misting as I teared up.

It's got to be now.

I released the chain, the whole hangar rocking from a sudden harsh gust, and jumped into the cockpit, flicking switches to start the motor and watching the blades on either side groan and whir into life, compressing the air that began to flow through them. Beside me lay the open supply hole of the mine, but I readied the ship without sparing it another glance. The dead planet had yielded treasure, as I'd known it would, but was no use to me anymore.

I'm coming for you.

* * *

The wind changed direction, howling over the low hills to the south and masking the popping, roaring ascent of a small dark speck into the sky.

The ship bucked and wobbled in the air, the racing white clouds catching its fins and tossing it between them. I'd piloted my own craft before, but they'd been nothing like this garbage-built toy, and I could feel the motor thrumming almost to breaking point through the plating of my padded suit, my wasted muscles squeezed hard against my bones by the force of the ship's ascent.

The ship plunged into a grey murk of cloud, the land obscured, no way of telling up from down. My heart squirmed, suddenly sure I was flying straight downwards, that I would end my life here, obliterated by a lack of proper instruments. I could have cobbled some together, but I was in too much of a hurry. So much haste. I knew then, as I peered into the mist, that impatience, more than anything else, would see my plans scuppered.

'They'll see my face again,' I said aloud in the confines of my suit, surprising myself. They were the first words I'd spoken in a long time: a gluey, staccato language that had never existed in this reality. 'My real face.'

The nose cone twinkled suddenly—a flash so abrupt and dazzling that I squinted and cried out. Sunlight.

The gloom was clearing.

The tiny ship roared through a glowering shelf of cloud and up into a pristine pink sky, tailed by twin streams of vapour. I screamed with delight, taking my hands from the controls and beating them together until the ship wobbled on its course.

I grasped the tiller and cleared my throat. My gums had begun to pour with blood, blood that smeared a wide and toothy smile.

43

PATTERNS

Whira half climbed, half floated to her room, scaling a much-repaired ladder past a sealed chamber filled apparently to the brim with icy sea water, to reach a boarded walkway that looked down over the open refectory (what Gnumph called *the commons*) with its rickety, tied and stuck-down furniture. The gravity inside Gnumph's belly was minimal, only existing in any appreciable way around the inside edge of its stomach wall, and she had to frequently swat at the air in front of her face to clear it of floating fluids, debris and mildewed food. They might have organised a vacuuming of the place, at least, before they set off, but His Majesty Phrail was apparently in such a hurry that no one had even thought to give the place an inspection.

Her room was larger than she'd expected, which was a small mercy until she'd realised that she was sharing it with something living under the bed. Whira had swiftly put an end to its tenancy and now the Glorish Peeper, a creature renowned for its shyness, lived in the corridor with what passed for its baggage, after whining softly throughout the first night.

She reached the door to her room, unbolting the Whisperlock she'd installed and slamming it behind her. Her first act after booting out the Peeper had been to wash the padding in the cradle (the creature hadn't even used the bed for sleeping, storing room temperature meat dinners in it instead), sweeping all the remaining filth into the corridor, where it still floated around in the hazy interior currents of the spore. Now she lay down as best she could, floating awkwardly in the covered cradle, her eyes flicking around the chamber, hearts pumping. There were no windows or screens to betray that they were in intergalactic space at all. A useless wooden calendar clock, divided into the ancient Dzull's nine chapters, was nailed high on the wall. It ratcheted steadily downwards into its casing, rising again with each new, meaningless day.

Exploring the interior she had found there were seventy-four separate chambers at least (more than half of them with their doors locked or jammed), a few supposedly home to extra, artificially inflated subdimensions hosting expansive play quests and adventures into which some of the long-haul passengers had simply disappeared, and another three filled with water and flame environments. There were also more inhabited cupboards than she could count. Creatures she'd never seen the likes of before gambled, imbibed, stupefied themselves with narcotic light and otherwise took their ease in the corridors and communal spaces, watching her attempts at counting them with interest. The palpitating thump of music was never far away. The place was a menagerie of iridescent life, Gnumph's stomach lining painted and scrawled over by dozens of generations in more colours than Whira's eye could process.

A hairy Speckled Larl named Scrapher, idly flossing his hundreds of teeth out in the hall, had told her that a swarm of tiny, fluttering things had come aboard some years ago and swiftly reproduced, resulting in a colony of young that had found the warm, damp, low-G interior of Gnumph's tummy rather appealing. As far as anyone knew they were still here, and further enquiries had led to the discovery of a storeroom packed with the creatures, though they were much too busy with their obscure and noisy religious rites to answer her questions. Scrapher had also introduced her to the small population of aquatic passengers living in a windowless water tank near the toilet, creatures Whira had presumed lived in darkness until she unscrewed the tank's lid and was confronted by a blaze of mesmerizing colour cast by the phosphorescence of their eyes.

We have to be in Waeziro's Landing for an appointment, one of the things said to her in colour-speak, having learnt of Gnumph's course diversion. She'd issued them a compensation chit, felt distinctly queasy after inhaling the fumes rising from their glowing water and headed for the bathroom, only to find it occupied, as usual, and knowing full well who the culprit was. The writer she'd heard the passengers gossiping about was given to snoozing the days away in the darkness of its broom cupboard of a chamber, and Whira heard the rumbles of his snores from her own room day and night, broken only by long-winded trips to the toilet that seemed to last for hours. He was a Great Zabbas, they said, a species that produced some of the finest extragalactic pioneers alive, setting course for the neighbouring galaxies and living long enough to make it back. Why this creature had chosen one of the cheapest services in Yokkun's Depth, though, Whira couldn't fathom, and it was only later that she learnt he was roughing it deliberately to produce a book on the lesser-known shipping lanes.

One or two of the passengers she supposed weren't so bad. Earlier this very day she had met Phathor, the inhabitant of a giant chromium shell plastered with advertising pamphlets, who had been squatting near the commons table and shovelling seedbiscuits through a fluted hole in the top of his carapace. The being—which seemed to consist of a headless tangle of warty crimson feelers whenever he popped out for a look around—had no room of his own, and appeared to wander the inside of Gnumph's belly perpetually, chatting amiably with the other passengers and retreating for naps inside his shiny shell wherever he pleased. Whira knew she would need Phathor's muscle to help her with the only resident who gave her any real concern: a distant relative of the Throlken called a Jhahzang, one of dozens of known branches in the sprawling family tree of the Designed. It seemed content enough in solitary confinement in its chamber on the uppermost floor, and made no reply when Whira knocked on its door, her free hand resting on the hilt of her Iliquin pistol. She was certain that, had her superiors known something of the Throlken line was living aboard they'd never have hired the spore, let alone allowed it anywhere near Salqar. She would have to force her way in.

It was supposed to be a dignified entry, a simple smashing of the lock. Instead the whole door split up the middle under Phathor's blow, cracking without breaking, and the giant had needed to bash another three or four times before the door clattered into two halves, revealing a room in motion.

She made her way tentatively in, gripping the pistol tightly in her pocket.

The Jhahzang had certainly been busy: machinery bobbed and gyrated and pumped up and down in every spare volume of space, with only a slim walkway between the incomprehensible equipment allowing Whira access at all. Some of it had clearly been pilfered from Gnumph's communal area, or was fashioned from bits and pieces left by other passengers and never claimed. She paused in wonder amongst the forest of metal and plastic, unable to spot a single instrument panel, number or readout that would afford her any clue as to what these things were supposed to be doing. Whatever it was, they had been left to their own devices—she had reached the end of the room, and the Jhahzang wasn't here.

'Go and look for it,' Whira said to Phathor, who was still waiting at the door, too huge to even consider entering. 'Check the cargo hold.'

It turned, hesitating. 'I've never seen one before—what do they look like?'

Whira ignored it, not about to admit that she didn't know either.

'It's doing *something*,' she whispered to herself. She craned her neck to gaze at the looming machinery overhead, but could not see any kind of product being manufactured.

Whira thought long into the night after that, wondering whether to command Gnumph to return, but the Jhahzang weren't known to communicate with their cousins in the stars—or with anyone else, for that matter. They, like their forebears, operated at a remove from the quicker life in Yokkun's Depth, and Whira couldn't begin to imagine how the Throlken line thought. Nobody could. The Throlken were said to have solved all the mysteries of existence, spending their first five million years in power picking the locks of the universe and then sitting back, so to speak, to luxuriate in everything they'd discovered. Whira was aware that the structure of her simple mind precluded her from ever grasping what she might be missing, and the Throlken apparently agreed, sharing only scraps of their wealth of knowledge with the population of the galaxy. There were persistent rumours of mortal species trying to make deals with them in return for a little more of this knowledge, presumably to no avail—what the Throlken could possibly want in return, Whira had no idea.

Music blared abruptly in the room above, which she'd thought was empty. Whira groaned, turning in the cot. Something smashed down below, and a loud, slobbering cheer went up. She wished she had a window to look out of; there wasn't even a sense of movement. Her mind worked in the foul-smelling darkness. For all she knew they were broken down and drifting, or stationed in orbit somewhere while Gnumph let people off. She might as well have been locked in a tunnel a hundred miles beneath the ground. She felt very far from home. She tossed and turned, imagining this was what it must have been like aboard one the first voyages that crossed the galaxy billions of years ago, before it had unified and relinquished most of its mysteries: ships that would have been entirely animal, or built from simple plastics and fibres and alloys. It must have taken them generations, whole species' lifespans, geological ages. In the darkness she felt their ancient loneliness, their fear.

There was a rapid knocking at her door. She opened her itchy, exhausted eyes.

'Whirazomar?'

It was Nodo, the spore's resident Igmus. As the only other bipedal symmetric aboard he'd taken it upon himself to be her assistant and guide, and seemed overly eager to please—perhaps hopeful of some sort of tip for his services, which she had resolved not to give him.

'Not now, Nodo.'

The knocks paused, before resuming. 'Gnumph says to come down... He's got as many passengers together as he can, if you want to talk to them.'

She leaned onto one elbow to kick-float out of the cot, beckoning irritably at the air and waiting a moment for the Myriad in the room to swarm together against the surface of her wattled skin, first scrubbing every centimetre of her colourful body clean before repurposing her waste molecules and whisking up a monochrome article of opaque vacuum-wear that drifted about her for a second as though she were underwater. She yanked open the door as the Myriad applied a fresh coating of white paint to

50

her coiled horns while the last of their number formed a constellation of Lazziar runes of office particular to her station that floated above her head and around her four small ears. 'Fine.'

Nodo stepped back, taking in her cold glare. He was fairly typical of the Phrailish folk of Salqar: a jowly, hairless, long-nosed, glossily cream-skinned creature with bulbous pink eyes of quite different make and size from her own and a forked, stubby tail. He wore a dark, tight-fitting gown of papery material—some fashion of theirs that Whira, having only visited Salqar a couple of times, knew little about—that showed off his pudgy stomach to good effect. But since both of them had two arms and two legs, a collection of (differently) jointed fingers and toes and stood upright at roughly the same height, this coincidence had somehow brought them together, just as it had their respective Alms. They could even interbreed (though the notion made Whira's skin crawl), both being descended from the all-encompassing lineage begun in the first age of the Throlken. Nodo smiled uncertainly in the Igmus way, puckering his lipless mouth. He had no teeth at all. Whira did not return the gesture, pushing past him to float into the corridor. The Glorish Peeper was nowhere to be seen, though the remnants of its campfire marked the floor.

They went out onto the balcony, loping in clumsy strides, and she saw a host of absurd creatures peering up at her from the commons. A curious feature of the majority of life in Yokkun's Depth was its scale: excluding a smattering of aberrations, most thinking beings—Whira included—measured no more than a foot or two in height or length, presumably because their ancient postbiological forbears had once been of a similar size themselves.

Public speaking, she thought, endeavouring to hold her horned head high and not swing upside down in the frustrating lack of gravity. *Wonderful.*

'Alright,' she said as she descended the ladder one-handed. 'Everybody here?'

They were not all here. That much she could see at once. Phathor, the chrome-shelled giant, squatted like a monolith beside the table. He gave her a small wave with one red feeler, sending wafts of debris and cooking smoke this way and that. Standing amongst his many limbs or lounging around the table other passengers watched her with interest. The crystal-eyed Qathis folk bubbled and hissed irascibly from inside their floating coldglobes. The Great Zabbas, patterned with whorls of gold, swam in sluggish circles in the air, his five large eyes staring dolefully at her from wrinkled hollows. Whira could see his brain (amongst the many golden organs visible inside his serpentine, partially translucent body), nestled safely in a thickened pouch, flickering away at its own silent computations. Scrapher the Larl polished the profusion of ebony teeth in his long snout, combing the fur of his glossy black potbelly with another of his three free hands. The Glorish Peeper peeped, its luminous eye fronds pulsing. Something scuttled across the table's stained sticky-fabric on pale, segmented limbs, sampling the cooking on the pan at the far end and fetching a bowl. Some passengers had their feet up reading pamphlets and spoolbooks and seemees of various kinds and not looking at her at all, with those whose cultures practised inter-species modesty clothed in a variety of flesh, shell, feather, synthetic and gel attire, elaborate moving screens, or creatures that were paid to follow their employer at all times and obscure any parts they wished to keep mysterious. Others chattered away apparently oblivious to her arrival, played with slaved Microscopia kept in ornamental pouches about their person, or tended the allotment, munching seedbiscuits and snapmix and peeling the clear suspension film from all manner of perishable fruits and delicacies bought in Salqar.

Anything that wasn't tied or stuck to the table, assorted chairs or perches free-floated around the communal space, including a few of the smaller beasts that seemed quite happy to live without any sense of up and down. Whira watched them all, waiting for silence.

'Alright. Thank you.' She cleared her throat and looked around, noting Gnumph's pale cluster of interior eyes gazing down at her from above the concentric rings of the various wooden floors. Some vestiges of childhood self-consciousness, reappearing now after years buried, tied her tongue. All the passengers saw was a self-important Lazziar busybody sent by some unrelatable Alm who didn't give two shits about them or their journey. The long limbs that sprouted from her narrow torso were altogether too gangly to be considered powerful by anyone but the spore's tiniest passengers, and her four-eared head—strange even to most other humanoids in that it contained one nostril, a pair of three-pupilled golden eyes mounted on the curve of her bulbous forehead, and a profusion of painted horns that curled from the back of her skull—would be almost unreadable to those not well travelled in Lihreat. She could feel herself freezing up at the thought, and willed herself forward.

'We've been off course for some time now,' she began, 'and I thought, since many of you wouldn't accept my compensation and, er, *alight,* as prompted'—here she glared at the Peeper, which whimpered and ducked behind one of Phathor's limbs—'it was high time to explain where we're going.'

Whira unrolled one of Gnumph's grubby galaxy charts halfway across the table, waiting only semi-patiently for the long-limbed thing to move its dinner before spreading the map all the way to the end so that they could trap its edges with sticky-bottomed cups and bottles, and pointed to a hieroglyph containing a cluster of more than two hundred and eighty-five thousand stars branched by a frenzy of coloured trade routes.

'Jumalar cluster—the southern cape of the Almoll of Plitipek,' she said, reaching *into* the chart and cupping the tip of the kingdom in her hand. 'Still about nineteen thousand lightspans away.'

A Spotted Gholkar cleared its sinuses and raised a shimmeringly scaled limb. Whira glared until it dropped its hand.

'Questions at the end,' she said, stabbing the location with her finger, stars glimmering up her arm. 'Now, Plitipek happens to contain a wonder of Yokkun's Depth.' Here she saw one or two nods from creatures who already knew of it, and met their eyes. 'Simply known as *the Well*. Nothing like it has been found anywhere else.'

Another limb shot up, waving in case she hadn't seen it.

'Questions at the *end*,' Whira snapped, and the many-jointed limb hesitated before disappearing again.

'It is thought to be the ancient impact crater of an unknown class of bomb,' she continued, taking a sip of metallic-tasting water Nodo had brought her, 'though no records survived of when it was used, or what long-extinct weaponry fired it. To the best of our knowledge nobody today can produce anything powerful enough to permanently damage the skin of a reality, and if it *is* the remnant of some long-ago war, no other craters like it have ever been found.'

Someone began to mutter something and she folded her arms, gazing steadily at them until they were silenced. The lack of a language barrier, once a blessing, now seemed more of a curse; since they all spoke a variant of the *Pattern*, the ancient Throlken-designed root language of the galaxy, a trillion or more languages, flickers of light, alterations in skin pigmentation or even pheromone expression could be spoken and understood by any resident of Yokkun's

Depth without any major difficulties, besides the odd embarrassing grammatical mistake, glaring cultural faux-pas or double entendre local to the dialect. But all that was pointless if they wouldn't listen.

Whira rapped on the table a few times before the murmuring subsided entirely and reading material was put away (or at least lowered).

'We don't know how old it is,' she continued, 'but it almost certainly predates the Throlken, since there are mentions of something like it in the Gigaverses. The Well was only listed as a site of special interest recently, and is presently surrounded by the Obaneo Nest Installation, a listening station run by an aquatic species known as the Bellowers. Signals from below can be heard more clearly there, and surveyors from across the galaxy use the place as a convenient entry point into the Well and the topmost Phaslairs.

'Which leads me to the reason for this detour,' Whira continued, sticking herself onto a wobbly chair. 'Some years ago a message filtered up from the deep Phaslairs. We get millions of transmissions every day from operatives and surveyors, on top of all the general noise. But this one... stood out.'

She looked around, daring anyone to speak, then glanced up and to one side, signalling the invisible Myriad. They replayed the signal, converted into multisense audio.

It was a *shriek*: the formless, heart-bursting terror emitted by an animal being eaten alive, designed to drive a pulse of primal panic through everything that heard it, regardless of the gulf of time. Whira had barely acclimatised herself to it, and watched with satisfaction as a dozen passengers cowered, hackles raised, paws and claws and feelers covering their ears.

She nodded to the Myriad, and it ceased.

'What in the sun's dead eye was that?' cried Scrapher, recovering first and glaring angrily up at the ceiling.

'They think it took an entire interstellar civilisation's resources to produce,' Whira said. 'A fifth, perhaps even a quarter of a galaxy's worth of energy. A concentrated blast designed to travel as far as possible. And it is followed by an addendum.'

The Myriad played the next part, a vocal file forwarded by Obaneo's counterpart station at Thundra.

The signal shifted to a wail, then a moan, dopplering into something their ears could process more easily. It petered out to be replaced by staccato, gobbling plosives, faint and scratchy with age and clearly patched together. Long blank sections—filled only with the word *Insufficient*, supplied by the Translators—interspersed the signal. Whira's ears twitched restlessly with a mixture of agitation and excitement. They were the most ancient recordings she had ever heard, from a time when some of the stars that formed the planets that birthed the first computers that became the Throlken hadn't even coalesced. The operators at Thundra had determined that these sounds had originated here, on Whira's home Surface: they had been fired downwards into the deep Phaslairs, to rebound like an echo in a cave over the course of all those years, available for all with the means to listen.

The file ended.

'We couldn't translate a single word of it, if what we heard there *were* even words.' Whira said. 'So the signal went into storage for a while, before it was passed on, just another oddity percolating up from the Well.' She took another sip of water, glad to have their full attention at last.

'But someone at the Obaneo station took an interest, decided to keep digging, collating and comparing every signal they had in their stores.' Whira pointed to a few places on the map again, her finger moving across the systems that ringed the Well. 'They started finding other signals, originating from very deep Phaslairs and following the precise path of the Scream. And once they'd put these signals together a pattern emerged.

'They found a *presence*, moving through the layers of reality, behaving oddly enough to be remarked upon as it went.' She fell silent for a moment and looked at them. 'We've checked and rechecked and checked again, and this thing, this entity, isn't moving downwards. It's travelling *upwards*. Towards our Surface.'

She met the assorted polished jewels and feather-structures of their eyes: a light of understanding was dawning here and there. 'This,' she continued, 'is not permitted by any current model of the laws of Phaslair physics.'

Whira sat back in the sticky chair, the whole thing creaking dangerously as if it were about to fall apart. 'We've estimated its closest approach, which happens to be in the vicinity of the Well, and I have been tasked with descending to meet it, whatever *it* is.'

Silence from the assembled passengers. Their questions seemed to have evaporated.

'Alright,' said Scrapher, slithering his tongue across his teeth, his tufted, multiply-ringed ears pricked. His little red eyes, situated at the very end of his snout, blinked. 'So? Why does it matter? Who cares that this thing can come back up?'

Whira scowled at him. 'Our reality,' she replied, choosing her words carefully, 'our Surface, has been engaging in... *experiments* on the Phaslairs below. If just one, younger iteration of Yokkun's Depth learns the secret of this entity's talent then they could use it, perhaps against us. They could ascend and exact revenge—'

Whira hesitated. Scrapher was grinning at her.

'But is it not *also* the case, Whirazomar, that their highnesses Thelgald and Phrail would dearly like to learn the secret themselves, so that they could—oh, I don't know—travel upwards, neutralise any threats from above? To become the *only* Surface, isn't that the dream? And why are the Throlken so keen to put an end to this mission, anyway? It's almost as if...'—he cast his beady gaze around in a pantomime of innocence—'they don't approve?'

She glanced at her audience, shifting in her seat as she realised her mistake. She shouldn't have indulged them, should have been stricter, should have locked them in their rooms for the duration of the voyage.

Scrapher's smug grin returned, and he looked amongst his fellow passengers as he picked between his fangs with an ornamented toothpick. 'I propose a vote. This has nothing to do with us paying customers. Who thinks we should kick *her* out, make *her* find a replacement service?'

Whira pressed her palms to the sticky table, wrestling with her temper. She travelled under the protection of Thelgald the Only, a conferred power not lightly ignored by anyone in Yokkun's Depth. The Alm had sent her the Jewelship she wore in one of the cluster of pendants around her neck, and she wondered what would happen if she switched it on now. She'd be fine, of course, contained within a fully operational crystal vessel that had grown to full size around her in a fraction of a second, but poor Gnumph would burst like a rotten fruit, its passengers flung into the void. It was tempting.

She opened her mouth, but Gnumph beat her to it, its voice grumbling through the floor and walls.

I'm afraid I can't allow that, Scrapher.

'Oh can't you?' retorted Scrapher, holding up his ticket for all to see, a plastic disk stamped with miniscule writing. 'You are bound by the statutes of thirty-five Almolls to drop us off at the nearest system or continue on your promised course, Gnumph. It says so in the small print.' He gazed around. 'And instead we are being held prisoner while you do neither.'

Whira glowered at Scrapher, wishing she could Drop him then and there.

Why can't I? she thought. *I'd be within my rights.* She watched Scrapher as he spoke animatedly to the others. He was supposed to be employed in some legal capacity between Salqar and Phorlmazuur. *Or so he says.*

'You give me no choice, then,' she said, rising from her chair and clasping her Arqot pendant, selecting a gleaming Iliquin pistol from the hollow bubble that appeared around her neck.

Scrapher snarled, stepping into Phathor's shadow, his teeth bared.

Whira pointed the pistol at him. A sculpted silver portrait of Thelgald's horned head gazed calmly from the front sight. 'I will Drop you, I swear it! You are hindering the task set for me by Salqar—'

Panic erupted amongst the horde of passengers, their voices gabbling over one another as creatures scrabbled to push themselves beneath the table, bury themselves in the allotment or float back up to their rooms. A misfire could cause all kinds of damage.

Scrapher flattened his ears. His tongue slithered over his teeth again. 'Let's calm down. How about a compromise? You let us off us early in Jumalar cluster, with chits for, say, a free open return anywhere in Yokkun?' He spread his hands. 'Do that and I'll be on my way, no fuss.'

Whira didn't lower the pistol. 'That's not something I can promise,' she growled, 'without sending a message back. And we can't send messages.'

'We can't?' asked the Great Zabbas sleepily from above them, blinking his eyes. 'I have. I just sent a manuscript to my publisher in Ampo.'

'*What?*' Whira hissed, staring at it. 'Didn't you hear me when I came aboard? No signals!'

'It's nothing to do with your little mission, don't worry.'

She wanted to grasp the Zabbas by the tail and swing him until his teeth fell out. 'Every transmission is *noise,* idiot!'

Some hands and limbs and digits were rising.

'I've been sending letters to my sisters,' admitted Mobe, a glistening, flat-faced Horphopede. He floated upside down above the table, a host of parasitic species attached by suction to his undercarriage.

'And I've been filming my seemees,' said Shumholl the Xaal, sucking in its transparent eyes to blink. 'I've got over a hundred patrons back home; if I stop filming they'll forget about me.'

Maybe it's for the best, interjected Gnumph softly through the soles of her feet. *We're playing the role of a normal shuttle service, after all. Wouldn't it look a little strange if we weren't signalling other places as we went? Everyone else is.*

Whira stared at them all, fists clenched, before paddling ungracefully back up to her room.

I'd be in Szoddul by now, if the Alm hadn't hired me, Gnumph said, rumbling through the wood of the table Whira sat at with the Qathis as they munched their way through a twelve-course dinner of rubbery meat caught in Gnumph's exterior traps, their yellowed, crystalline eyes watching her with interest from inside their coldglobes.

We were supposed to be in Maarl harbour for a birthday party, supplied one of the Qathis in frost-speak, exuding a rapidly growing tendril of branching icicles from an orifice between its eyes. The neighbouring Qathis seemed to consider this, some crystals of frost forming and melting, replaced with different patterns. *We've missed it now.*

Whira peeled the suspension coating from a puffseed, inspecting the fruit for rot and blowing into one of its chambers to inflate some of the fleshy, edible bulbs, barely listening to their chatter. She was thinking for the thousandth time about what she had in storage, kept separate from Gnumph's cluttered cargo hold (already full to the brim with luggage and possessions and things she hadn't been able to make out with her weak light, as well as the chuckling, muttering echoes of yet more stowaways). Something so special that even she wasn't allowed to know more than the bare minimum about it, in case the Throlken somehow got hold of her. What Whira did know was enough to keep her awake into the small hours of ship night, her mind shooing it away at every turn.

Plausible deniability. Phrail and Thelgald and whoever else was in on this would have systems in place to stop anything ever reaching back to them, should the Throlken find out, and this shouldering of the risk was simply the price of Whira's employment.

She stood abruptly, ungluing herself from her seat and floating up past the various floors towards the collection of lenses in Gnumph's ceiling, to gaze through the scope at the cerulean vault of the galaxy and the distant spray of stars they were headed for. Plitipek, where she was due to rendezvous with the station and its giant guardians before vanishing into the Phaslairs below, knowing all the Throlken in the sky would stop her, if they could.

RUINS

Like the surface of the planet they'd left me on, the system's atmosphere was pearlescent, oily white. A rainbow-hued, debris-thick fog of drifting shape and shadow, the accumulated guff of a galaxy long settled, it seemed, and now rent asunder by some war inflicted upon it from above.

My ship drifted slowly across the system. Some planets were crowned, their globes garlanded with colossal crystalline spires that branched into fluting candelabras to cup the wandering moons. Others were smashed entirely into gravelly stretches of waste and slag and still-glowing coals, an unceasing shower of hail that dashed past the ship's nose as it ploughed onward through the mist. And all were lifeless, as far as that word meant anything: microbes and slime had won the day, blossoming on the shores of irradiated seas, caking the windswept crags.

I tried the basic spectrum channels, hopping the empty static for days at a time, my supplies of skin leather and gristle running low. My suit—which I could not take off inside the unpressurised and freezing interior of the ship— was filling up with excrement and vomit, a vile chowder that sloshed from legs to chest and up my nose when I tried to lie down and sleep, the cause of all the infected sores now crusting my skin. In the days of my youth you could sail the void and never starve, catching vacuum swimmers by the bucketload as you swept through shoals of life, siphoning water from frost-catchers in your hull. Now I was reduced—once the boiled pit-mummy cartilage was finally gone—to peeling and eating the rubber from the soles of my boots (inserted into a heated feeding canister and connected to the bodged airlock in my faceplate). It was only then, whittled by starvation, that I encountered my first spinning hulk, hidden in the shattered orbit of a half-obliterated world.

Food, my thoughts babbled as I piloted the ship carefully through the reef of drifting rubble and made my way inside the ruin, burning through the tunnel port with my improvised welding blade and shouldering my way through, scattering popped plates of mail from my suit.

All was dark, still smoke and death air, lit only by the sputtering spark of the blade, connected to my suit generator. My helmet had no audio feed, no microphones—I hadn't known how to make them—and so all was quiet save for the churn of blood in my ears. Deaf, shit-coated, piss-filled; I waddled like an infant. But to remove my helmet in here would be instant death, of that I was certain. A war had raged some time ago; this was like those realities my ancestors had left, decimated and sealed off, never to be revisited. This ruin could have been here for one hundred thousand years at least, its bottled chambers of air as deadly as the lingering, pan-spectrum radiation outside— radiation that was already making me ill.

Doesn't matter, need food. Food, then medicine, then escape.

I plunged forward into the embrace of the black smoke, the waste sloshing in my legs, stumbling over unseen debris, bumping into the bulkhead until I found myself in a space that suggested great depth. I flared the blade, squeezing a trigger on its hilt and sending out a spatter of drifting sparks. They floated in the blackness, illuminating nothing but the soup of smoke, before winking out.

But one light still shone. I turned at the reflection, staring through scummy eyeholes down the corridor I'd just come through, at the smashed doorway. It was coming from my ship.

I half swam, half cartwheeled, the shit upending into my mouth and eyes and nose, coughing and spluttering into the remains of the airlock. I knew that light. A frequency.

I fastened myself in, vomiting up the last of my meagre meal as my eyes searched the surface of the dead ship and the white, glowering sky of space above.

Oh, yes.

VERSES

Whira had given up applying stick pads to her fingers and toes, and spent dozens of hours simply floating, often upside down, in her room. She had cleared the curved wall of debris, scrubbing away as much of the graffiti as she could, and now used it as a projection screen while she sifted through the Alms' ephemeral libraries. She put her Myriad to work, forming a fleet of microscopic pumps to suck pigments from the dirt in the air and fashioning moving inks that floated and fluttered across the wall in huge banks of scrolling text and three-dimensional video.

What she was searching for lay far beneath the accreted dump of galactic and intergalactic history, in a body of disparate records, stories and oral histories known collectively as the Gigaverses. As far as anyone could tell, the verses hailed back billions of years into prehistory, beyond the fabled pre-Throlken Gyilong and Dzull lineages, when all life had been chaotic and biological. It was a task, Whira knew, that had kept many a long-lived Zabbas busy for their entire career, only to discover that they'd barely scraped the surface of what lay beneath. Luckily for her, translating ancient texts, documents, and ancestral, preserved records of long dead civilisations (sometimes in the form of effectively immortal creatures programmed to tell their stories over and over again until the end of time, written histories poured like marbled calligraphy into the strata of planetary crusts, planted forests that spelled out words in indecipherable languages or even messages carved into the interior of glaciers) were her specialty, and the very reason she'd been hired by Thelgald's Interpreters in the first place.

She began once more at the only logical place: the history of the Well itself. It was a subject that had been rigorously scoured by every Sovereign agent already, but Whira flicked through everything she knew, diving past the discovery and study of the hole in the Phaslairs and deep into the patchy history of the region. The Well did not move in the same way that the stars did, and she called up a galactic chronochart to wind back the millennia and positions of the suns, their dazzling spray of light swirling and coalescing like boiling gold, her chamber filling with pulsing light. Whira would never tire of watching the motion of the galaxy in time lapse—it was as if the creator had dipped its spoon into a glowing soup and stirred. It was not, perhaps, an original angle of investigation, and many a scholar had already plotted the position of the Well over the last few million years, but she spooled backwards anyway, peering at the minuscule points of light as they revolved and danced around the metaphysical crater of the Well.

She read, muttering commands to the Myriad to call up potted histories of species and worlds, scanning through the records of the fourteen thousand, eight hundred and sixty-one notable kingdoms, states and hierarchies that had, at one time or other over the last few million years, dwelt in the vicinity of the Well. Pictos and seemees of a dazzling variety of life (most of it rendered by the Myriad in three dimensions so that she could push off from the wall and float around inside the scenes, should she wish) filled the confines of her chamber. Something with a lustrous magenta carapace seemed to notice her intrusion and she flinched, floating to one side, only to realise a moment later that the sixty-three million-year-old rendering was reacting to whoever had taken the video. It extended a feathery black proboscis and vibrated it rapidly, showering Whira with droplets she couldn't feel, perhaps their equivalent of a smile.

Whira spooled further until she was now, at more than one hundred million years BPD, in what was considered the *Classical Era*, in a time when nearly all the life that abounded in the galaxy was different: an alternate cast of species that would go on to become the societies she knew today. The Throlken were by then in their middle age, she supposed, an entrenched fixture on the galactic stage, busily spreading the fingers of their branching family tree out into the darkness while converting themselves into ethereal helium spirits to claim their thrones inside the stars, as self-elected lords of the galaxy.

But still she had to go deeper—five times deeper, by her count. The age of the first signals that had filtered up suggested that whatever was down there had been trapped for five hundred million years. Whatever *it* was had existed before the Throlken were even thought of, in an age Whira simply couldn't imagine.

The map had spooled back to the verses of the region from this time, when a thicket of elderly stars surrounded the Well entirely. Their spectra, mass and colouration were mostly guesswork, gleaned by the Myriad's real-time reading of the verses, but their positions should be accurate. Whira brushed her fingers against the floor, floating cross-legged towards the arm of the galactic map, her downy skin glowing golden green with reflected light. The Myriad had brought her to a time the verses remembered as the *All*, when the galaxy was divided into five sprawling kingdoms. The Well, then thinly translatable in one of a few intelligible local star-dialects as something along the lines of *the Inescapable Hole*, lay in the kingdom of South-All. Whira's eyes moved across the precis, knowing all this already. She had set the Myriad to work as soon as they'd set off, trusting in their innate, insatiable curiosity, but this deep all they had for her was a pile of educated assumptions, a blur of maybes and possibilities generated by the vaguest of data.

'Bring up the verses from South-All,' she commanded. 'Divide between Songstream, timeline and map, 520 to 480 million BPD.'

They did so, spinning colour and light from the molecules in the air, microscopic reactors powering their work. The constellations drifted over forty million years, the files of generations of scholars cycling beneath, accompanied by a fat stream of raw, unprocessed data collected and hoarded long ago. Whira was looking for the relative proximity of star clusters to the Well, and paused the map when they came close enough to overlap, their worlds orbiting into its path. The problem was that there were too many to choose from: she'd already exhausted a few days back on Salqar spooling a map back and forth only to discover that over a hundred groupings of stars had swirled into the path of the Well during that age.

'Overlay with localised verses, colour-coded to time.'

The Myriad stippled the clusters with coloured tags, each indicating—according to the Throlken's colour arm of the alphabet—a relative proximity to the present day (blue being the oldest, ultraviolet most recent). Whira sifted the tags, bringing up spools of transcriptions, footnotes and images, not to mention a few intrusive biographies of the more self-important—and mostly long-forgotten— scholars who'd studied them.

She spent the next day or so hardly eating, hardly blinking. These were fossil records, made by a lineage now gone entirely, and constituted some of the oldest Gigaverses she'd ever studied. There was no visual data for large periods of time; either the various civilisations from the stream of star clusters were all blind and hadn't used it, or—more likely—it simply hadn't survived the great, eroding span of entropy. What she could find was more abstract: vocal recordings etched like musical notes into chasm walls that, when played, moaned and hooted into her chamber as though from the bottom of the sea. Whatever made those sounds was long lost, with no images, remains of infrastructure or genetic information surviving at all. Indeed, she could only find one pictographic recording of a species from that time at all: an image from a spoolbook dredged up from the library of Ird-Cur-Im, claimed to have been found scratched into a lump of semi-melted lead. Whira expanded it, dubious.

She looked for a long time, trying to convince herself that she was reading meaning into nothing. It probably wasn't a face at all, but it certainly looked like one to her Lazziar eyes.

She swallowed, minimising the image. The snarling face wouldn't stop staring at her, so she cleared it away. There were myths from every Phaslair strata of evil spirits—beings that seemed to climb the realities at their leisure, tormenting everyone they came across. One such demon was known amongst a scattering of realities as *the Hermit*, and was said to desire an end to existence itself. The Myriad had flagged the legends of the Hermit, noting that they occupied roughly the same vertical Phaslair volume as the Scream, but Whira had no time for superstitions.

'Weren't there any Machine Ancestors there at the time?' she asked the Myriad, hoping for something more concrete. Wherever machine life evolved there tended to be better records, as if a compulsive urge to catalogue dogged their early steps, before they blended inexorably with the populace and all life's consciousness grew muddied and chemical all over again, like the ecosystem of Yokkun's Depth today. As far as Whira knew there had been four major blendings in the history of the galaxy, though only the Throlken's had lasted for any great stretch of time.

The Myriad fussed, generating flowering diagrams of a machine emergence from a period five hundred and nine million years before, but it was all curiously incomplete. With it came a sump of raw data: keening, wailing speech or music, the clicking and popping of something that sounded like sonar linguistics, even colour patterns programmed into the evolution of a more recently mummified species' gut flora (discovered by accident) that directly referenced those times. Whira shook her head at the swathe of information pulsing and screaming across her wall, remembering how it had taken her almost a year to tease apart the basic orthography of post-Throlken Residual Waleem, a language only half the age of all this nonsense. What she'd already spooled through represented many lifetimes of study, unless she appealed to her Alm for Extension, and she wouldn't get that if she failed her first major job.

Whira gazed at it all, a headache budding behind her eyes. *Something* was coming back, something that had driven that awful scream before it like a great bubble rising from the deep.

Something.

They began their climb back towards the populated currents, though there was nothing to indicate any change inside the stale, weightless interior of the spore besides their position on the plastic constellation map being continually redrawn, as though by invisible hands, as the Myriad documented their rise. Whira stowed her

72

Sovereignty tech back inside its Bubbles, clicking shut the silver sheath on her Arqot pendant to snap the little subdimensions closed. She was forced to trust the shifting map if she wanted to plot their course without bothering Gnumph, who had a natural aptitude for navigating by the textures of the currents and patterns of the starfields, ignoring the confusing highways of the shipping lanes (which were still named after mysterious pre-Throlken stars, peoples, places and legends that had long since vanished or drifted away) and scooping up great mouthfuls of vacuum fauna as it went.

Their ascension to the Star Apse of Obaneo would take the best part of another five days: five days in which they became a much more obvious target. Re-entering such a dense volume also slowed their approach, since the Mode-Eleven worked most efficiently in the absence of interstellar atmosphere. Since the vast artificial play dimensions operating inside room six and nine were a drag on the engine they had to be shut down. Any travellers left inside would be trapped.

Room six had been taken by a passenger travelling between the Almolls of Zengo and Ehlullaph some years ago, and the door had remained locked for weeks before the chamber was broken into by new travellers eager to secure a bed. Inside, they'd found a procedurally generated infrasphere, spanning dozens of virtual lightyears, and it was like stepping through a doorway into another world. The infrasphere, which was one of the few places the Myriad could not enter, ran off Gnumph's own electrical field, winking out of existence whenever it came to a stop. It was filled to the brim with players able to access the great game from other points all over Yokkun's Depth, and perhaps—it was speculated—even such off-limits places as the Forbidden Almoll or Galactic Centre. The enterprising soul who'd eventually claimed the room had managed to monetise access to its wonders, charging fellow passengers for playtime inside.

Whira appeared inside it now, her fee oleaginously waived, stepping down from the wonky doorway and through the thickened field barrier, a no man's land of swirled, faded glints of colour like spilled oil.

The cold hit her at once, sinking into her lungs as she looked out upon a bright, snowcapped range of impossibly tall mountain peaks. Letters, twinkling in the glow of three white suns, hung above the mountains. Whira squinted and read the spiralling Throlken characters in the sky: *Here And There Pass*. Across the valley and beneath the cold shadow of the mountains stretched a manicured woodland, the auburn leaves heavy with snow. A thin, drifting smear of smoke rose from deep inside the woods.

Whira studied the backs of her hands, conscious that she had come through in the default infracharacter template of a heroic-looking Wumo, the species that must have designed this particular set of virtual worlds. She cupped a pair of translucent webbed claws to her mouth, screaming into the blustery middle distance. 'We're shutting down now! This door is *closing!* I repeat, shutting down!'

There. Nobody could claim they hadn't had fair warning, especially since the very presence of this virtual land contravened the scrawl of house rules on the back of every ticket Gnumph issued. Anyone trudging back to the spore's interior for dinner would have to wait in the cold, maybe out at that dwelling in the woods, until her mission at the Well was done.

Whira glanced back at the open doorway, eyes narrowing as she saw Scrapher there, peering in at her. From beyond his grinning, toothy head floated the distant clatter of other passengers settling round the table for the evening.

'Don't you even *think* about it—' she began.

His grin broadened, and he slammed the door.

'Bastard!' Whira howled, sprinting through the snow towards the outline of the doorway. She scrabbled at the virtual inside handle, her new hands rattling it back and forth, unable to make it budge. 'Scrapher!' she yelled, thumping on the wood, which was nothing but a layer of imaginary texture and sensation. 'Nodo!'

It was useless: no sound escaped the infrasphere with the door shut.

'Throlken's glare,' she hissed, staggering in the snow and gazing out at the mountains. The wind was picking up, driving a dry gust of sharp, identical little ice crystals across the valley. Whira threw one last punch at the unyielding door and wandered a little way down to the edge of the woodland, looking to the rising column of smoke. Misted lettering, carried up and through the smoke, spelled out words as it rose:

Izred Plain supplies.

Ready? Gnumph rumbled through the wood of the table.

Nodo looked at Scrapher, who nodded. 'All clear—Whizzo's gone to her room. Told me to shut it off, like you wanted.'

Alright.

In the gloom beneath the galaxy's lowermost currents—a dim wasteland of habitat webs occupied by everything and anything capable of withstanding the chill silence of real void—Gnumph rose, a pallid ring glowing into life around it. Inside the drive's radius every law in the universe became soft and supple, mimicking the chaos at the heart of a star: a place of strange and even occult visitations where the principles of reality blurred. The drive shut down for a full second, its halo drifting, before restarting as Gnumph swept back towards civilisation. They were on their way.

*　*　*

Whira looked over her shoulder, undecided, just in time to see the doorway completely disappear. She trudged to where it had been, hurled some snow at the empty air, and got to work marking it with some perfectly sculpted polygonal rocks.

They'll realise their mistake soon enough.

She finished piling the rocks into a cairn that she was confident she could spot from a distance, before worrying that some sort of cleaning programme would reset the landscape. Whira went over to a tree and snapped a twig experimentally, watching it closely to see if it would reset, but it did not. She arranged some more rocks into a circular Throlken sentence facing the spot where the missing door had been.

GONE TO THE HOUSE IN THE WOODS—WHIRA.

She looked at what she'd written, grabbing more rocks for an addendum:

SCRAPHER DID IT.

It had grown uncomfortably cold. Whira had to remind herself that she was, in reality, still aboard Gnumph and sitting cross-legged inside a small chamber, afflicted by suggested stimulus and a hyperreal projection of tactile perspective that would allow her to travel thousands of miles across this artificial world and beyond, if she wished. She had never played in one of these places before, though, and had no idea what would happen to her if she got lost, or injured. She made her way warily into the forest towards the column of smoke.

She pushed through the woods, snow slipping down the back of the heavy, scaled clothes the simulation had clad her in. The silence was permeated with a soft, tinkling music, and it took Whira some time to work out that the music pervaded the whole artificial realm, presumably hotting up a little when the quest got serious or danger came near.

The ramshackle home appeared between the trees: a bodged, patched-together heap of mud-brick and timber, the snow piled upon its pointed eaves. The chimney smoke, though it carried sometimes on the gusting wind, held no smell. Nothing did. Whira stood watching the place, taking in how empty and abandoned it looked. It must have been built by a player waiting out here for customers: travellers coming down over the pass or across the wide river at the base of the valley. But a primal need for warmth had brought her here, as well as a new, sickening hunger—a crude and exaggerated approximation of normal sensations that didn't feel like anything she knew in the Real. She considered the dwelling for a while longer, her breath misting in artfully rendered curls and coils, wondering whether she was walking into some sort of trap. She tried the door.

It wasn't locked, but the snow had piled up against it, wedging it shut. Whira cleared the ice roughly from its base with her bone-capped boot and pulled with all her might until the wood began to creak and splinter and she had an opening through which she could peer into the dark interior. She slowly squeezed her way through.

Someone must have been here recently to light the fire, which roared away to itself on a scale-tiled hearth at the far end of the lower floor. Unless it stayed lit the entire time, without any need to replenish the fuel. Whira hesitated as she stood before it, watching the licking flames for signs of a repeating pattern, interested to find she was warming up. She glanced about the place, moving her face very close to the carved timber beam above the fireplace until she could discern the tiniest hint of what might have been a sharp-edged polygon gracing its pattern of knots and whirls. This was a clever little place, made with real artistry. The scales that made up the floor were verdigrised with apparent age, and the bare brick walls blackened with a layer of carefully applied soot. She had once snorted in derision at the sort of folk who played these games, but she had to admit the love and care that went into them was something to behold.

Whira waited until she could feel her hands again before creeping over to the wooden shelves that lined one wall. Players could buy whatever they needed here, she supposed, but unless someone came to serve her soon she'd have no choice but to help herself.

She waited another few minutes—hugging her simulated arms to her and listening to the wind howl through the eaves—before she did just that, taking a hard, branched crimson vegetable (its skin tattooed with what must have been a price: 12) from a basket and biting experimentally into it. It tasted of nothing, but she was filled with a sense of wellbeing just chewing on it, and almost instantly her burning hunger was gone, replaced by an internal warmth. She wondered if that was how Gnumph felt when its belly was full of paying guests. The price on the skin of the vegetable, now that it was missing a chunk, had fallen to 8.

But taking it had tripped some kind of alarm, and a tinny, wailing scream arose from the flames of the hearth and went careening up the chimney. Whira could hear it issuing out across the woodland until it was swept away in the gale. She stared at the fire a moment longer before the sensation that she was not alone brought her head around to the counter.

Something long and narrow stood there, sparsely lit by the distant glow of the hearth. Whira met the being's faded blue eyes.

'Can I help you with something?' asked the figure behind the counter, in a voice that was clearly hurrying to synthesise the words of the player that controlled it. It stood on a pair of trousered, stilt-like legs, its four hands resting on a

78

pudgy stomach. Its face, once her eyes had adjusted to the gloom, appeared as a wrinkly droop of nose and mouth, the pale eyes set very low and far apart, so that they seemed to melt downwards to either side. 'Did you come over the pass?'

Whira pointed in the rough direction of the woods. 'I'm on a... ship, they locked me out, I needed warmth and food. I'm sorry if—if I needed money to pay for it or something...' She wasn't explaining herself very well. The person's low-slung eyes darted around the shop, appeared to evaluate the stock instantly, then snapped back to her.

'You came in here and *stole*?' he screeched, sending a shiver down Whira's non-existent spine. 'Who do you think you are?'

'I'm sorry,' she repeated, stuttering. 'I've never been in this place before—'

'You thought you'd just jump in, take a bite out of my prize Loveroot and run off home again, is that it?'

'Look,' she replied, translucent hands held out in front of her, still clutching the Loveroot, 'I can pay, when they get the door open again. I just needed to keep warm.'

The figure was nodding viciously. 'Oh yes. I see. This shop gets plundered every winter by players coming down from the *Here And There*, but you're different, are you?'

'I'm not a thief!' Whira roared, straightening her back.

'Says the thief,' scoffed the shopkeeper. 'With a bellyful of my stock.'

'This is hopeless,' sighed Whira, turning to leave. She'd just have to wait out in the cold.

They both stopped then, ears pricked, midway through shouting at each other. Someone was wading through the snow outside, cursing and grumbling, the crunching of their steps growing louder.

'Hello in there!' called a jolly voice, and a gloved, six-fingered hand appeared around the edge of the door and thrust it open with a grunt, pushing a drift of snow across the floor. A yellowish, bearded face with large black eyes peered at them. 'I saw the smoke; you open?'

'If you have money,' the shopkeeper said, looking him over icily. The visitor pushed his way in and shouldered the door shut again behind him. He was bipedal symmetric, his short legs and long arms shod in what looked like thick, toughened glass, ice crystals and flakes of snow carpeting the crimson furs that lined his throat. Whira saw that the side of his yellow skull was tattooed with an artful pattern of writing and numbers—his name and player stats, plain for all to see. The numbers changed even as she looked at them, rising and falling hectically.

'My flyer hit turbulence over Bormao Peak, came down in the foothills,' he continued, nodding brightly to Whira. He went straight to the fire, calling over his pauldron for a bowl of something she'd never heard of, and pulled off his gloves to warm a pair of clawed hands. Whira joined him, hoping for strength in numbers, glancing at the shopkeeper as he came over with the drink.

'One more,' said the newcomer, passing Whira the small bowl. The shopkeeper opened his mouth to object, closing it again as he was handed a glowing handful of tokens.

The ice on the newcomer's furs was melting to a puddle around his boots. He turned to Whira, his glass armour clinking.

'Tiliph,' he said. 'Playing from Oublish, in Deephrull.'

Whira took a sip of the warm, viscous drink he'd given her, recalling that the lands of Oublish were populated by a truly colossal species of eight-winged, cavern-dwelling predators who spent their long lives almost entirely upside down, and that the character standing beside her was, in reality, probably as big as the Well station she was travelling to. She looked him over. 'I'm not a player,' she said. 'I got shut in here by someone. Someone living on borrowed time.'

Tiliph frowned. 'Goodness. How are you going to get back?'

She shrugged, leaning to warm her hands again on the fire. 'They'll realise eventually and come looking. The doorway's just beyond the woods.'

'So *you're* Whira,' exclaimed the traveller, running his claws through the fine black spines of his beard. On one of his fingers he wore a glittering ring, and for a moment Whira fancied she saw lights dancing in its band. 'I wondered what all that was about, with the stones.'

The shopkeeper returned with Tiliph's change and the second drink, leaving the bowl on a table that Whira was sure hadn't been there before. 'Watch yourself with this one,' the snide thing said to Tiliph. 'She can't pay her way.'

'Of course she can't,' he replied. 'Didn't you hear her? She's lost!'

Tiliph gazed at her contemplatively, the infrasphere running a swift proxy of what must have been a quite unreadable expression on his vast face, out in the Real.

'I'll pick up her tab, anything she needs,' he said to the shopkeeper. 'And give her a bed for the night, will you? She's waiting for her friends.'

The shopkeeper hissed, sloping off back into the shadows.

'Probably playing from some cramped little bedroom,' snorted Tiliph. 'Who'd want to run a shop in here, anyway, hiding from everything and everyone?'

Easy enough for you to say, thought Whira. Outside, in the Real, Tiliph was the size and strength of a thundercloud, with the confidence to match.

Tiliph laughed out loud, patting her on the shoulder. The warmth and pressure felt real, as did the effects of the drink, which must have been faintly narcotic. 'A tip— when you think in here, a thought bubble pops up over your head.'

'What?'

'See?' he closed his eyes and a pale mist drifted from his fan-like ears, spelling out a word as it joined over his head. *Hellooooo.*

'You have to train yourself to hide it,' he explained, the cloud drifting away up the chimney.

'So you've been playing for a while?' she asked.

'Years,' he said, taking up his bowl. 'Lost count. I love it in here. I suppose there are better, more realistic spheres out there, but this one just feels *right*. Won most of my stats fighting in the Flesh Campaigns.'

Whira glanced at his suite of changing tattoos. Even immersed in her studies as she had been, she'd heard of those. The Flesh Campaigns, which had begun over a request for more playable species, character bodies and outfits, were one of the longest running virtual conflicts anywhere in Yokkun's Depth, spreading across all the worlds of the Wumo infrasphere. In some places they were still raging, consuming newly designed planets and systems almost as soon as they were birthed.

'But I've retired from all that, got too many points, too much stash to lose. Now I get my jollies from treasure hunting—the losing side left a lot of rare loot behind when they abandoned this world in a hurry a few years back, kicked out by us. I've been back and forth trying to find it, mostly on commission.'

Whira knew you could make real money on the outside, in the Real, from in-game treasure. Some folk did just that, funding their entire lives from in here. It made sense, she supposed, that some of the more reclusive species would prefer to live a simulated life. The Throlken had outlawed war in Yokkun's Depth for millions of years: infraspheres were the only places where the bloodthirsty could get it, where they could revel in it, glorying in all the virtual destruction they could muster.

'What did you find?' she asked, not particularly interested, but sensing she owed him some conversation. His ring, she saw at last, held what appeared to be a miniscule living ecosystem, its shadowed underside stippled with the lights of cities. Another game, perhaps, within this one.

He eyed her by the fire, an uncertainty hovering in his horizontal pupils, and Whira realised she'd gone too far. She held up a hand. 'None of my business.'

'It's not that,' he said, staring into the synthetic flames and cocking his head ever so slightly in the direction of the shopkeeper somewhere behind them in the gloom, 'but you never know who's listening.' Whira nodded, imagining the great winged thing muttering to itself in its dark lair, paranoid from its years of solitude.

'Anyone from this galaxy,' Tiliph said, 'or even *another*.'

She looked at him askance.

'I mean it,' he said. 'This Sphere's popular. There are players from everywhere. You can always spot the truly exotic—those who've come in from outside Yokkun's Depth—because they do everything with a slight lag. But that just means they have to up their skill level, and more often than not they end up quite formidable.' He drained the last of his drink and set the cup down. Whira noticed his throat did not work when he drank, the liquid simply disappeared at his lips, topping up some hidden meter. 'I met a few laggers on the battlefields at Munzoan-Elaeyii, gave them a wide berth.'

Whira noticed that the flames were finally dying down. The shopkeeper didn't seem interested in replenishing the wood. He brought his selection of goods over to Tiliph inside some kind of glowing orb. Tiliph leaned forward in his chair, scrolling through the orb's contents with a fingertip to find what he needed for his damaged vehicle, while the light faded outside.

'I'm going out to check whether they've been back,' Whira said, rising.

Tiliph made his choices (pointing at what he wanted, only for it to disappear in a flash—winking, Whira presumed, straight into his baggage) and stood with her. 'I'll come with you. Then I'd better be off before someone steals my flyer.'

They left the sour-looking creature to his own devices while they trudged outside, the sky darkening further as a landscape of bruised clouds rolled in across the mountains. Whira looked out towards the river, and was entranced to see planets floating in their thousands in place of stars, the speckled traffic of millions of players drifting between them.

'I've left some more money for you, just in case,' said Tiliph, waving away her muted thanks. He gestured to the house. 'Make sure he escorts you out again in the morning, if they haven't come by then.'

'What do you do on the outside?' Whira asked, mainly in the hope of changing the subject. She'd always felt uncomfortable receiving unasked-for gifts or acts of kindness.

He looked surprised, and smiled shyly. 'I farm transistor berries. It's a slow business, coming up with ways to pass the time while they hibernate, so I wait out the fattening season playing in adventure realms, like this one.'

Whira imagined such a powerful beast idling its time away in the dark. 'Are you happy?' she asked, bluntly. It had always seemed to her like a curious waste of life, playing around in artificial realities when there was a real one, as it were, right outside your window.

He tilted his head to look up at the artificial worlds and their multicoloured webs of traffic. Their names, made wheel-shaped by Throlken lettering, hovered like bracelets around their atmospheres. 'There's no single reality to life—as long as you're enjoying yourself in one, does it matter which?'

Whira digested this while they walked. Her spirits fell when they came to her mound of rocks. Her message remained, and no footprints marked the fresh snow.

'A night with that one, then,' she muttered.

'Don't let him treat you badly,' Tiliph said. 'In fact...' He rummaged in his pack, which, like Gnumph, was much larger on the inside than it appeared. He found what he was looking for and passed Whira a thick spoolbook. 'Here. It's the rulebook. If he tries anything nasty, thinking he can get one over on you just because you're new, throw this at him.'

She took it, embarrassed once again, and they looked at each other for a moment. 'Well, I'd better be off,' he muttered, checking his pack. He cocked his head. 'What, um, what species are you, by the way? I forgot to ask.'

'Lazziar,' she said, smiling. 'I suppose I'd fit on the tip of your finger.'

Tiliph glanced automatically at his virtual hand, and beamed at her. 'I think you probably would! Here—' He snapped his fingers. 'My details, in the Real, should you ever want to look me up—I've just sent them to the addresses page at the back of the rulebook.'

She checked, opening the origami structure of the book and spooling quickly through to the last section until she found his name:

Drethenor Tiliph Zelt Friest of Oublish, Within
Deephrull, *Subject of Izzogath*
The Berrycaves, Oublish Under Vounel
The Underside
World Two, Zingost
Zingost Star
Deephrull Wild

Whira rolled the spoolbook closed, patting it to show his address was safe and sound.

Tiliph's eyes flicked to his boots. 'Well then, see you, Whira.' He trudged back in the direction of the mountains, fading in the falling snow.

When she returned to the shop the awful owner had closed and barred the door, and after much cursing and screaming through a snowed-up window she went around the back. The ginger trees had sunk into the ground as darkness descended, withering from lack of light, and through the drifting snow she saw animals lounging in the shelter of a stable block. They each had names and numbers rising in the mist of their breath, and she realised as she stood there that they were players, too, apparently content to sit and wait for riders to come down from the mountains or across the plain to hire them.

'Hello?' she said, creeping under the eaves of the stable, her hood filled with snow once more.

The gazes of a host of three-limbed, woolly black beasts drifted in her direction. She stared at them. Did they really just stand here, day in, day out?

Then she noticed the shopkeeper's silhouette in the falling snow. Watching her.

'I have the rule book,' she cried, holding it triumphantly above her head. 'You *have* to let me in!'

The long-legged form turned in the snow and stalked off towards the building. Whira hesitated for a moment, glancing at the animals, then followed.

He had left the back door open for her, and as she closed it darkness swallowed them.

'Beds are upstairs,' said the voice of the shopkeeper in the dark.

* * *

She snapped awake in the pale light of morning, her senses attuning at once, terror and panic flooding her. Nothing was right. It was like waking up underwater, slapped out of unconsciousness inside an environment she had no business being in. Then Whira remembered—she had woken inside a game. She stared out of the window at a field of snow unspoiled by footprints, the trees risen once more to drink in the imagined rays of three virtual suns.

This wasn't how things were supposed to have happened. She'd left her lover back in Lihreat, rejecting the dormant embryo he'd given her, quite aware that she was unusual, unfeeling in some way, longing for adventure over anything else. It was a waste of life to sit hemmed in by walls, when there was a galaxy out there to see.

'So, you're awake.'

She turned from the window. It was the shopkeeper, ghostly pale in the light. His blue eyes appeared to have drifted even further apart over the course of the night. 'Are you ready to go back now?'

She nodded, rising from the bed and following him downstairs. He'd opened the door already and was waiting for her, standing against a dazzling backdrop of snow. One of the three-legged pack animals sauntered alongside, a star motif shaved into its thick wool.

No breakfast then, she thought, then called ahead to the figure marching through the snow. 'You don't have to come with me, you know.'

He continued pushing his way through the trees, with no indication that he'd heard her at all. Something large and feathered red and gold sailed overhead, pursued by tiny ships. They watched until it had soared out of sight, its thin screams drifting away with the tinkling background music.

'I want to see this doorway,' the shopkeeper said at last, waiting for her at the edge of the small, purplish forest. 'Show me.'

She pointed up at the rise, about to explain that he could see perfectly well without following her, but then her hand froze.

Someone was up there, skipping anxiously from foot to foot, apparently unwilling to cross the threshold. Nodo.

'Nodo!' she called, wading through the snow. 'I'm here!'

'Whirazomar!' he cried, staggering down the slope to meet her, his form snapping into the default shape of a Wumo as he sunk up to his knees into the snow. 'We thought we'd lost you!'

'Scrapher—'

'Yes. He hid himself in his room when people noticed you missing.' He paused, glancing over her shoulder. 'Who's your friend?'

Whira didn't answer, instead grasping the handle of the door that had reappeared on the snowy plain and pushing it open. The same twinkling sheen of oil seemed to coat her body and then she was through, back in the warmth and light of Gnumph's interior, her senses reawakened.

'Scrapher!' she raged. The thump of feet and a door slamming distantly was all she received by way of reply. Whira scrabbled for the ladder, rising awkwardly to the next floor and somersaulting, Gnumph's stomach wall becoming her floor. She arrived at the cursed creature's door and slammed her palms against the wood, then drifted to her own room and retrieved a whisperlock, planting it with a satisfying thump on Scrapher's door. It grew tendrils of pinkish, brittle light, blanketing the wood. There. He was locked in now, her prisoner until she could bring him before a Lihreat magistrate.

She returned to the doorway with the intention of saying a grudging farewell to the shopkeeper. The cold, mountainous landscape, when viewed through the doorway, looked suddenly unreal. Whira could barely remember being there.

She tried to meet the eyes of the shopkeeper as she went to the door, the virtual cold unable to penetrate her warm interior world, but he was gazing instead with an intense curiosity into Gnumph's belly, eyes shimmering as they took it all in. The animal, still at his side, stared blankly in at her, as if possessed.

'We should let them go, Whirazomar,' said Nodo at her side, grasping the handle of the door. The shopkeeper made no sign that he had heard. Nodo closed the door in his face, the three-legged creature peering avidly around the edge until the infrasphere disappeared with a click.

Nodo turned and leant his back against the door, breathing heavily. He squeezed his eyes shut.

'What was that about?' she asked him, not particularly upset that she never got to say her goodbyes.

Instead of answering her he pressed his skull to the door, listening through the wood. Whira knew that was pointless: the infrasphere could not penetrate the solid, real world; they could not be heard from inside. She whispered when she spoke, nevertheless.

'What is it?'

Nodo looked at her at last. 'Shut it off now. We need to shut it off.'

She stared at him.

He cradled his head in his hands, muttering and whimpering, and it was only after some repetition of the same word that she finally caught his drift.

'That thing,' Nodo said. 'That black animal in there.' He glanced at her. 'I've played in the infraspheres before, I know the codes people use.' Nodo pointed at the door, his pink eyes never leaving hers. 'It didn't have any. Just the symbol of a sun.'

She waited for him to stop shaking his head and muttering. 'You mean the star? What does that mean, Nodo? What does a sun mean?'

Nodo was staring fixedly at the closed door. 'Sun means *Throlken*. That was a Throlken in there.'

FLICKER

Since the enforced shut down of room six and nine's virtual dimensions—the infraspheres winking out to reveal bare rooms filled with skeletal, dust-caked cadavers, the remains of infrasphere junkies who'd chosen never to leave—the passengers had to make their own entertainment, staging shows and Myriad-generated plays in the commons and gambling with real live money, the meagre stocks of Flickerfolk brought on board in everyone's purses.

Whira watched Nodo pouring a measure of his glittering fluid currency for Mobe, who appeared to be raking in quite a share throughout the extended trip. She hadn't ever made use of the living currency herself (conducting all her transactions, like any civilised creature, in Promise), and watched with mild interest as they were bet, lost and won.

Though the Flicker couldn't reproduce, they were effectively immortal, and most of the miniscule silvery things traded tonight would have been gambled and lost in ages gone by. They were organised by size and species into special denominations, were impervious to fire, radiation, vacuum and every known poison, and let out a shrill and glass-busting scream if they were stolen or mislaid. It was a form of slavery, Whira supposed; that the Throlken were the ones responsible for the Flicker's inception spoke volumes of their cruelty. The tiny creatures were farmed on a single, prodigiously fortified world under the direct protection of the Throlken themselves, the trade in decillions of imprisoned beings forming a crucial mechanism of Yokkun's Depth's economy. Physical transactions of any other nature were formally forbidden across the galaxy, but Whira had nonetheless heard of every conceivable currency under every sun being used in a pinch, from the carved cubes of frozen nitrogen exchanged on the water moons of Plothe, to the molten Horag sap that cooled and hardened at different elevations, to the burning, scented stick money of Udablo, which dealt with the trade of fine smells alone. She was sure the variations and inventions across Yokkun's Depth, its neighbouring galaxies and the Phaslairs above and below were uncountable, and felt her mind uncomfortably dilating at the thought of such an infinity of permutations. Whira rubbed her eyes; she needed this journey, this mission, to be done and finished, so that she could go back to her far-away home and think on lesser, saner things once more.

Tonight it was the musician Oldro's turn to perform, and Whira applied stick pads to her fingers and toes once more to lean at the railings and watch the rasp player—a gangly, six-armed being whose protective orange hotglobe occasionally billowed with smoke, as if it were leaking— tune up. Oldro had mostly kept to its room until now, but had dragged the huge instrument out at the other passengers' insistence. The rasp, which Whira had never seen the likes of before, was built from two large combs of treated cartilage, the surface of each tooth buffed and sanded to make a different texture. An elaborate machinery of levers allowed Oldro to swiftly scissor the blades together in hundreds of different combinations, snicking back and forth between them like a loom, its two-dozen clawed fingers (gloved in a shimmering, protective extension of its atmosphere) flitting between the strings. When the teeth came together they produced a shock of loud, atonal growls and groans that didn't sound much like music to Whira at all. Passengers covered their ears and sensory organs, scowled and grimaced and threw things until Oldro was finished, nodding contentedly to itself and snapping the toothy machinery of the rasp closed.

Whira remained on the balcony while Oldro packed its things away, eyeing the instrument's great jaws. She opened the palm of her hand and called up the Myriad.

'Show me again what they found.'

The microscopic entities did as she asked, sketching moving images a centimetre above the skin of her palm; true-colour, three-dimensional footage of the five-hundred-million-year-old bone pits found on the Nutolush moons. Whira had sent word to Lihreat some days ago recommending that they deliver agents to a handful of nominated planets that could conceivably be the homeworld of the signal, but the emissaries she'd spoken to seemed uninterested. Her mission was one of thousands ordered by the Alm Thelgald every day, and hardly a top priority—for all they knew this being would never appear, or bypass the Surface entirely, or arrive charmingly flummoxed, peering at its map and asking directions. Only the prospect of the secret it possessed interested anyone much, and the creature's history and lineage was viewed as largely inconsequential to the mission. Nevertheless, teams had at last and somewhat begrudgingly been sent. The fossil beds they'd located were the graves of an ancient species that had once lived close to the Well, and traces of their patchily translated literature revealed they had known of it and even used it, once upon a time.

Was this what she was looking for? Was this being one of them? Whira stared at the tracery of flat, mineralised bones, seeing what might have been an eye socket, or perhaps a mouth. She knew that time worked differently down there, in the deeper Phaslairs, but could it really have been wandering for all that time, alone, hungry to return? At times like this, she wasn't sure she wanted to meet it after all, and was momentarily glad of Thelgald's secret weapon, still locked away in the hold.

HOMEMADE

In the drifts—what was called an Estuary on the seven-hundred-year-old charts—beyond the shattered outlying moons of Zira's Gate, they heard what might have been a voice. It wasn't in any language they knew, and a lengthy consultation of the index told them it wasn't in any language in the hard stores, either.

The garish shanty-shape of the homemade, studded with dishes and turrets and improvised towers, altered its course, rising with a burst of its great exhaust through the waste cloud of wreckage and pulverised rock to home in on the signal, which originated somewhere in the ruins of the system.

Look, said the navigator through a shadow pattern cast onto the inside surface of her translucent wings, peering into her readouts. The signal operator came flitting over to join her in the glow of the plastic screen, perching with all four tufted arms and rasping rancid breath over the navigator's shoulder. *It's reflecting all over.*

Hard stuff? Impossible.

It's got to be.

Metal. Since the tax, such things were unheard of.

They powered into the system, heading straight for the strengthening signal.

The crew readied the hatchway, fluttering up and down in the spun gravity of the homemade's interior, a swarm of multicoloured shapes bobbing about in the warm, pungent air. *Iron, steel.* The rumour had spread through the dingy, rubbish-stacked hallways, up into the wooden, plastic-sealed lookout towers. They were rich.

Eighty-eight miles out from axis south, said the signal operator, flicking a dial. *Should be able to see it in—*

A spot of darkness in the flecked white void, the ruined globe of Zira rising hazily below to port. The spot grew in size until it was a shard beneath them, a drift of smoke wreathing its fins. Part of it lay open to the cold, and for a moment before the tiny ship fell under their shadow the navigator could see a suited figure in there, gazing up at them.

Live occupant, said the navigator, arching the frilled edge of one wing and wriggling the digits on her third limb to create complex, coloured shadow-words against the membrane. *I saw it. Looked bipedal.*

Bi—you mean a Maleurin? The signal operator withdrew his arm from inside the sail-shaped flap of his wing, replacing it a moment later. *No. They'd be long gone. The Maleurin worlds were near the epicentre.*

The navigator thumbed the picto with her muscular first arm, momentarily lost for words. The ship really was metalloid, constructed like an infant's block toy of crudely salvaged parts and pieces, with what looked like twin ramscoops bolted to its stubby wings. An escapee from somewhere, possibly, ostracised or shipwrecked. But the fuselage and engine cowling were patched together with hard stuff, of that she was certain. The find of a lifetime.

Cut all signals and let it in, the navigator said, bobbing her long neck and splaying her wings to shield her naked hand signals from the others. A broadcast about this from any of the crew and they'd never make it out of Zira's Gate alive. She plugged into the comms, flicking through the dim, patchy readouts on the screen. A few precious drops of tin for the circuits were all they were allowed. The navigator's fingers hadn't touched the stuff for years, she could hardly remember the feel. Cold, she thought. Smooth and slippery, like glass. The idiot occupant of that ship didn't know the pain it had brought upon itself by opening its channels and calling for help.

It's a fool—it deserves to die, she thought, the pulse quickening in her clammy fingers. *And we deserve to be rich.*

The navigator and the signal operator looked down at the sleeping form. It had stumbled aboard leaking all sorts of pungent, horrible fluids. They'd had no choice but to gas it with a haphazard pan-species sedative, before strapping it to a couple of pushed-together medical perches.

So, they think it will die, the navigator said in shadow puppetry from behind her backlit wing.

Soon? The signal operator unfolded his wings and sat forward on his haunches, angling his frilled node of a head closer to examine the beast. They had pulled the crude helmet off to reveal a bony, elongated face stippled with wiry outgrowths of fur and angry sores. An eyelid had torn free, leaving one perpetually staring eye. The mouth, missing a great many teeth, was pouched at its corners, like a deflated sack. The eight-fingered hands were scabbed and scarred.

Any moment.

The signal operator shrugged a wing across his body, playing out the words with flickering, light-emitting fingers. *I say we wake it, then, before it can take its secrets with it. Wake it, and keep its answers for ourselves.*

The navigator stared at her colleague for a breath, then turned to glance at the door. There was no surveillance in the medical pod.

We have all we need here to cause it maximum pain, the signal operator said. *Let's do it, quick as we can.*

The navigator swayed on her haunches, thinking. *Give me a moment, I'll heat up some tools.*

The signal operator clapped his four hands together softly and watched her rise and flutter out of the pod. He turned back to the dark body of the creature, leaning slowly over to peer into its face.

A sound like clapping must have woken me.

One eye opened, the other wouldn't. Glued shut by something. Scents I hadn't smelled before, sharp and sweet, lying just atop the miasma of my own waste that was almost unnoticeable after so much time spent sloshing around inside my suit.

The first thing I saw was something winged and colourful hovering over my face. A four-fingered hand, its tufted fingertips glowing, appeared at the edge of my view.

Food.

I struck, opening my extendable jaws and snatching it up.

The thing didn't have time to struggle. I sat up, popping my shoulder restraints and hauling the creature towards me by its arm. My own hand darted out, seizing the creature's stubby leg and digging my claws in. Only then did it recover from its shock. Three remaining arms emerged from beneath leathery, translucent wings, slapping and clawing. Besides its ragged breathing, it made no sound.

I bit down hard, wrenching the creature's arm from its body, and burst out of my leg restraints. Only a thick, padded section still held my waist tight.

The creature in my grip was making frantic patterns with one hand behind its wing. I paused, watching the colourful shadow display for a moment, then took its wings in both hands and ripped them off.

I was still trapped, though my legs and arms were free. I dropped the twitching thing and glanced around at last. The spherical chamber was moulded from translucent plastic, the walls lined with racks of rubbery instruments.

Another of the hovering creatures appeared in the doorway, carrying a tray of gently smoking wooden implements in two of its arms. The thing saw me sitting up, noticed the remains of its colleague and made an about-turn in the air, dropping the tray as the door snapped shut behind it. The smouldering tools fell, scattering on the floor of the pod.

I twisted to watch as one came rolling over to rest beside my makeshift bed, the ember at its tip still glowing.

I waited, detecting the first waft of melting plastic. The other tools had started their own miniature fires all around the pod, but none had come to rest so close to a large, flammable object as the perch I was strapped to. It flickered into flame and I willed it to climb higher, the stink growing stronger, watching until it licked the edge of the bed, sooty coils of smoke rising from it. I rolled my body as far from the tongue of flame as I could, watching over my shoulder as my waist restraint began to bubble and smoke where the flame had caught its edge.

By now one side of the bed was aflame, and the pod was filling with smoke. The curved wall caught, sagging and melting into pooling, soot-dark stalactites. I waited, feeling the warmth caressing my back, then wriggled my waist, sensing more freedom of movement. Finally I attempted to sit up. The plastic restraint, now soft as warm wax, stretched with my body. I grasped it in my hand, scalding myself, and tore it loose.

I was free.

I sat up fully, lifted an aching arm and poked my unresponsive eye, feeling it loosen and come away in my fingers, dragging as I tugged on the optic nerve. A prick of pain and a flash of colour and then it was gone. I tossed it away.

They had tried to open the suit, but only succeeded in releasing my helmet and peeling back some of the treated leather on my leggings. I shifted on the flaming bed, peering through my single eye at the mess of my exposed leg. At the far end of the pod was a plastoid mirror, and my hazy reflection.

It was not encouraging: brown, dripping beard, one livid red eye socket that wept blood and clear fluid, pus-florescent sores sprouting from my bald, scabbed head, nearly every tooth missing.

I levered myself painfully off the melting remains of the bed, staggered and almost lost consciousness. My one remaining eye was blinded by dancing spots. A flash of terror like vertigo struck me then, for the first time since my incarceration. I was going to die. All that I had done, all of it would have been for nothing. An emptiness crept in at the fringes of my vision, a sudden and complete awareness that there would be nothing more, for ever after, and that it was coming soon.

I had built a weapon out of parts scrounged from the mine, and I searched in vain for it, peering in a circle. A puddle of browns and yellows had spread across the flaming floor from the opened leg of my suit, and I almost slipped.

The pod was melting, its ceiling drooping overhead. I watched a dribbling hole appear in the wall, revealing a passageway beyond. A hint, I hoped, of things to come.

SLARSEGORN
PHASLAIR 17,039

Slarsegorn's Home looked, from a distance, like any other small, bright planet: a relatively young, ringed world, orbiting one of a cluster of stars inhabited by this Phaslair's iterations of the Throlken and Irraith. But the vessel Draebol had chartered into the system was not like others he'd piloted in other realities: the starsteel bulb was spined all over its chassis with mile-long, electrified antennae that dragged behind it in the solar currents as it approached its destination, at which point the first hint of what it was protecting itself from became apparent.

The planet was not fully whole. It had been bitten into like a ripe fruit and inhabited by something more enormous than Draebol had ever in all his years encountered: a coiled parasite that had bored its way into the crust of the world and settled inside, ensconced and dozing and open-mouthed for many millennia, the rubble of its excavations now encircling the world in the form of wide, russet rings. Draebol made out the gappy rows of country-sized, rotten teeth that lined the hole in the world like mountain ranges, their worn peaks whitened with frost, a jumble of broken incisors towering like spires amongst them. The mouth's interior dropped into a void, a dark throat many thousands of miles across—so vast that great weather systems churned and flickered inside.

The planet Slarsegorn had taken for itself had been ruined by its invasion, and what was left now as a shell around the beast had become a frosted wasteland too frail to hold onto much of an atmosphere. But life somehow abounded on the world of Slarsegorn's Home in its millions, a thriving network of trade and industry uncommon in these wild parts.

It was the creature's gargantuan teeth that had been inhabited—a wormy network of fissures and bore holes in the range of stained ivory peaks becoming visible as Draebol drew closer, their mathematical regularity and rule-straight lines all that gave them away from orbit.

Draebol took an unpleasantly vertical room inside the outer layer of a tooth, paying extra for additional height, as well as a circular window that looked out across the gulf, the far teeth almost invisible in the haze. Moisture collected on the window's pot plants, watering downy white succulents, and now and then a chilly wind moaned through the pores in the enamel wall. He looked at himself in the polished surface of the wall for some time, before climbing awkwardly to the clothes rack.

His new body was tubular, silver-furred and beaked at one end. His three ruby eyes, arranged vertically, were mostly hidden amongst the wispy tufts that carpeted his belly. Two joints of his elegant single limb were suctioned so that he could stick to the sunlit wall—only after a few nasty falls had he understood that one furred suction cup must remain always in contact with a surface—and endowed with several long fingers at one end, which he used to sort through the few articles of leathery white clothing he'd bought earlier that day.

He was middlingly intoxicated, as was usual, hovering in the sweet spot where everything was as rosy as could be, the future ripe with possibilities. Doubtless this place would have been just as wonderful experienced sober, but Draebol had long accepted his lot as someone who thrived under the influence, and since a well-timed Drop rendered hangovers or any kind of bodily damage obsolete, what harm was there in a life of indulgence? Oh, he supposed he might accidentally overdose on something *one* day—as his brothers and sisters had warned, long ago—but until then he planned on damn well enjoying himself on every level of reality he could find.

Once he'd selected an outfit, Draebol went to work trying to put it on without unsticking himself from the wall and dropping twenty feet to the bed shelf, wondering—while he cursed and fiddled with the hooks of his new shirt—just what he'd got himself into. Phaslair 17,039 was a curious place indeed, and this volume was home to a menagerie of outsized species that Draebol had never encountered the likes of on his travels before. Their groans and howls had reverberated from his ship's sensors as he flew, vibrating the equipment with haunting song. Most settled planets and habitats here had long ago equipped themselves to deal with these goliaths of the void (throwing up flexible orbital barrages of electrified spines longer than a solar system that irritated anything sweeping in with its mouth open for a gulp) and vast pan-species corporations disported themselves around the systems, engaged in hunting the creatures to extinction, their flesh and blubber fuelling entire interstellar civilisations.

There, outfit on. It felt a little tight, and he hoped he had it on the right way round. Draebol scrabbled down to the mirror again, inspecting himself. The only way to know for sure was to go out and socialise, he supposed.

'Slarsegorn has fasted a long time,' the black-furred female said as she dangled from his balcony. Draebol had forgotten her name almost at once, and it was now far too late to ask. 'He must be getting hungry,' she added, shifting to change the track on the wall-mounted speaker so that another squealing, jangling piece of music began.

'How long has it been?' Draebol asked, wincing as the chorus started up.

She shrugged, her second, narrower tongue darting out to polish the silver-shod tip of her beak. 'Something big must have come close to sniff around in the times before the city was founded. We still find seams of fossilised flesh here and there in the molar ridges, down deep.'

Draebol couldn't quite imagine it. He passed her the bowl, his three-eyed gaze drawn to her tubular, principal tongue as she drank, guessing from his own interest in it that the organ served more than one purpose. He was now quite thoroughly sozzled, and things were going well.

'Doesn't he get tooth rot?' he asked, refilling their drink and selecting as a garnish some deep frozen, brightly coloured little creatures. One or two were still moving, blinking sluggishly and uncurling tendrils as they were submerged into the room temperature liquid.

'Hmm?'

'How does he clean his teeth?'

'We do it for him. The Dhimhall founders hunted his natural cleaner beasts to extinction, so it's our job if we don't want to deal with fractures. Mining will do that soon enough, though, if they keep drilling.'

Draebol gazed out at the view, a cold wind tickling his fur. The sprawling kingdom of Dhimhall was completely self-sufficient, extracting every mineral, fuel and element it could ever need from the substance of the teeth it bored its way ever deeper into. Weed forests grew in abundance amongst the molar ridges, their wild occupants hunted for food, and power stations glimmered in the valleys of the creature's receding gums.

Out amidst the suggestion of the rings, he could see thousands of twinkling sparks, too bright to be stars in the daylight. They were orbital stations, each watching the heavens for any sign of the leviathans that prowled beyond the heliosheath of the system sun.

Draebol took the empty bowl when she handed it to him, setting it down on the sill beside his charts. It was a relief to be able to talk again. His excitement at finding a Lawless Phaslair had faded rapidly. They were dangerous places, and whoever was sending his surveyor's fee hadn't yet acknowledged his tip off. Perhaps it was an automated system. Perhaps it wouldn't reply at all.

'You know,' he said, slipping a finger around her hunched back and gazing up at the twinkling stations, 'I spoke with a Throlken once, in another world.'

She rolled her three midriff eyes at him. He'd already told her about the duel with the Invisible Viddar, the black gas Phaslair and his journey to the edge of the Forbidden Almoll, and was clearly pushing his luck.

'It's true,' he protested, and it was. 'I spoke with her, or him, or whatever, for quite some time.'

'Oh yes? I suppose you just strolled into a star, did you?'

He thought back to a time some thirteen years before, when he was just beginning the lifelong task of chronicling his fall through the Phaslairs. He had Dropped into a black-and-white-spotted gas giant orbited by a profusion of life-abundant moons, opening his eyes as one of the mile-long digestive tendrils that floated from kite-sacks amongst the cumulus.

'The species I lived with had a special deal with the Irraith, the plasma beings.' He glanced at her. 'I don't know what the deal was—they would never tell me—but I did them a favour that they couldn't pay for, and I was eventually taken before the Irraith themselves.'

He hadn't known what to expect. Vanishingly few had met the Irraith, and even fewer a Throlken. Rumours abounded about their appearance, none in any agreement. Some

Throlken were even said to have taken up residence beneath the bedrock of planets, spreading through the fissures and cracks and into every molecule of chlorophyll, filling jungle biospheres with their unblinking gaze. Others told of Throlken who inhabited certain favoured mountains, snoozing in the black gaps between mineral seams.

He remembered a month of hard bargaining bringing him before the gas giant's Irraith contact from the local star. The light the Irraith cast burnt a violent sunset through the clouds long before Draebol came close enough to see it, squinting against the glare.

And then there it was, blazing brilliant through the flags of the floating harbour. A flourish of colour, bright as stained glass, burnt from the corona of a form too bright to make out. The Irraith existed inside a sunshell—a soap bubble of agglomerated fields swirling with fiery convection— protected from the planet's own comparatively freezing atmosphere. The sunshell dimmed as he came before it, and he saw at last the suggestion of eyes—spots of glaring red that danced and smouldered, never quite in the same place from one moment to the next. The thing drew him forward with nothing more than its massive gravity, wisps of fire arcing inside the sunshell, and still all he could see were those glaring, baking eyes.

'How about you take me with you, then?' she asked, interrupting his reverie. 'Or do you just like spinning your tall tales to any female who'll listen?'

He smiled a smile that did not reach his eyes. 'It does get lonely travelling the realities,' he lied. 'But you know if you left with me then you could never come back here.'

'Here isn't so special.'

He nodded, another lie.

She gave him what appeared to be a searching look. 'We're agreed then? You promise? You're not just leading me on to get inside my beak?'

He held all three of her ruby eyes. 'Let's go, tomorrow morning.'

His plastic translator ring woke him up two hours later, pre-set, with a sharp buzz on one finger. Draebol rose quietly, still considerably intoxicated, and searched the vertical darkness for his luggage, bumping into things as he clambered. The sex was always disappointing for them, he was sure—in each new form he was a virgin, clumsy and untrained—but he hoped it was never dull. He glanced at the darkness where she slept, all ready to go, then remembered his charts.

He had opened them up so she could look at them the night before, and they still lay carelessly on the windowsill. Draebol scooped them up, glancing at a page as he buckled the spoolbook shut. The arrangement of the Phaslairs was charted in numbered loops and whirls, like a topographical map of peaks and valleys, labelled with warnings like dangerous reefs. He had noted every line and digit by hand, in hundreds of local inks and pigments, after conducting a series of brief physical and chemical experiments in each Phaslair he visited (buying and copying a local map of each iteration of the galaxy, if he could). No copies of his work existed, and if he lost these charts—as he almost had, many times, under the influence of countless drugs and stimulants and general overexcitement—he'd lose *years* of work; the notion chilled him to the pit of his alien stomach. Draebol stowed the atlas carefully away, locking it inside its wooden case and stuffing it beneath his folded, stretchable environment suits and emergency bottle of something strong at the bottom of the bag, glancing one final time at the range of mountainous teeth beyond the window.

He had tried exploring his own galaxy, his own Surface, once upon a time. But by the time of his birth there had been very little space left uncharted in Yokkun's Depth (where nearly every rock formation, lake, forest and lonely mountain road had already been named, forgotten and renamed a hundred times already), and Draebol wanted above all other things not just to make a name for himself, to leave a lasting legacy, but to actually step where no other had been, to look upon things that nobody else he knew could ever see. He could have set sail for another galaxy, he supposed, turning his sights to Salga Ehothalong, Zotulast or even Yokkunphirelleng (also apparently named after the mysterious Yokkun, whose influence must have been considerable), each fixed equidistantly around the branching, connected cluster of the Olas. Beings from Yokkun's Depth regularly made the journey across, but it took time, a span of thirty standard years or more, just to reach the closest, and only the most long-lived species took such pursuits seriously, developing a monopoly on the news and knowledge and wonder brought slowly back. And so instead Draebol had concentrated his attention on the peculiar science of the deep Phaslairs, and all the infinite mysteries they held, deciding that he was prepared to turn his back on his home Surface, family and friends forever in an effort to glimpse as many as he could.

He opened his elongated suit of Iliquin-coated armour, which had come through into this Phaslair in the shape of his own bizarre form. Draebol shrugged on his pack and climbed inside, locking himself in as quietly as possible. The interior was furnished with a clutter of life-support and heating systems, emergency supplies, musty blankets and communication apparatus. He pushed his arm into the gauntlet of the suit, activating the switch on the inside palm.

His sudden weight popped the membrane of existence in an instant, crashing like a meteor through the thin wooden floors of an infinitely tall building. As Draebol fell he remembered the story of some would-be adventurer swallowing an Iliquin pill once and boring a hole straight through herself. As far as he knew, that pill was still dropping—a bullet strobing through realities, piercing anyone and anything it happened to meet—and it would be falling until the end of time.

PROXIMITY

Outlying star cluster Baelziad now within signal range, Gnumph muttered through the walls.

It had been so long since they'd been in the vicinity of a single star, let alone any number of them, that Whira's entire body now tensed involuntarily, breathless as her hearts drummed. She used to gaze at the night sky and think of the minds that lived inside every speck of light, wondering if, in turn, they contemplated her. Now they had become spots of eerie, unfeeling intelligence that she must hide from, at all costs.

Could they defend themselves, if they were spotted? Whira didn't know what would happen if they used their Iliquin weapons to try to Drop a star. As far as she knew it had never happened, even in the Experimental Phaslairs. That wasn't something anyone—even the ancients, as far as could be discerned—had dared to try; displacing such a colossal mass of energy into the unknown depths below was a recipe for genocide, let alone the single fastest way of getting the Throlken's attention. It was, however, one of the higher spectrum orders both Thelgald and Phrail had issued—leaving nothing in writing, of course. Everything Whira and Gnumph did, they did on their own.

Her eyes flicked around the crowded amphitheatre of

Gnumph's stomach. Tatty washing had been pegged, weightless, from the balconies. It floated amidst the smoke and smells that rose in the updraft, and was getting dirtier by the minute. A few passengers milled around in the absent gravity, floating on their backs as they read or chattered to one another before supper. The Zabbas, coiled around the legs of the commons table, was scribbling his notes, smoke curling from his pipe. She would have to confiscate his work, she supposed, when this was all over.

'Is Scrapher in trouble, then?' asked Phathor, his shadow falling over the table, along with a steady stream of water droplets. Someone had spread their washing over his shell to dry.

Whira looked up from her drink, making a show of mulling the matter over. 'We'll see how he behaves when we dock.'

'They are taking this message very seriously,' Phathor said in a low rumble, after waiting for some of the other passengers to drift off.

She took a deep breath, inhaling steam from her mug. 'So it seems.'

'And how will you find this... being, when you have passed into the Phaslairs below?'

'The Myriad are following a Surveyor's transmission trail,' she said. 'According to my sources he's been down there a long time, and might have something in his possession that I can use as bait.' Whira rubbed her eyes and shrugged. 'All that's required of me is that I get close enough. Then we'll see if our masters are as clever as they seem to think they are.'

Around them the bustle and clamour had gradually increased as passengers quarrelled and jostled for access to the cupboards fixed along one curving wall. Iihi and Immonod had been nominated as onboard cooks, but that didn't stop some of the more antisocial passengers—many of whom never left their rooms for any other reason—from preparing their own exotic foods at the same time, and five times a day the commons became a seething mass of jabbering, floating life.

This evening they celebrated their return to inhabited systems, and Immonod had raided Gnumph's supplies for all the finest things he could find, delicacies purchased in Salqar before Gnumph left port: a box of leathery, long-forgotten munsillor hides, a glowing cask of Ubranese twinkle nuts preserved in larvas oil and some old, low-pressure bottles of gwar, many with pickled, unidentifiable things floating at the bottom. A few of the nicer passengers were even contributing their own stocks in anticipation of being able to resupply at Obaneo in a few days' time.

Immonod, a scarlet-scaled aquatic being festooned with bristling antennae and encased in a milky globe, did no actual cooking, preferring instead to hover high above the commons and grunt his orders to anyone who would listen. He never partook of whatever they created, either, keeping his own supply of food inside his globe. He grew excited now as the Sukopral was escorted in, lumbering on two thick, fleshy legs. Its small mouthparts, dangling somewhere in between its legs, munched from a nosebag while the rider, Nurtil, sat where the thing's thorax ought to have been, steering its course with careful taps of a wooden rod.

The milling passengers cleared a path for the waddling Sukopral, which came to a stop amongst them. Whira could smell it from where she sat.

Nurtil patted the thing happily and took a knife from her utility belt, clambering down. She began scraping away the fine downy hair around the Sukopral's haunches.

'Gently now!' chided Immonod from his place above them.

Nurtil sheathed the knife and produced a brush, dipping it in a tin of something and basting the shorn flesh on the back of the creature's legs. Sukopral had no pain receptors, and could be harvested for their living meat all day long.

'Not too much,' muttered Immonod.

Nurtil nodded irritably, putting away the brush and hefting a tool half her size, its ends carbuncled with a mass of attachments. The tool emitted a sudden, high-pitched whine, and the Sukopral snorted, startled. The rein slipped from Nurtil's grip as the Sukopral set off at a canter, bounding through the crowd and into one of the adjoining rooms. There was a rare silence as the massed passengers stopped to listen to Nurtil's distant cries, followed by the bangs and crashes of the Sukopral as it careened around, and then everyone went back to what they were doing.

Immonod grunted a laugh, returning its attention to the preparations by the table, where Iiihi and Mobe were tackling a large, quivering black cube of congealed singing sauce.

Obaneo is very beautiful, they say, said Iiihi with a flourish of painted writing from inside her environment case. *A Star Apse, quite rare*. Her casing was made up of a cone of clear glass filled with smoky-grey atmosphere and set atop a gimbal on which she rolled around all day, her interior form quite hidden. She assisted Immonod with his cooking almost every evening, and Whira had begun to catch some form of chemistry blossoming between the two wildly incompatible creatures. To cook, Iiihi employed a set of Every-Gel fingers that could set hard and reform to suit the task at hand, her hands warping between tools, the singing sauce squealing as she sliced.

'I can't even remember the last time I was in port,' said Immonod. 'Crowds! Strangers! I never thought I'd miss them. The occupants of this spore are testing my nerves.'

'You'll have your wish soon enough,' said Whira. 'I'm throwing everyone off at Obaneo, whether you like it or not.'

114

She flinched as something whizzed over her head, narrowly missing her horns. Though it possessed real weight and texture it was composed entirely of Myriad, its form changing into something new and random with each toss, transforming back into a fuzzy reddish ball of a few trillion Myriad, ready to be thrown again.

Snatching fearful glances up at the game was Wirrit, a flabby, white-furred triped clad in expensive antique woodware. He was scribbling something over by the fire with his pink trunk of a nose, filling sheafs of sticky notes with hurriedly scrawled messages and stuffing them into the flames.

'What's he up to?' Whira asked.

Iiihi glanced over. 'He's afraid. Writing benedictions to the Zilble.'

Whira studied the fluffy creature as he pursed the prehensile lips of his trunk, picking up the stylus once more and scratching away at his notes. He finished a page and held it to the flames. The Zilble was a mythical, all-seeing particle said to be more than fifty universes old. Untold generations had spent millions of years in this universe alone attempting to communicate with it in some way, unsuccessfully petitioning the Throlken (who were thought to know it intimately, though nobody knew where that rumour had originated, either) into providing an introduction. It was written that the Zilble visited each atom in every Phaslair once every zeptosecond, building up a near-perfect image of everything and everyone in existence, seeing all, hearing all, witnessing every microscopic thought as it birthed in your mind. It knew you, they said, infinitely better than you yourself ever could. How it had survived so many seventeen-billion-year cycles—rising and falling beats followed by eventual heat deaths and crunches—of the universe's continually regenerating heart was just one of the volumes of questions the various mystics and religious sects wished to ask it, if only they could get the damn thing to reply. Offshoots of these religions had become convinced that the Zilble lived a vibrantly social life, interacting with a host of other particles and nanoscopic beings whose existence was also mostly hypothetical, from the Ambient Svesh and Qom to the larger scale Myriad (who would neither confirm nor deny that the Zilble spent any time amongst them, or if it existed at all).

'Should have left when I gave you the chance, shouldn't you?' Whira called over to Wirrit.

His six eyes darted to hers. 'Are you sure the Throlken can't see inside here? What if they lied?'

Whira sniffed, finishing her drink. 'I think we'd know by now.'

Wirrit finished another note. 'But what if it's a trap?'

It was possible, she supposed, but she wasn't about to admit that to the passengers. Subdimensions—known widely as *bubbles* or *shallow Phaslairs*, like Gnumph's belly and those her lump of Arqot projected into being— were supposed to be beyond the Throlken's sight. Only one test had ever been proposed—something tried before, with middling success: to commit murder inside one.

Whira considered the lurking prospect of Scrapher, still locked in his room. The perfect test subject. Subdimensions remained a grey area when it came to Throlken observation for the simple reason that only the bravest dared try killing anyone, and when it *had* worked (apparently without retribution) conspiracy theories abounded that the Throlken had simply turned a blind eye. Why play their full hand, when they had effectively convinced the galaxy that subdimensions were hidden to them? Whira could imagine playing a similar sort of game were she a similarly omniscient entity, lulling her subjects into a false sense of security so that she could watch them unawares.

She frowned as she observed him writing his prayers, the smoke making her eyes smart. 'Stop burning those damned notes, for a start.'

Wirrit glanced at her, his pen poised. 'What? Why?'

'Well, the Throlken are made of fire, aren't they?'

Wirrit gulped and withdrew his trunk from the page as if it were infectious. 'I can see it now,' he whimpered. 'My brain zapped to... to *mush* as I set foot on Obaneo, just for being complicit, no matter that I'm a hostage in here.' He looked at Whira with frightened little eyes. 'Is it true you can't be resurrected? If I changed my death wishes and left you my what was left of my brain, in a jar or something, to be rebuilt one day, somehow—'

'I couldn't go near it, Wirrit,' she said, enjoying his look of abject hopelessness. 'You know I couldn't.'

Wirrit nodded sadly, filling his flask from the pitcher and floating away. Whira watched him go.

'There was no need to frighten him even more,' said Phathor.

Whira shrugged. 'I spoke the truth.' As a child she had seen one of her classmates struck down for swinging a blade too close to another. Their tutor had opened up the little Lazziar's horned skull there and then to confirm it, all of them crowding around the corpse, and Whira vividly recalled stepping back as the liquid remains of the poor thing's mind spilled out across the floor. Brains, once pulped by the Throlken, were cursed objects that nobody wanted to get within a few meters of, let alone touch. As a deterrent, people who did anything other than flush the brain-waste away were targeted by the same invisible pulse of terminal energy—a lesson it had not taken any species long to learn. Whira supposed it was perfectly possible that a Throlken-liquified brain could be reanimated (the way anyone in civilised Almolls who happened to die from massive accidental trauma—falling from a great height, for instance, or being eaten by some wild creature—could be fixed and sent on their merry way if found in time) but the act was forbidden.

The Great Zabbas snickered to himself from beneath the table, the fat, serpentine lower half of his body draped over a chair. He uncoiled with a wheeze of effort, his neck rising at the far end and looping around another chair for purchase. Like Wirrit, he had been scribbling his own spiralling notes, though one of his five independently moving eyes seemed to be watching the Myriad play going on in the background. Another eye twitched to study Whira.

She gazed calmly back.

'I suppose I should thank you, Whirazomar,' said the Zabbas. His voice creaked like a warped plank of timber. 'This detour is just the sort of thing my readers will like. Something a bit different.'

'I'm glad to be of service.'

The Zabbas brought his jowly head closer. His sunken cluster of eyes were also, upon closer inspection, transparent. 'The last time I had a delay like this I was on my way to Salga Ehothalong. The Wanderer I'd booked passage aboard became unwell and had to find a rock to go to sleep inside. Took us a year to locate anything suitable, and then another three while the beast regained its strength.'

Whira had heard of such famous delays: the Ehothalong galaxy, though it was the nearest in the Olas, was by no means an easy journey. 'You found a way to pass the time?'

'You can go anywhere if you're not in a hurry, and I had my notes to write up, my drawings—which of course you will have seen if you've read my book...'

He eyed her, waiting.

'It's on my list, I'm sure.'

The Zabbas sighed theatrically, waggling one of his stunted limb flaps in the direction of Shumholl. 'Go and fetch my copy of *The Road to Na* from my room.'

When Shumholl had returned with the chunky spoolbook, the Zabbas rolled it out for her. Whira leaned across the table politely. Sketches of celestially beautiful creatures interspersed with dense, nested circles of text decorated the plastic pages.

'No trace of the Throlken over there,' said the Zabbas, circling the air above the table, absorbed in his own work. 'They do as they please in Ehothalong.' He gestured with his pipe stem and Shumholl unrolled another page. 'But there is chaos there, and I grew homesick for order. I didn't stay the full term.' His gaze drifted to a contents page, littered with more fabulously coloured drawings, before snapping back to Whira. 'See that you order a copy when we get to Obaneo. Better still, the series—I went to Salga Izadrijjin too.'

'Quiet!' someone croaked from over by the far wall, and they turned. The epic had reached a suitably emotional act; the two leads (composed completely of Myriad) were embracing. The Myriad characters turned to Whira, their three-dimensional faces glaring at her. It was a remake of a sequel that she hadn't seen (every original idea in the galaxy having been rehashed several hundred thousand times over, at least), but she knew the gist. One of the lovers was secretly a disembodied Irraith, one of the star folk descended to live amongst mortals for a day only to fall head over heels for its host. Whira thought the whole genre was quite the most childish entertainment imaginable, and was rather disappointed with the Myriad for indulging their audience. Said audience, however, was loving it, and could only be peeled away by the smells of dinner, which was now very close to being served.

Whira propelled herself to a nearby cupboard, searching for the condiments, which were always being misplaced. The cupboard swung open to reveal a hovel stuffed with tiny furniture and books. A small bald creature shrieked and threw a shawl around itself, disappearing into a hole in the wall. Whira wrinkled her nose and closed the door again.

A dinner that was broadly acceptable to most of those present had been set out: a carved heap of roasted Ghomut (caught in the vacuum), sauteed unzo pods, Braelish soup and fried vurmsprouts, all stuck or tied or weighted down, blobs of this and that floating across the scene. There was no sign of either the Sukopral meat, or Nurtil.

Everyone descended to their places—stained, bowl-shaped depressions arranged along the length of the table—more than a few hovering overhead or grabbing what they wanted and rising again to stick themselves to the balcony railings. Those already sitting reached and floated across one another, drifting up out of their seats to catch thrown morsels and pots and cutlery, the smaller passengers darting amongst the crush. Whira observed with interest as some of them performed their various incantations before digging in, a small cross-section of the countless superstitions practised in Yokkun's Depth. Some made no sense at all, and were merely cultural hangovers: Shumholl the Xaal, for instance, dabbed the top of his skull with a wet finger before he ate, which accomplished nothing at all—the original mannerism came from a long-extinct species that had once occupied the Xaal homeworlds, creatures possessed of mouthparts on the top of their head. The two civilisations must have met and socialised in the Very Long Ago, she assumed, and the superstition was preserved. Others like Nodo, who possessed no teeth, swallowed a handful of small stones—prized treasures the Igmus kept on their person like personalised cutlery—before each meal, to aid digestion. Whira tried to avoid imagining Nodo passing the stones out again and rinsing them, ready to be swallowed afresh.

She let the Myriad cut her food for her. A few passengers

watched with barely concealed interest as a cuboid chunk of meat rose to her lips, as though by magic.

The diminutive Master Zees and his wife made their usual late appearance, floating over the table and depositing themselves at its centre, where they could most easily hold court and hear what everyone was saying (making sure to turn their backs on the charnel breath of Little Yith, which Whira could smell even from the head of the table). Zees clambered from his wife's nostril—where he seemed to live on a semi-permanent basis—and bowed ostentatiously to Whira. The small winged humanoid was a distant relation of the Igmus, and was travelling to one of his properties on Varamore in order to evict a late-paying tenant. Not surprisingly he had won little sympathy on board Gnumph, few of whose customers owned their own homes, or even had any permanent address at all. Zees had demanded his own room, despite being smaller than one of Whira's front nip-teeth. His wife, fat and taciturn and a hundred times Zees' size, slept in the hall.

Lucky arrived last, as always. The Orawi, an obese mound of mottled black flesh clothed in innumerable layers of foul-smelling rags, reached without ceremony into the heap of dishes and platters and swept Zees, along with a considerable amount of crockery and food, aside. Lucky, who had some unpronounceable real name that none of them had bothered to learn, was fumbling for something that had been eaten years ago and was certainly not there anymore, his great paws groping past pots and bottles, demolishing everything in their path. Whira moved her drink out of the way as Lucky found Zees' wife and lifted her experimentally to his wide green eyes, eyes that could see the past as well as the future. His irises contracted, the dark bowls of their pupils flattening as he inspected the squirming thing in his grip. Up until that moment, Lucky had been ambling around in a world that hadn't existed for some time, amongst travellers who had long since reached their destinations. The signals that arrived at his brain did so more slowly than in most other species, drifting through his hibernating ocular and acoustic nerves so that he lived in bygone days, listening to remembered conversations and occupying rooms that no longer existed. The delay had seemed to suit him just fine, aside from the odd catastrophic accident, but now, with Mistress Zees in his grasp, Lucky was summoning all his energy to accelerate the signals to his brain. Whira watched as his pupils swelled further, his ears pricking as he took them all in, and she nodded a hello. It was the first time, she believed, that Lucky had seen or heard any of them. His pupils continued to inflate, widening until his eyes became globes of shimmering black, and Whira knew he was drawing in a wealth of signals faster than any of them, effectively witnessing everything in advance.

Little Yith's rasping, phlegmy cough brought Whira back to reality, and she moved her drink once more as the spongiform being expelled a cloud of floating particles into the already dirty air. The swarm of detritus spread across the table, slipping into people's mouths as they opened them to eat and issuing back out of their nostrils or ears. Once the cloud reached Whira she saw that it was in fact made up of miniscule, curly-tailed seeds: baby versions of Little Yith.

'Even *Littler* Yiths!' cried Mobe in delight, scooping up a handful to admire them. They gazed up at him and wriggled in his fingers until he released them to their father, who gulped them back into one of his large mouths.

Whira was still trying to wave away the stench of the swarm when she felt the rumble through the soles of her bare feet. She glanced at Iiihi beside her.

'Was that you?' she asked her.

Iiihi's machinery swivelled and straightened, a painted scowl appearing on her casing as she realised what she was being accused of. *Certainly not. I think Gnumph's trying to say something.*

Whira listened again, sitting still amongst the riot of talk and music, then pressed her head to the sticky table. Nothing.

'Silence!' she yelled, thumping her fist down and sending scraps of food and blobs of liquid sailing in slow arcs into the air.

The table fell gradually silent.

'Gnumph?'

I said—I see flares, Gnumph said.

'What?' Whira asked, tipping her head up to the faraway eyes on the ceiling.

From the cluster.

The panic bubbled through her, rising with her body. She pushed herself out of her chair and then away from the wall, ascending to the magnoscope, her hands trembling as she grasped an eyepiece.

The distant, fringe stars of the galactic belly came into focus, their clustered light dazzling her for a moment. She blinked and pressed her eye to the scope again. Twinkling flares were dropping like fireworks from the cluster. The Throlken were firing plasma into the void. They had been waiting, calculating the most likely approach. It had begun.

She watched as the great fizzing trails of light poured through a misted gulf eight light-years across, their trajectories curving in the gravity of the stars. In the volume's planets, night had turned to day, all diurnal life snapping awake.

Detonations in the vicinity of the star Jomurus, said Gnumph through the walls. *I'm getting warning or distress signals, cut short at source.* Their pursuers from other Almolls, caught up in the distant rain of plasma, never suspecting that Gnumph would be going the long way round.

Whira swam down to check the map again, determining that they had passed below Plitipek's borders and were already on their way beyond the Well Station, with the intention of rising and looping back. They would be ascending sharply within the day.

Plasma ceased, said Gnumph, and Whira looked again. The belly of Yokkun's Depth, though still dazzling, was quiet once more.

Everything coming this way must have turned tail.

They were going to have to leave it until the last moment before they signalled the Well Station. Whira felt herself trembling uncontrollably, exuding spent adrenaline, and floated silently down through the haze of cooking smoke to the remainder of her dinner.

THELGALD

It was long past supper, and Thelgald was often tired when the time came to have their daily conference. Phrail, though he was some twenty-four thousand light-years away, operated within the shared time zone of the Exthis Accord—a grouping of four humanoid Almolls who had synced the days of their ruling habitats some time ago—and preferred to talk during the evenings (the Igmus were more productive at that time, he claimed). Thelgald looked forward to their agreed swap to breakfast calls next month, as long as the Igmus Alm didn't change his mind again.

Thelgald Zunusa Zelt Eryo of Silitahlm was only, at seventy-one years old, a decade into her rule as Alm of Lihreat, and understood she still had much to learn. The Throlken kept their anointed rulers on their toes, and things seldom went precisely to plan; for all she knew, her time as ruler was almost done, and she'd be cast back to her quiet little life before the year was up. She missed that old, vanished life so keenly that she often hoped the Throlken *would* find someone, anyone, else; the next ruler of Lihreat might not even be a Lazziar, despite their status as the most common intelligent species in the immediate volume. Barring complete self-sabotage, however, the chances of release were probably not in her favour. Her predecessor,

Orbinezamar, now happily retired inside an infrasphere somewhere, had lasted just under eight thousand years on the throne, and her counterpart Phrail boasted—regularly—of his solid tenure of five and a half millennia.

Just as nobody knew the full extent of the Throlken's laws (even after millions of years of deadly trial and error), the methods by which they chose their Alms remained an enduring mystery. One moment Thelgald—then a maker of bespoke wind chimes—had been out in her garden collecting a few sprigs of something for the pot, the next she was surrounded by a faint wisp of pale flame. She'd wondered at first whether she was dying, but the flame—though warm to the touch—had not harmed her. She remembered glancing skyward to see it rising into a tapering column, all the way to the sun. It had taken her more than a week to ascertain that the tongue of flame that connected her to the local star was not some long-winded joke of the Myriad (they were known for similarly cruel pranks, usually on people they thought deserved taking down a peg or two), and the reality of the situation had begun to sink in. Her old, quiet life was over. Phrail, the neighbouring Alm, had welcomed her to Salqar with great ceremony, showering her with gifts and proclaiming a new era of prosperity for the two humanoid volumes. From the Throlken, however, there was never a single word.

Speaking of the beast. There Phrail was, waiting for her as she walked into her office, a grand hollow bubble of intricately carved echowood a quarter of a mile in diameter. The seething-generated image of the Igmus Alm and ruler of all Salqar turned to examine her, his puffy face exaggeratedly pale in an angular grey tent of stiff, papery robes. As Thelgald closed the distance they performed the Yokkun standard humanoid greeting of spreading their arms apart in a proto-embrace, her own light, transparent skin-gown belling in the ever-present breeze that circled her huge chamber, and settled on their respective thrones; hers a squidgy lump of malleable and supremely comfortable doughstone, his a mirage of the ancient mirrorwood chair back in the vestibule of Salqar. The thrones drifted together into an uneven symmetry so that they could talk as naturally as possible, despite Phrail's considerable half-second lag (it was like speaking with someone who was ever-so-slightly distracted with what they were doing, minus the *umming* and *erring*). Then Thelgald summoned the Orrery.

It sprang into existence before them, filling the hollow space as snugly as a brain inside a cranium: a dazzling, rainbow-hued globe of influence encompassing not just Yokkun's Depth—caught silently at its centre like a vast, glowing sea creature—but also the few thousand outlying star clusters that clung like bubbles to the Olas's branching, thorny upper limb, and were therefore still under the Throlken's eye. The seven other galaxies in the chain appeared at the edges of her vision as floating symbols, enlargeable—if in somewhat reduced detail—if she desired to view or talk with them (though at a considerable delay and with every court translator working overtime), while only the very closest of the eternity of galaxy clusters beyond were represented by contact symbols—a few scant addresses she could call upon, this time with a lag of some years and in languages her specialists had only begun to get their heads around.

Salqar and Lihreat, both occupying the same limb of the galaxy, glowed into life and enlarged, rising above the churning blaze of star clouds to occupy a higher tier, followed a moment later by the thirty million or so information tags that sprinkled into life across the scene and swiftly nested inside one another for ease of navigation. Thelgald pushed at a node that sprouted from her seat, bringing the second tier—that of their respective Almolls—into focus for their preliminary talk, and turned to Phrail, who had already placed his small hand protectively over hers, the Microscopia hardening it to give a sensation of touch.

'I'm late for something,' he said. The voice from his toothless mouth was liquid and claggy. 'We'll have to keep it short. Talk to the others for me, make my excuses.'

Thelgald shrugged, irked by the way Phrail constantly assumed supremacy. At least the Microscopia were no friends of his: a life-sized image of him naked and dancing around the room flickered into existence beside him, followed a second later by footage of him saying unpleasant things about her.

'Enough,' groaned Phrail, hunching his body and turning away from the images. 'I haven't the time.'

'Neither have I,' said Thelgald in a gently scolding tone, tapping one of her horns to beckon them back to her. They were not wild Myriad, precisely—she had not yet won the favour of that enigmatic group—but the finest slaved Microscopia it was possible to purchase, known collectively as a seething. They swirled rather slowly back into place around her head, reforming as her Sovereign star high above the polished tips of her horns. She had seen the worst of her colleague a thousand times already, and the insults no longer stung. In fact, he had asked her more than once if she might consider unifying their two thrones, perhaps to produce a crossbreed child, but she'd turned him down every time, aware that she might have thought longer on the proposal if any union between them could have made a difference. The Throlken chose the succession, and nothing as primitive as genetic lineage had played a role for time out of mind.

'Now my darling,' said Phrail, settling back in his chair and turning his gaze to the Orrery, 'I hear the stars are acting up in Plitipek.'

Her pulse quickened; she hadn't expected it to be the first order of business, but supposed that was necessary if they wanted to throw anyone (or any*thing*) watching off the scent. Thelgald ordered up the volume in her Orrery, dropping back to the lower tier of the greater galaxy and scrolling spinward. A jungle of clusters were glowing pale green, signifying a mass eruption of plasma across more than a few light-years as the Throlken reacted to a perceived threat. *Acting up* was certainly one way of describing the situation.

Now it was her turn to play casual.

'*Something's* got them excited.'

'Mmm,' grunted Phrail at her side, apparently distracted by a person out of sight that the seething hadn't deigned to render. 'Perhaps we'll find out what it all means later. Perhaps we won't.'

Thelgald swallowed. The mission didn't have a name. It wasn't allowed one. They weren't even supposed to *think* about it, outside of their official subdimension meetings, which happened only every second month, and Thelgald had trained herself as best she could with the help of her court seer. The Throlken were not known to read people's thoughts, but it would be perfectly within their powers to observe the accumulation, encoding and manoeuvring of neurons or their equivalent inside most mortal brains. As such, the hiring and deployment of five different spores (two of which had already been destroyed by star flares) and an experimental crystal Sovereignty ship in different volumes of the galaxy had been arranged without actually discussing it overtly, and the assembly of the immersion materials organised in tedious slow motion and sent amongst innocuous shipments of parts so as not to draw attention. In the event that any of the agents were caught, their orders were to dismantle their cargo themselves without delay and commit suicide by whatever means available. Other Almolls had almost certainly also sent covert missions out to the Well Station, but luckily for her they all appeared to have done so on their own initiative, and couldn't point any fingers in Thelgald's direction in the event they slipped up.

'And,' said Phrail, 'in case you haven't seen it—new arrivals reported at Forbidden Edge, Ghort cluster. Salqar is observing them from half a lightspan out, standard hails ignored, as usual.'

Thelgald brought up the Forbidden Almoll, still reeling from their little display of playacting and hoping the thumping of her hearts wouldn't betray her. *I am being watched this minute, by who knows how many stars.* She stamped the thought down as the Ghort cluster sprang into focus, the projection extending almost to the membranes of her eyes so that it was as if she swam, god-like, amongst the drifts of the galaxy.

The Forbidden Almoll was one of the enduring mysteries of Yokkun's Depth, one of only a few decent riddles left in such a long-settled and comprehensively tamed galaxy. It was a volume apparently filled with planets and stars just like any other, and yet different in one crucial way: nobody was allowed within half a light-year of it. Anyone venturing closer simply disappeared. Or, more accurately, was never heard from again. The ships they travelled on continued to sail off into the distance between the stars, unresponsive, as though all aboard had simply vanished. Even the Myriad, famed for being able to squeeze into every nook and cranny in the galaxy and beyond, weren't exempt. Scholars of the Forbidden Almoll had been gazing at it for millions of years, peering as far as they possibly could and watching the seasons change on pleasant-looking but apparently uninhabited worlds, mystified.

But sometimes, every once in a while, things came *out*. The beings usually took the form of teardrop-shaped balls of dully-glowing light, and zipped here and there at the edges of their realm, engaging in bizarre and wholly incomprehensible activities that resulted in lots of light and noise and radiation, before disappearing as swiftly as they'd arrived. Any and all attempts to catch or interrogate them failed, and the beings had so far managed to slip through the grasp of every species who'd tried. Mentions of the beings and their odd realm could be found throughout the Gigaverses, and a great many theories abounded, the most common amongst them that everything glimpsed inside the Forbidden Almoll was a projection thrown across that region of the galaxy to conceal the last bastion of truly organic life (perhaps a stalemate reached during an ancient war with the Throlken or their predecessors, the Dzull); the lair of a colossal creature able to generate a protective globe around itself while it slept; or a great Throlken laboratory similar to other off-limits areas of Yokkun's Depth. They maintained a number of these, including the many experimental star nurseries (where the sun gods were believed to be tinkering with new generations and variants of stars to live inside), the Vusm Contraptions, or the incomprehensible Throlken machinery that surrounded the galaxy's central, long-evaporated black hole. Another popular theory was that part of Yokkun's Depth was simply missing, and a huge curtain of ersatz heavens had been slung across it to hide repairs being carried out. Nobody (least of all Thelgald, the ruler of nine billion stars) knew for sure.

Inside the Orrery, a ruby field of influence flecked with splashes of brilliant white opened like a flower at the edge of the mysterious volume—the competing interests of the Alms Faisstel and Ozulmorp, who had sent seething portraits for her that stepped from the mists of the galactic projection to speak. They had also lost ships at the edge of the realm, and wished to hear her thoughts. She switched the jabbering, exotically alien things to mute, to be heard later, and they watched, apparently sullen, as she turned back to Phrail.

'So, what's so important that you've got to cut me short?' Anticipating one of his customary obfuscations, she added: 'I'll hear it from my seething, one way or the other.'

Phrail sniffed, adjusting the origami edge of his robe. 'Well, you'll ruin the surprise then, won't you?'

She flicked a hand, not in the mood today. 'Go on then, be off with you.'

Phrail smiled an oily, puckered-lip kiss of a smile, and lifted himself off his throne, his image growing murky.

'Before you go,' Thelgald said, reaching out across the edge of his mirage, 'the Olas race.'

Phrail rolled his pink eyes and sat back down, puffing out his considerable belly and glaring at the galactic bubble, which zoomed out by orders of magnitude to reveal its seven neighbours, all bound together by the mysterious Olas. Salgas Zotulast, Gemit-Galazaph and Izadrijjin flickered, an array of data stippling into life beside them, denoting their entries in the race. Thelgald leant forward in her moulding seat, the weight of ornamentation her seething had layered onto her horns almost tipping her head. She surveyed the images of the other galaxies as their racing entrants were announced.

'Time to relay our best wishes?' she asked Phrail.

'Mmm, *quickly*.'

It was a grand spectacle; hundreds of competing craft from each galaxy zipping down into the depths of the Olas and back up again, a journey of centuries for most, though the record of a shade over two hundred years there and back had been claimed in the last race by a Mootpherl homemade.

The seething recorded them in full length as the two Alms sat side by side: an awkward message to an ungraspable number of subjects. They finished up quickly, knowing it was being edited as they spoke.

'Well, that was painful,' muttered Phrail, standing again. 'Until tomorrow.'

He dissolved at her side, evaporating before she could say a word. The spare few million Microscopia employed in rendering his form rejoined their fellows amongst the Orrery. Thelgald dealt quickly with the glowing pulses of petitions and requests across her realm, ordering up copies of herself and sending them with a flick of a finger into those volumes, where her portraits—complete with full scans of her brain—could answer any and all correspondence individually. The images of her counterpart Alms came forward again, tired of waiting, and while Thelgald conferred with them she zoomed idly on her own position, scrolling inwards until it was as if she flew faster than any ship ever made, soaring through a hailstorm of stars towards a great roiling landscape of tropical thunderheads and into the volume of Lihreat. The constellations that she knew so well resolved before her eyes, swirling past more slowly now as she lifted the pressure of her finger and slowed to only a few thousand times the speed of light, a flurry of bright pinpricks slipping to either side of her vision until the first suggestion of architecture rose out of the blue-green mist: the palaces at the centre of her Almoll, worlds garlanded long before her time with jagged petals of pale, self-replicating crystal, their planets sitting small at the centre like the luminous pistil of a great, glittering flower. The petals joined to form a monumental cupola, and it was in the crowning spire of this mind-bogglingly huge structure that she now sat, poised above her own home planet. Thelgald nodded absently to something someone said, scrolling out and up and travelling through the vast halls of her palace to the apartments of the Alm and zooming for almost a minute until she located her own echowood chamber. Her finger tapped the armrest, stuttering closer, until the seething painted everything she saw in absolute real time, and she was looking at the scene as though through their own eyes.

There, at the far curve of a room dominated by a riotously coloured swirl of information, a tiny blob of white. Her throne. And there she was, peering intently at a view of herself, a reflection within a reflection.

Her own face, staring vacantly into the Orrery, hovered before her. It was wattled with youth and still black around the eyes, her little upturned nose with its single nostril prominent in the fold of colourful flesh beneath the slit of her mouth, the bald top of her head embellished with a web of globular runes that wound their way up her horns to the glowing star of her office. Never had she seen anyone look quite so idiotic.

'Alm?'

The trance broke, her finger guiding the view back into the heavens by the twitch of a reflex, and she looked up. It was Ozulmorp, a massive, jowly underwater face that loomed out of the Orrery like a sea monster, still waiting for an answer.

She replayed what he'd said, blinking quickly as Microscopia whispered the particulars into her ear.

Thelgald sat forward again once everyone had gone, rolling her shoulders as her ornate headwear disappeared; the weight of real, conjured runes—a physical reminder of her duties—lifted, their atoms repurposed elsewhere. Her gaze flicked amongst the Orrery's depths, a roaming, silent map blossoming wherever she looked, but edged carefully away from a volume near the Obaneo Well Station, in Plitipek. When her eyes did chance to hover over that area, they did so only for the briefest of moments, before moving on.

APPROACH

The green expanse before them rose into eternity above and below, the stars swimming into focus as Gnumph slowed to a crawl and rose sluggishly through the warming volume of Plitipek. Here, closer to inhabited systems, the view was once again of a roiling emerald ocean merging with the muddy delta below. Uncountable generations of life had left their mark, filling the emptiness that once, Whira had heard, must have been black.

Gnumph was enjoying the renewed warmth of the stars, and hummed and groaned softly through its walls like someone slipping into a steaming bath after a night spent out in the cold. Whira found herself smiling, glad to hear it happy and cautiously hopeful that they might have weathered the storm. The spore, at least, had fulfilled its end of the bargain. She had no idea what they were paying it; for all she knew it was doing what it did for free.

They wouldn't see the thirteen-thousand-mile-wide structure of the Well Station until they were almost upon it, but ought to expect a blink-hail long before then. Whira watched, waiting. The Throlken had gone abruptly quiet, and any signs of being followed had vanished as Gnumph rose beneath Thron and doubled back, looping below the volume of Plitipek to rise once more.

The journey had taken seventy-three days. Seventy-three days of stink and filth and discomfort, as far as Whira was concerned. At the price of being a slightly easier target, she could have taken a crystal Sovereignty vessel and got here in less than thirty, swaddled in luxury every moment of the trip. If all went to plan, she would return that way, in glory.

'How long until—?' she began to ask, before the answer flashed across the scope.

The Throlken had awoken again. The inner stars of Thron flickered with a glitter of green-gold light.

'They're just guessing, now,' she said as she watched the detonations, a tremor in her voice.

Clever, mumbled Gnumph. *That's the route I almost took.*

She felt suddenly cold. 'Why didn't you?'

Because when I crossed from Zisayeph to Thron last, they'd started charging a toll.

Whira kneaded her knuckles, considering this, her eye still pressed to the scope. 'It won't be long until they turn their attention to the Well, will it? Should we make a dash for it?'

That's what they're watching for, I imagine. They're trying to flush us out.

She swallowed. 'Slow down, then?'

Gnumph seemed to hesitate. *I saw once, at a travelling show in Salqar, an approximation of how the Throlken see. I feared I would go mad where I stood, and a few others had already run out to void themselves in various ways. They'd warned me that I wouldn't get my money back outside—*

'Please, Gnumph, your point?'

Oh, well... You see, the Throlken's views of the heavens are linked, Whirazomar. Chattering to one another, their observations become one, capable of taking in the Without and the details of the neighbouring galaxies at the same time as they observe a scrap of rubbish cast out of a window in Silung. Very, very little escapes them, indoors or out, not least any irregularity, since they see always and entirely, without the need to blink.

She waited. 'Meaning?'

Meaning they will almost certainly have a picture of the motions of Yokkun's Depth as they see it, the course of every craft, every drifting body. They are watching even myself, you see, though so far with apparent ambivalence, watching and waiting to see if any of us change course or fluctuate our speed at the first sign of violence in Plitipek. We must stay our course, and keep calm.

Whira considered this, conscious that she would never fully comprehend the Throlken's reach, even when one had stood right at the threshold of the infrasphere, looking in at them. Alms of the past had tried all manner of tricks and distractions to avoid the Throlken's scrutiny, some conducting their affairs in deep fortresses drilled into the cores of planets, or at the very edge of the galaxy. It was only comparatively recently that the Alms had learned of the exotic photons the machine gods cooked up inside their stars, able to penetrate any and all materials, no matter the thickness or depth. The only place of refuge for the guilty appeared to be subdimensions, like Gnumph's marvellous belly, and even then, who knew for sure?

Gnumph swam up within the outlying worlds of Obaneo. The Well Station was still invisible from inside the system. The spore narrowed its many eyes against the glow of the star and opened its channels. The planets here were under the stewardship of a species called the Numongumuea, who had built, over millennia of careful secretion, a spined, nautiloid conch of glimmering material around their worlds, known as a Star Apse. It was an unusual arrangement, since most of the star systems in Yokkun's Depth relied

137

on sentinels to keep out the raging weather of the galactic currents. Sentinels were cohesive, layered colonies of wild Microscopia that mostly slumbered their lives away, rarely in the mood to converse with the flock of planets they contained. What they got out of the arrangement was not fully understood, though the sentinels appeared to function like giant digestive systems enclosing their islands of worlds, perhaps feeding off the waste products that the planets released from their atmospheres. Because they had evolved in orbit and were nearly impenetrable, a translucent peeling of dead sentinel flesh—known as slar—was much prized by the shipping industry, and guilds of merchants snipped and grafted vast fields of the patchwork to sell on.

Whira gazed out at the Apse, as large as a solar system, each planet lodged in the nacreous wall of the structure like gently rotating jewels. The star, Obaneo, lay deep inside, and its reddish glow shone through the shell walls, a sump of contained heat. It was a wonder the resident Throlken had allowed itself to be walled in like that, Whira thought, as the Apse grew before them.

I'll be docking at Obaneo's Daughter, Gnumph murmured through the walls. *For anyone wishing to alight here, please make sure you've collected all your belongings—*

Whira rapped on the wall. 'They're *all* getting off here.'

My apologies, rumbled Gnumph's voice throughout its innards. *All passengers—I repeat, all passengers—will disembark here, please.*

The planet in question drifted slowly into view, lodged inside a canker of worked, pearlescent calcium in the surface of the Apse. A corona of sunlight glared around its circumference, peeping through the mile or so of void where the housing encased the jewel.

Whira's eyes tracked the neon contrails of ships above the planet's atmosphere, her retinas stinging in the light that lanced from the Apse's reflective wall. She realised that

138

they were orbiting upside down, since the magnoscope was situated in what Gnumph would call its belly. It had been so long since she'd seen much beyond the claustrophobic interior of the spore that only some coughs and grumbles from other passengers reminded her that they, too, wanted a look. She floated reluctantly to one side, allowing Shumholl a peek, and propelled herself down towards the communal area. The chaos and bustle of passengers squabbling their way down to the cargo hold surrounded her, and she found herself smiling as she hung there, almost upside down, watching them prepare to exit her life—and the mission—forever. She would not miss them as she continued alone into the deep Phaslairs. Scrapher, still banged up in his room, would need to be taken down to Obaneo's Daughter and sentenced, not to mention that Jhahzang, wherever it had got to.

Whira opened her mouth to say as much to Gnumph when a gasp filtered from above. Some passengers, clustered around the eyepieces, were whispering frantically.

'What?' she hissed, flinging herself up to the ceiling and waving them aside.

Her pupil shrank in the glare of new light.

They had found her.

'Gnumph?'

I know, the spore rumbled, *taking measures*.

Whira pressed her eye to the scope again, watching the vast bulk of the Apse shift and rotate above them as Gnumph manoeuvred out of its orbit. Obaneo's Daughter shrank until it was one of many set into the great shell that surrounded the star. Her eye found its range, looking past a blur of nauseating distance and beyond to the surrounding stars, three of which had loosed a cannonade of blazing, curving light trails. They had timed it perfectly. They were waiting.

* * *

The closest star detonated like a cobalt firework, trailing slow, blazing tendrils, until all the milky green space around them was stained with falling sparks. As the spore dropped further, a forest of showering colour fell to meet them, surrounding them in light. Gnumph, soaring until it could use the Apse as cover, unhitched its Drop rifle and clasped it tightly in its fist, thinking fast. It could try to Drop as much of the incoming light as possible, but it would be like shooting individual raindrops in a storm. Gnumph aimed at one of the flares glaring above it, and squeezed the trigger.

The Iliquin warhead crackled as the charge ran through it, mixing with the glittering avalanche of Throlken light. Rivulets of falling plasma blinked out of existence, leaving molten emerald drops still dashing down. Gnumph accelerated and fired again, blazing a charge across the pale cloud overhead and vanishing more of the descending fire. A fresh, luminous shower fell in its wake. This wasn't going to work.

Gnumph fired rapidly, targeting and dropping, clearing a path through the deadly light and banking. The Star Apse took a first hit, blooming as an invisible current repelled the Throlken fire and sent it spraying back like bright, splashing water across the heavens, complicating Gnumph's dive with an influx of rebounded plasma. The spore darted, zipping along a lightning bolt's course of branching choices. Three stars opened into concentrated fire above; at last they knew where to direct their attack. Everything brightened, unbearable. Gnumph flew blind, spinning as a shockwave detonated nearby, a peel of armour flaying open.

We're Dropping. I need someone outside to help me with my suit.

The passengers stared at one another. Whira's breaths seemed to slow to nothing. It was happening too early, before they could reach the station.

140

No time! growled Gnumph, a vicious rumble they felt in their bones. *Someone has to help me mend my suit.*

'Alright,' roared Phathor, staggering up from his sitting position and lumbering over their heads. 'Open up, Gnumph.'

A whistling and popping assaulted their ears as Gnumph opened its secondary mouth and the barrier between dimensions thinned. Whira turned and gazed up at the third floor, half expecting to see the void. The crease that had been Gnumph's other mouth had become a tunnel above the balcony, a swirl of something that looked like snow drifting in.

Phathor was already on his way out. Whira opened her mouth to say something, but he was gone.

Phathor clasped the inside of Gnumph's lips and clung on, peering out at the blazing eternity as they dived between two great waterfalls of green light. The spore fired a shot, clearing a swathe of plasma and soaring expertly through the brief hole in its trail.

Much appreciated, Phathor.

'Don't mention it,' the giant muttered, crawling onto the stained green plating of Gnumph's outer armour and hooking his feelers into the crevices. He took a great gulp of air from inside his shell and poked his single eye stalk out into the freezing mist.

It'll need repairing, can you see?

Phathor tapped a claw to signal that he'd felt Gnumph's vibration, and climbed up to the rent area on Gnumph's upper back. Occasionally he glanced up at the vista stretching beyond, the distant glimmer of Obaneo and its mounted planets drenched in reflected light, a vast sea of trailing cerulean falling all around. The stars had spread out their electric tentacles, hoping to catch whatever they could.

Phathor stepped carefully over Gnumph's exposed eyes until he came to the buckled plate, straining to pull the peel of Iliquin-coated metal back into place while they swerved another trail of plasma, everything rushing and whirling overhead. Phathor hinged the metal tear closed.

'I'll have to crimp it closed. Let's hope it holds.'

Phathor took another gulp of air from inside his shell, spreading his bulk over the tongue of torn metal and hammering its edges down. Try as he might, he couldn't make it stay in place.

'I'm going to have to hold it together!'

What do you mean?

'I'll have to use my weight.'

Are you sure?

Phathor released the edge of the plate, which snapped back again. He knew enough that anything less than a full Drop would result in gruesome disfigurement, at the very least. 'I'll hold it shut, you go.'

Gnumph's vibrations stopped for a maddening interval as they wove through a gleaming forest of falling flares, seemingly as tall as the heavens. At last it spoke.

Tell me when. I need to get as close as possible to the Apse.

They darted, spinning, Obaneo rising closer. Phathor felt the momentum without the force, his joints aching, as light and colour swirled around them. He pulled the torn section shut once more.

'You're ready,' Phathor said when he was done. 'Drop.'

Thank you.

And with that, Gnumph simply ceased to exist.

Phathor spun, alone, tumbling amongst the pillars of green flame. He clutched the stump of his missing limb, having used it as a peg to keep the metal together, feeling the fearsome heat of a descending tentacle blistering his shell.

Phathor's slow thoughts led him to the only possible answer, and he closed his eyes.

BED AND BOARD

Draebol didn't like to wander too far from where he'd first Dropped, a place which had been known—on his Surface at least—as the Obaneo Well Station.

He'd chosen it for the simple reason that leaving from Obaneo was a considerably cheaper trip; you needed only a very thin coating of Iliquin to pass through the already frayed membranes of the Phaslairs there, where the Well cut the realities like a crack through layers of rock. The downside of this was that every other fool and would-be explorer took the jump at Obaneo too, congregating at the Star Apse for a week-long queue, and the day he'd departed for the worlds below the single air habitat in the water-filled station had been heaving with excited Droppers saying their final goodbyes to loved ones. In place of friends and family, Draebol had arrived with more baggage and useless equipment than he knew what to do with, most of which he'd since lost along the way.

The officials of his Surface station had issued him a chit for food and lodging at every Iteration of the station he might come across further down, and Draebol had dutifully used it at almost every Drop, approaching the local guardians of each Phaslair's Well and waving his credentials. The inside of any variant of the Well station was traditionally a place of sanctuary for Droppers far from home, loosely bound by the uneasy (and frequently violated) statutes of the interconnected Phaslairs and containing everything one might need to send messages back to your own Surface, and to collect monies or post sent from above. Any funds Draebol had once possessed had long since been imbibed and pissed away, and he relied now on the handouts of anonymous brokers whose messages were always terse and unfriendly, as if they suspected him of trying to cheat them.

He stepped into the cool darkness of Dobu-M'sira station, waving the pass on its chain to a member of staff. The being shuffled aside, using one of its palps to direct him towards the dining room, which was still serving their approximation of lunch.

Draebol thanked it and used the toilet first, reading a set of instructions on the back of the door and hooking half a dozen tubes into his large furred ears. The multi-purpose organs began to dribble at once, the building pressure eased, and Draebol sighed, gloriously happy and looking forward to the comforts of a private room and the bottle of Norbese spirit he'd hidden in his bag. After three nights spent sharing a filthy, cramped compartment on a desert train, he needed it.

He went in for lunch, selecting a decanter of sweetworms and surreptitiously adding a measure of contraband under the table. The Well Stations were traditionally dry—he'd been thrown out of more than a few—but this place looked nice and relaxed, even if the sensation of being watched grew stronger by the minute.

While he waited in line for the terminal he noticed a shapely female with the full complement of arms and orifices glance his way, and smoothed his ears back with a couple of palps.

"'Scuse me, is this the right line for calling home?' he asked, trying his best impression of a suave Dobu smile. He

144

could feel it coming across as a twitching leer, and smiled wider in an attempt to correct the problem. The Norbese spirit had struck hard already.

'Draybol Naglish Zit Thurn of Eldra?' she asked him.

'Er, it's pronounced *Nayglis* but yes—'

They came for him from all corners of the room, diners standing and unfurling their legs, servers clambering over the bars. Draebol counted six rushing towards him before a lightning bolt of energy erupted in his ten legs, the spirit roaring in his veins.

He reached the nearest window and clambered out into the heat of the desert, locking it shut behind him. A hairy, long-eared face appeared at the glass, its mouths open. Draebol's room looked out onto the little oasis in the Well's courtyard. He scampered up the wall and reached the balcony, swung inside and grabbed his things, running an eye around the room to make sure he hadn't left anything. He began to giggle as he heard the drumming of their feet in the corridor, hurling everything inside his ten-legged suit and vanishing from existence.

The sudden gravity well generated by his activated Iliquin pulled all the dust into the centre of the room in what was known as a Traveller's Disc. Only the strange ring on the floor and the echo of Draebol's laughter lingered under the vaulted ceiling, before that too disappeared, as if the Phaslair had realised that it didn't belong, after all.

Another world, another station. Draebol pushed the door open to his minimally furnished chamber, thumped into the room and sat heavily on the bed, five times his Surface size and more than a ton in weight. He was furious; there was even less money waiting for him this time, and the slap from the androgynous thing in admissions felt like a slab of rock had shattered across his face. He opened a canister of the bubbling stuff they liked so much here, drained it, and began to undress.

'Breaking through' wasn't really an accurate term for what he did. What actually happened was that the skin of the new Phaslair vacuum formed over its sudden interloper and coated them (as well as anything they brought along) from head to toe, altering them to fit into their new existence. As such Draebol usually appeared as a reflection of whatever sentient creatures were nearby, and this was the largest he'd been in some time.

Sounds outside his door. He turned, cocking his muscular, toothy head. He'd have invited them in for a drink if he wasn't already half naked.

But then he remembered the people waiting for him in the last Phaslair, that sensation of being watched.

The door burst in, splinters flying. Three heavily armoured officials pushed their way inside, finding nothing but an empty room.

FALL

Gnumph had never Dropped before.

It began with a sensation of instant, vivid vertigo, the senses inverting, and swiftly levelled to a crushing, rushing pressure that poured from every direction. The distantly analytical part of Gnumph's unusual brain knew that this was in fact the weight of the Iliquin armour forcing itself through the Phaslair membrane, and even had time to wonder whether there might not be easier, less violent solutions. After barely a second more Gnumph detected a change in pressure and then a subtle *elongation*, a thinning of itself as it drained through the hole in the membrane. And then it was through, birthed inside and coated by a new, ever so slightly younger Phaslair (which, truth be told, looked mightily similar to the last, barring the glaring disparity in the positions of the starfields around it). It had all happened in the space of half a second or so—more than enough time for the Throlken in this Phaslair to detect the Drop.

The stars targeted them once more, dazzling Gnumph with green-tinted light. It Dropped again.

And again.

* * *

Gnumph plummeted through cloud, the air thrumming and snapping at its tumbling body, spinning end over end until a forest of towering trees rose to meet it. It dropped between their thorny canopies, whipped from all sides, slapped and cut and scoured until a branch broke its fall and it thumped ungracefully onto the ground.

Gnumph swam in and out of consciousness. When it opened its eyes fully, it registered that the light here was very bright and dappled. It fancied it could see fewer colours than it usually could, though the memory of those colours was suddenly fuzzy. It checked its body, and was not surprised to see that this was not the one it had budded inside seven thousand years before. Its new self was something four-legged and bald, with a long tufted tail that twitched on command. There was nothing reflective enough nearby for it to see its face, though its skin was patterned with a mottling of bluish spots and freckles, and Gnumph had an idea that it was now about the size of a standard Salqar chair, unless it was very much mistaken. The lovely green armour it had been loaned in Salqar (doubtlessly now moulded to fit Gnumph's present form) was gone: lost somewhere amongst the trees, or still falling on its own.

Gnumph tried to stand, staggering on its newly acquired legs, and leant against a tree to spit a mouthful of thick, sweet black blood.

'Anyone in there?' it asked its own stomach experimentally, hearing nothing but the sigh of the wind in return. Its voice slipped out as a squeak. 'Hello?'

This wasn't ideal.

'Gnumph?' Whira called, floating up to the eyes in the ceiling. She usually felt the spore's intelligent gaze settling on her, but not now. There was still no sense of motion inside Gnumph's belly—they could be travelling at speed, or stopped dead: nobody could tell the difference. She peered into the scope, but all was black.

'What about Phathor?' asked Nodo in a whisper, rising to meet her. Below, a swirl of passengers had begun issuing from their rooms, an assembly of distant, colourful faces staring up at her.

Whira didn't answer. She didn't know. They could be anywhere, or nowhere. Perhaps Gnumph had already been taken by the Throlken.

Or killed.

Trapped inside the belly of a corpse.

Gnumph made its stumbling way through the woods. It wasn't the first time it had been in scrapes like this, but Dropping to a younger Phaslair was a new experience. It could only assume Whira and the rest of its paying passengers were still alive in there, trapped but safe in the subdimension bubble. To think anything else would be counterproductive, and wouldn't change the fact that it needed to find a way across this world to the local iteration of the Well Station, which had not been more than a couple of million miles off when Gnumph had first Dropped, and was moving ever closer as it continued to accelerate between falls. It thought it had a good sense of which direction the Well Station ought to lie, and could think of no better plan than to follow its instincts.

The forest was a dry, baked brown tangle of skeletal trees, and the walking—even once Gnumph had got to grips with its four ungainly legs—was slow going. There was no sign of animal life at all, just withered branches and desiccated brown brambles that crackled underfoot as it trudged onwards, following a vague sense that the Well station was somewhere—perhaps many hundreds of miles—up ahead. Night did not fall as expected, and a bright light fell through the canopy for what felt like days until Gnumph succumbed to tiredness and curled up at the base of a tree.

Hours passed, then a full day. Questions drifted upwards from the commons while Whira sat with the use of stick pads on the second floor railing, her legs dangling over the side, consulting the Myriad. Like her, they were unable to see anything beyond the limits of Gnumph's belly, but at her command they sketched out all that was known of the Phaslair laws, and the air in front of her was filled with opened documents of moving script and diagrams. Whira barely understood a tenth of it, but with the Myriad's help she soon came to a conclusion the other passengers weren't going to like: they *were* trapped, at least for the time being.

Her guts churned as she swept the information away, the reams of text drifting in the breeze, and she wondered how many lost souls must have found themselves in a similar position, their mummified remains locked for all eternity inside inaccessible dimensional bubbles. It was certainly not a death she'd ever imagined for herself. Truth be told, Whira had half-fancied she might live forever. It was certainly possible these days to live for thousands upon thousands of years, but you had to fundamentally change almost every structure in your mind to help it cope with the strain; whatever amounted to your original self was wiped away, regardless.

Instead an ignominious death, never to be heard from again. She wondered what it would be like to starve. The muscles in her legs trembled at the thought, and she desperately tried to unstick herself from the railing, perilously close to tears. She couldn't let the passengers see her cry.

Of course, she could Drop. Just her—leave them all. She would have to. But to who knew where?

After fumbling with shaking hands to unpeel herself, she

wiped her eyes and drifted down to the commons, waving away the garbled questions and making her way to the adjoining storage tunnel. She had made sure, upon leaving Salqar, that they had sufficient supplies to last them at least a hundred days. That number, however, had been dependent on a good portion of Gnumph's passengers leaving at—or before—Obaneo.

She propelled herself into the softly lit space, pushing past chillspheres and floating urns to get to the great shelf of cupboards. Doors were already hanging ajar, their empty shelves quite visible as she floated across the space.

She came to rest against an empty compartment, some crumbs still drifting inside, and wept quietly in the dark.

The trees were thinning, the heat intensifying. Gaps in the trunks revealed an expanse of light beyond, and then a sullen world of rusty-looking sand.

Gnumph had come to the edge of the forest. It stopped, sitting in a tangled heap of legs and gazing out across the wasteland. A pawful of the sand proved to be made up of oxidised grains of wind-eroded metal, not sand at all. A few tiny crawling things scuttled in the mixture, oblivious.

Gnumph's eyes turned to the sky, revealed at last.

The brightness that had fallen through the trees was not uniform, but a dazzling collection of rising towers of light; stars, Gnumph surmised, but streaked upwards as though the world it sat upon was plummeting amongst them. A single column of starlight enveloped this planet, wrapping its soft glow around the horizon. The more Gnumph stared the more convinced it was that the world lay *inside* its own streak of star, like a bubble inside a straw. This was an odd Phaslair indeed.

⁎ ⁎ ⁎

Even the most exuberant passengers were acting sluggish now, keeping to their rooms for most of the day, and only a few met around the table to play a few desultory rounds of whichever game sets still had all their pieces or boards. The Myriad had done their best to extract organic matter from the dusty air, cleaning it and fashioning it into edible wafers, but these had lasted only a couple of days, and now the warm currents of the weightless space were spotlessly clean, filtered at an atomic level for anything that might possibly be of use. Arguments had died down with the last of the food, and there were mutterings that Oldro, the musician, was at death's door.

Whira knocked at Oldro's door, waiting. The Myriad had already drifted in to have a look, and said that they could help it with its respiration and blood flow, but the leaky, smoking hotglobe that kept the musician alive could not be breached without risk of an explosion. It was a torture they had brought upon themselves, Whira thought while she waited, feeling the protrusions of her bones through her skin: the Myriad could keep even the most stubborn of them alive long after they really ought to have died. She gave up knocking and drifted off. The swarm of machines and microbes would live almost forever in here, she assumed. Would they eventually go mad, cooped up in this finite space? She would never know.

She drifted back down to the table, currently occupied by Shumholl and Mobe, who were slouching with their heads in their hands. Mobe's parasitic hangers-on had disappeared somewhere; Whira suspected he'd eaten them. Immonod floated above them like a diaphanous red kite surrounded by a watery bubble, his eyes closed. A beat of music drifted from a distant room, but their little world was otherwise silent. Even Scrapher's raging curses, emanating weakly from behind his locked door, had ceased.

Shumholl noticed her at last, and waved languidly

to a chair. The Xaal, a glistening, rainbow-hued tree-climber, raised his long neck to look at her. Whira met his transparent eyes, which flicked to the locket of yellowish crystal around her neck.

'That's a ship pendant, isn't it?' he asked.

Whira instinctively closed her palm around it. 'What about it?'

'Can I see?'

She shook her head. 'I'm *not* using it.'

He stared levelly at her. 'Never?'

Whira took a deep breath, tipping a jug in her direction to discover it empty. Her belly growled, loud enough for all to hear. 'Not until we're out of options.'

'*Options?*' drawled Mobe, his little flat red face still buried in his hands. 'What options? Gnumph's dead, it's obvious. You won't be doing him any harm.'

'He's right,' said Shumholl, licking his parched lips with a long white tongue. 'One touch from you and that locket crystallises, yes? Explodes into a fine Sovereignty ship? *Use* it. Say the word. We can't go on like this.'

The weight of the pistol was a comfort in her pocket. She had kept it on her person in case of eventualities like this. 'Or I could just Drop you right here? How about that?'

Shumholl straightened his neck, eyes narrowing, but said nothing.

'Piss off back into that infrasphere and leave us to it then,' grumbled Mobe, burping into the table, his face squashed into its surface.

The silence of a slowly dying population descended once more, thick and glutinous and suffocating.

The infrasphere. She glared at Shumholl and heaved herself out of the chair, propelling herself with her last stocks of energy into the air and heading for room nine.

She swung into the room, now occupied by Iiihi, Swerlk and a permanently dozing cluster of Qathis folk, not caring how much noise she made as she rummaged beneath their coldglobes and luggage for the sphere projector.

What are you doing? Iiihi asked blearily from under the covers.

'Go back to sleep,' she whispered, switching it on. A garishly pink floating display blossomed into being and she skipped through the options until she found a list of accessible spheres, unbelieving. This shouldn't work, not from a distance of dozens of Phaslairs. Whira navigated the menu until she found a previous save from her last trip, reaching and grabbing it. It showed her, wandering in the snow. She shook it, and the world opened up around her.

She was back in the snow-blanketed land at once, accompanied by the room's other occupants (now in the form of Wumos, too). Iiihi stared groggily around her. The Quathis folk squatted together, jabbering excitedly. Swerlk still snoozed.

'Wait here,' Whira said, and trudged in the direction of the merchant's hut. She only needed a matter of seconds to access a terminal, and could be in and out before the proprietor knew she was there.

Whira pushed her way through the low forest, the sharp combination of hope and cold energising her wasted brain. It seemed to take longer to get to the shop than it had before, but she attributed that to her weakened state. Whira pushed on, searching the forest, the panic rising as she doubled back. She had a thought and gazed into the sky, looking for the telltale plume of smoke, smoke that used to advertise the name of the store for all around to see.

There wasn't any. It was gone.

Whira sank to her knees, burying her webbed Wumo hands in the snow, too exhausted to scream and shout. She pushed her fist through the compacted surface of the snow, drawing a line, her strength almost spent, then rose slowly to her feet for the trudge home.

*   *   *

The rusty desert seemed home to little but a dry, biting wind and the teeming sand creatures. The vertical blaze of stars, hovering always overhead, forced Gnumph into a stooped trudge, its eyes lowered to the rust. It wished for night and darkness, but supposed it should be glad of what meagre warmth this peculiar arrangement offered: it was cold enough now—if night ever fell it would surely freeze to death.

Again and again it wondered how it might get in touch with the people inside its belly. It knew that they weren't physically there—it could cut itself open and find nothing but steaming guts—but trapped in a limbo between the Phaslairs, here and *not* here. It hoped they were alright, but knew deep down that they likely weren't. There simply weren't enough supplies for an extended jaunt like this. By Gnumph's calculations they would be running out already, assuming the time it experienced was relatively similar for them. Perhaps that wasn't so, and they were already long dead, or—and it thought this less likely—maybe time moved so slowly inside their cut-off realm that they hadn't even noticed Gnumph gone. All it could do was keep on walking, relying on a natural instinct for direction that had survived the Drop.

Thoughts of impending retirement kept Gnumph going. After an exhausting century and a half as a spy for the Alm Nuzimir it had hoped for a period of rest, but as soon as that job had finished it was activated by Phrail and kept on standby for almost three years, plying the routes around Salqar to earn a little money on the side until being called up. They had told it very little besides that it would be ferrying a linguistics expert to Obaneo, a journey that, due to a few minor misunderstandings here and there, the Throlken would most likely disapprove of. It was the recording of the Scream that had convinced Gnumph to accept the job, and that shipping Whirazomar out of the Phaslair was likely in the galaxy's best interests. Besides, it enjoyed the work: to be paid to roam Yokkun's Depth with a bellyful of interesting conversation was a fine way to live, and constant peregrination was in Gnumph's blood. Its ancestors had been travellers for millions of years, since before the first age of the Throlken, evolving eyes and basic propulsion to home in on nearby stars so that they could open their bellies and scatter their seed. Back then the journeys lasted tens of thousands of years, but soon clever species worked out that they could hitch a ride inside, making the place homely and comfortable enough to turn the sentient Ingaal spores into crude but willing generation ships. The practice had persisted into modern, more civilised times, and—because of their vastly increased speed and low cost—megaspores and seedpods were now the transport of choice for the galaxy's most desperate and impoverished. Gnumph seldom met other Ingaal spores on its travels, but when by happy chance their paths crossed they always had lots to talk about, and Gnumph kept in touch with thousands of ex-passengers; with friends all over the galaxy there was usually somewhere warm and dry to stop for the night, no matter where it happened to dock.

After an interminable period of trudging, its belly rumbling louder every few steps, Gnumph came across something: a huge depression in the metallic sand over forty steps across. Squinting into the distance Gnumph could see another two of the prints fading into the horizon, so that they wandered perpendicular to Gnumph's route and roughly parallel with the border of the forest it had left some days ago, leaving odd, pungent-smelling mounds of swirled sand in their wake. Gnumph peered, its wide-angle herbivore's vision making out a great deal, and fancied that the track curved slightly in the haze of distance, ultimately travelling in the same direction it was. It resumed its walk, keeping the same course, but looking every now and then across the desert to where it presumed the maker of the tracks ought to be.

Perhaps a day later it saw the first far away turrets trembling in the smudged haze. Gnumph quickened its pace, taking long strides and watching as the wonky spires of a small city revealed itself over the horizon. But something wasn't right. Whenever Gnumph slowed or stopped for a breath the towers receded, as if they were crawling away.

Gnumph broke into a canter, chasing the towers across the desert.

The team of seventy-two passengers worked through the infrasphere's long night, carefully inscribing a sentence more than a hundred feet across the snow. Nodo and Nurtil collapsed, and had to be dragged back through the game's doorway and into the warmth of the Real. Whira, working alongside, fainted at least three times without anyone else seeming to notice, slapping herself and staggering back to her feet, and by mid-morning the snow-bound plain was decorated with a message.

ECHO

Simurg wanted one last listen to the virtual planet Mondra before she left for good. A timer on her sonic HUD informed her that the Cheat were due in-system already, late for their own war.

She risked a low dive towards the abandoned world, hoping to hear of some hastily dropped loot somewhere. Being totally blind in the Real meant the game translated everything for her into soundwaves, and Mondra grew beneath the ship, its continents loading instantly and spreading out into a sonorous vastness of soaring mountain peaks and a dense timpani of forests.

The new Flesh Campaign had erupted about a week ago (in-game), and a handful of systems were already threatened as the Cheat restarted a virtual foundry, swarming into peaceful space. The new faction was so named because it was playing dirty; their rapid accumulation of territory was fuelled by an illicit code stolen in perhaps the most daring raid of the entire war. The code was a particularly nasty one, capable of melting anyone in its path regardless of the strength of their armour and defences, and turning vehicles, automata and livestock against their owners; Simurg was one of billions of players who didn't fancy getting caught up in it when it arrived. The closest thing anyone could liken it to was a directed supernova (a phenomenon thankfully extinct in the Real now for hundreds of millions of years, owing to the Throlken's taking of the stars), a force that bathed whole systems until all opposition melted away. The Cheat wouldn't have the codes for long—the sphere's adjudicators were already scrambling to switch them all off—but a lot of damage could still be done in a few days.

Simurg banked as something flashed up, the ship speakers reading it aloud into her sensory module. A message. She logged it as a side quest, noting that it contained an address to be forwarded to.

Leaning back in her seat, her node-studded, chrome sphere of a body rolling like an egg under virtual gravity, Simurg listened to it again while she cocked an ear at the world, detecting a faint tracery of lettering a thousand or so miles above the southern pole. The message wasn't really that big—the HUD told her aloud that it was only about a hundred feet across—but the atmospheres of the virtual worlds tended to magnify anything of interest to passing players, particularly an SOS.

Simurg skimmed the rest of the system, scanning for anything else of obvious interest, before checking her timer again and snapping away.

Drethenor Tiliph Zelt Friest of Oublish dozed for the best part of a month while his autumn crop ripened, his stomach waking him just in time.

He yawned a mighty, bellowing yawn that echoed like cascading rockfalls in the darkness, and stretched in the luxuriant warmth of the den, uncoiling and twitching his three miles of night-black tail before opening his eight tasselled wings to inspect them for any new flashes of colour. At six hundred years old and five miles from nose to tail, he was rather small for a Vorl of his age; branching bolts of violet iridescence were supposed to come in at five hundred, and he felt dowdy, underdeveloped.

He slunk, upside down, from between a chasm of guano stalagmites to find breakfast—a hanging cauldron that had bubbled nicely over suspended coals while he'd slept—and moved through into an adjoining cavern to enter the worlds of the infrasphere.

The transition was like the rapid melting of a vast block of ice, as his gargantuan body dissolved into the virtual world. Inside he was the same dashing bipedal being he always was, cloaked in diamond resin and cape, and he strolled through the wind-blown grasses of his chosen homeworld to check his messages in the pond.

The correspondence floated to the surface to be flicked through with the tip of a finger. Tiliph squatted at the pool's edge to read a few messages from fellow treasure hunters, an update on the Flesh Campaigns and the new threat from the Edgeforces (the early stages of which he was ashamed to admit he'd slept right through), understanding that he would lose many of his old hunting grounds when the Cheat swept in from the rim of the civilised map.

He was working out his losses with a degree of consternation when he noticed a message from a name he didn't recognise. Tiliph opened it with surprise: his was supposed to be a private address.

Sender: Simurg Hasenem Zelt Vhule Of Burosh, Within Traul.

Greetings! I happened across this scrawled in the snow at Mondra, addressed to your fine self. May your horde be ever bountiful!

Tiliph dismissed it, sweeping his hand through the murky water to the communication enclosed, his eyes widening as he read.

TILIPH HELP WHIRA CREW TRAPPED
STARVE FIND US THROUGH DOOR.

QAAL

The town drew closer, clarifying in the wobbling haze. A cluster of rusted orange towers, crowded with a mess of antennas, aerials and wind-shredded, listless flags, rose from a jagged outcrop—an outcrop that moved in juddering, lumbering steps. The place had been built onto the shell of a giant creature that waddled on two huge, splayed feet. The material that made up the turrets and spires was the same as the shell, as though the inhabitants had quarried it to build their home.

The lumbering creature's head was perpetually bent over the desert surface, its lips slathering across the sand. At its tail a wooden keel at least ten storeys high seemed to guide the beast's direction. Gnumph wondered whether it even knew what grew out of its back, or cared. As it walked, it siphoned the metallic sand, egesting what it couldn't process in a misted brown shower: the ruffled, smelly dunes Gnumph had walked over. A great net had been strung across a portion of the creature's slobbering mouth, presumably to catch food for the town's inhabitants, and Gnumph could just make out miniscule silhouettes crawling up and down its ropes.

It appeared Gnumph had been spotted, too. The twinkle of telescopes or binoculars flashed from higher windows, a faint alarm carrying distantly on the wind. The town didn't slow down, but Gnumph found that with a little extra effort it could make progress, its canter taking it into the groove channelled by the huge wooden keel.

Closer still and it could make out winding steps leading down to a series of patched metal platforms growing on either side of the keel. A few squat people sat with their legs swinging over the edge, observing Gnumph's arrival. Beneath the holey rags they wore Gnumph could see jaundiced, corkscrew-shaped faces that grew out of their torsos. Their small green eyes blinked as they leaned over the platform.

'What are you then?' said one, squatting and resting its two-fingered hands on its thighs. Though it spoke from twin holes in its drill-shaped nose, the fact that it was intelligible told Gnumph at once that this place, though bizarre, was almost certainly a Throlkoid Phaslair.

'Food,' gasped Gnumph, still running to keep pace. 'Water?'

The speaker sniggered, pointing at Gnumph as if it had said something funny. 'Where you come from?'

'Forest,' breathed Gnumph, on the verge of collapsing. The town was drawing away, the corkscrew-headed things growing smaller in its blurred, exhausted vision.

'*Forest?*' asked another, standing. 'Help me, pull it up.'

Gnumph felt their unpleasant fingers brushing against its skin, clawing for purchase until they closed around its forelegs and hauled it awkwardly onboard.

'This is Qaal.'

Gnumph looked around, panting. The sand slid by below the platform, the keel creaking in its mounts, a cooling breeze drumming the air.

'Come on.'

It was like walking on the deck of a ship, the rolling, gentle sway lulling Gnumph almost to sleep after its long journey on foot. Together they climbed the winding stairway that ascended the pockmarked slope of the creature's shell, until the view of the desert stretched out before them. There were no railings or balconies, and Gnumph almost lost its footing a number of times during the climb.

'Watch out, little feller,' said one of the corkscrew-headed things kindly enough, extending a hand and patting Gnumph on the rump.

They passed a field of boreholes drilled into the beast's mottled shell, and it occurred to Gnumph that these things could in fact be highly evolved parasites, erecting a city from the material of their host's body. Given enough time and experimentation, they had civilised themselves.

Gnumph's suspicions seemed to be confirmed as they crossed an unsteady iron bridge and arrived at one of the holes, entering a spiral corridor that burned with simple electric bulbs. Its walls were made up of mismatched squares of beaten iron, like a patchwork. Worm-like creatures slithered along the ceiling, following the spiral of grooves to the next junction and dripping a clear, viscous sludge that coated Gnumph's head and body; an ointment of sorts that the inhabitants slathered over themselves after any amount of time spent in the dry air outside.

They rose with each step until Gnumph sensed that they'd left the lower levels of the shell and were moving up through the base of a tower. Daylight streamed suddenly in, and Gnumph squinted at the horizon through an open window.

The young of a dozen different species scuttled and played, pausing thoughtfully at Gnumph's passing before carrying on, while their elders seemed to do nothing but sit and play with tiny electrical devices. Gnumph assumed they sieved fuel, food and building materials from the giant creature's lips, darning their home like an ancient sock, and appeared to drain their water from moisture traps the party had passed on the way up. They passed an endless succession of tidy dormitories and parlours, their walls decorated with the same peculiar portrait. Gnumph had time to reflect that the desert itself might be the crumbled remains of a civilisation—one whose metals had eroded to sand over some colossal span of years. The parasites, biding their time while the world rumbled on, had seized their chance after its demise, clambering aboard the remaining megafauna and beginning their own ascension. For all Gnumph knew they were only a step or two from spaceflight.

'Here we are.'

They had stopped at an elevator.

'Qaal's house is at the top. Say to him what you said about the forest, eh?'

Gnumph turned, surprised. 'I thought Qaal was the creature—'

But they were already ambling away, chattering to themselves, and Gnumph was on its own.

It took the elevator, weak with hunger and thirst and wasting some time dithering with the indistinguishable buttons. The lift ascended with a groan, opening many times for various glossy, sticky creatures to crowd inside on the way up, all of them eyeing Gnumph and whispering amongst themselves, and the compartment only began to empty as it reached the highest floors.

The door squealed open, revealing a tall, well-lit chamber that offered unparalleled views of the desert. Gnumph lurched out of the elevator and walked slowly towards the high windows and their source of cool, smoke-scented air. In the shimmering distance rose the towers of two other moving towns.

'What's this?' screeched an unseen voice. Shod feet clip-clopped out of the shadows, and another corkscrew-headed person arrived, thrusting a mop in Gnumph's direction. 'You're not supposed to be up here, get out!'

166

'I know where the forest is,' Gnumph said tiredly. The thing straightened, withdrawing the mop, and scuttled off. Gnumph followed at a slow stagger.

The scurrying tap of shoes ended, replaced with frantic muttering too quick for Gnumph to disentangle. Gnumph walked into the light of a tall open window, arriving at a star-shaped chamber that was apparently empty but for a thick central pillar. The person that had tried to shoo it away was standing just beside the doorway. They seemed to be talking to themselves, and periodically glancing upwards.

Gnumph followed the person's gaze.

The room's occupant loomed overhead, like a bulbous, towering seedhead, bent at the neck from the weight of its skull. Twin flaps of flesh tipped with stubby fingers dangled like earlobes from either side of its face. What Gnumph had taken for a central pillar was its fat, scaly stem, rising from the floor below. It must have evolved, Gnumph assumed, to snatch crumbs from the great creature's mouth: they had built their tallest tower around it.

The head's attention shifted to Gnumph. It was a bloated, whiskery thing with a wet pink orifice like a blowhole at its tip. Two miniscule eyes stared greedily from baggy folds of flesh.

'Get this on the daily,' said the seedheaded thing to its adjutant in a gurgling growl, the breath from its blowhole steaming in the air, and the person below lifted an electronic device, zooming in on Gnumph.

'Greetings, friend!' cried the seedhead, lowering its fat, whiskery face towards Gnumph. Its voice had changed in pitch, rising shrilly. A hideous smell wafted from its mouth. 'Are we to believe that you have seen the *Puirr*?'

'Er—' said Gnumph, looking uncertainly between the two of them. 'I came from a forest, if that's what you mean?'

'Aha!' the thing laughed stagily, waiting until the camera had zoomed back on it before continuing. 'It is not a forest, though you may be forgiven for thinking so! It is a buried creature that raises its fingers up out of the Kpiet desert, the better to catch the warmth of the sun. This is a stroke of great luck indeed! We have not had a Puirr for a world-walk, at least. Long has Qaal searched for this, long may we feed.'

Gnumph reconsidered. The trees had seemed odd.

'Come,' said the seedhead, lowering to clasp Gnumph in its flabby pink arms. 'Pose with Qaal.'

Gnumph allowed itself to be manhandled into the air for the camera. It noticed as it rose that a jumble of hundreds of very bad portraits dominated the walls, all of the creature Qaal striking various poses, just like those it had seen on its journey up through the simpler levels of the town.

'Look at this guest that has dropped in to see us,' Qaal said simperingly to the camera, jerking Gnumph around like a doll. The stench of rotting flesh from its blowhole intensified. 'It has heard of the artist Qaal, and come across the Kpiet to bring us the location of the Puirr! Today is a fine day indeed!' Qaal's fingers fumbled at Gnumph's mouth, pulling its lips away from its teeth, so that they both smiled for the camera.

The device shut off, and the adjutant bent over it to study the recording. Qaal's grip on Gnumph intensified.

'Where?' Its voice had lapsed back to a growl. It withdrew its fingers from Gnumph's mouth.

Gnumph grimaced at the taste. 'About two hundred miles north east, if you use those directions here.'

Qaal did not answer. It was looking at itself in a full-length mirror on the wall. It raised one stubby hand and stroked its whiskers, admiring its reflection.

'Chro,' it said sharply to the adjutant. 'Outside.'

Gnumph had just opened its mouth to ask for directions

of its own when it felt a curious sensation: a bright flaring of the nerve endings in its rib cage. Qaal's grip had tightened.

'What are you doing?'

'The truth now,' the thing grunted, the stench making Gnumph gag. 'Which direction was the Puirr?'

The nerves cried out once more, leaving a lasting glow of signals, perhaps implying damage. Gnumph, who had never in its life felt real pain, took another moment to realise that this was what it was like. The sensation wasn't as unpleasant as everyone seemed to make out.

'Why would I lie?' it asked Qaal.

The parasite squeezed harder, black blood welling around its fingers and dripping to the polished floor. 'The *Puirr*.'

'I told you—'

'No more *lies*. You work for Wazting, maybe, or Zusul. They want the Puirr for themselves.'

Gnumph rolled its eyes. This needless delay would cost the passengers, it was sure. 'Alright. Fine. It's ninety miles south of here. How's that?'

'I knew it! I knew you lied!' cried Qaal. 'You thought you could trick old Qaal, but Qaal is *cunning*.'

Gnumph nodded. 'Yes, you caught me out. Well done.'

'Chro!' Qaal screeched. 'More poses!'

The adjutant hurried back in, its camera at the ready. Qaal covered Gnumph's bloody sides with a hand flap and thrust it towards the camera.

'Now,' said Qaal in its nice voice, 'we change course.' It arranged its hideous bloated face, attempting to look thoughtfully out of the window. The camera crackled away to itself, taking in the static pose. 'Our friend here will be given charity to go on his way, such is the kindness of Qaal.' It turned to look into Gnumph's eyes. 'Am I not kind?'

'Very,' Gnumph muttered.

This seemed to please Qaal. 'Mmm. I am the kindest being in this land, or so they say. And I think I am not bad-looking, for one so old and wise.'

It seemed to be a question. Gnumph nodded its head. 'Oh yes, very nice.'

Chro scuttled off with the camera, and they were alone again. Qaal's grip relaxed and it dropped Gnumph, like a child bored with a toy, and fixed its attention on the view beyond the window. It was giggling shrilly and caressing its whiskers, its gaze darting every few seconds to its own reflection.

Gnumph staggered to its feet and limped from the room, the blood warm on its fur. Chro returned and ushered it out.

'Congratulations, you are famous now!' it said, pointing out of the window at a town which had lumbered closer during the interrogation. 'You may go aboard Wazting. Wazting will take you where you wish to go.' Chro turned away, then remembered something. 'But do not say *a word* about the Puirr!'

Day twenty-four. Whira marked it off, scraping into the surface of the commons table with a broken shard of crockery. She sat alone, exhausted, having floated for some time in the emptiness of Gnumph's stomach, dozing fitfully through a succession of feverish dreams. Nine passengers were dead: Mobe, Oldro the musician, Yannenast, Phibbot, four of the water dwellers (found floating upside-down in their tub), and Little Yith, whom the Myriad had almost saved. His pups still flitted about the place, searching for the sanctuary of their father's mouth.

Whira had spent some days considering alerting the Throlken in some way. At least then her death might be quick, and the others spared. There had always been a good chance that this was a one-way trip.

A bumping sound that must have been there for some time registered at last on the fringes of her consciousness.

'Shut up!' she drawled, not lifting her head from the table.

There it was again. Like someone slamming bodily into a wall, or door.

Whira's ears flicked. It was coming from room nine.

She sat still, listening intently, her head lolling back. The fever, soothed by the Myriad while they scrubbed her skin and polished her teeth, must have returned.

'Go and see, will you?' she muttered to them, hearing the flutter of their whispers. She waited.

They returned a moment later, streaming ticklishly into her ear.

Whira's wasted hearts thumped back into life.

She didn't have the fluid inside her for tears.

Tiliph smiled sheepishly back at her from the snowfield, raising a hand.

Whira stumbled through the door, gasping at the sudden cold, and he rushed forward to catch her fall.

'Careful,' he whispered, his breath warm against her forehead. She closed her eyes, content, delirious.

'I'm here. I got your message.'

He bundled her into his arms and carried her back to the warmth of the door, unable to enter with her, though he would dearly have liked to.

'Stay,' she whispered, leaning inside the warmth of room nine.

'All I can give you is this,' he said, moving out of sight for a moment and returning with a thin white sheet of bendy-looking material. It was dotted with flat, elongated buttons, and emitted a gentle humming sound.

'Here.'

He passed it through, careful not to let his fingers cross the divide between the Virtual and the Real, the contraption diminishing as though from refraction. Whira took it weakly, sluggish questions forming on her lips.

'It will print food, real food, sent from my home in Deephrull.' He nodded to one of the buttons. 'Switch it on.'

She fumbled at the top edge and placed it on the floor. The thing engorged at once, as if sucking in a lungful of air, and churned out a wad of pink, cake-like material. Whira stared at it stupidly.

'Eat!' he commanded, a note of desperation in his faraway voice.

She did so, first a small bite, then another, then a fistful.

He smiled, eyes glinting with tears.

She laughed weakly, pushing the button again to produce another oblong of the delicious, sweet substance, then another. They rose as the Myriad lifted them into the air, cut them swiftly into perfect pink cubes and sent them throughout the spore.

'And water,' Tiliph said, pointing to another button. She pressed it and a corner of the thing swelled into a ball, a spigot opening on one side. Whira lifted it to her mouth and drank, gasping. The Myriad returned with jugs, dipping them into the flow in between Whira's pauses for breath and sailing out of the room.

When her stomach could take no more she looked at him. 'How did you do this? I've never seen anything like it.'

Tiliph shrugged, squatting in the snow just beyond the doorway. 'They're expensive, I'll tell you that. Had to sell a lot of loot.'

Whira stretched her hand out and passed it through the membrane, so that it was suddenly webbed. They touched fingers, and, though the sensation felt false to Whira in the Real, it was heavenly still.

172

'But how? Transmissions can't—'

He was nodding, anticipating her question. 'You were lucky. This infrasphere is not part of *your* Surface, Whira. I think I live some way below your home, but now we must have passed each other.'

Her befuddled mind, now awash with chemicals from the food, struggled to take this in. 'You're—'

'From another Phaslair, yes.'

She swallowed, noticing the scores tattooed on his skin had dropped almost to zero. 'I don't know how to thank you.'

Tiliph smiled, shaking his head. He nodded to the machine, still bloated with food. 'Keep printing it out, there's a year or more's supply inside.' He peered past her into the hallway. 'So what's going on? I haven't notified my local magistrate yet, wasn't sure I was supposed to. Just say the word and I'll get them to register your situation—there must be a Deep Eye contact somewhere from your Surface who can help.'

She held his hand tightly through the divide. 'We don't know where we are. Gnumph, our transport, Gnumph—I don't know if it's still alive, or—' Her eyes filled with tears again.

Tiliph winced, gripping her hand. 'Take this, and I'll put the word out.' He fished in his pocket, producing a small, button-shaped device. 'Reinforced tracer, for under the surface tracking. Don't lose it.' He tossed it through.

Whira caught the thing, which appeared more solid once it was in her palm.

'Now I'll always be able to find you,' Tiliph said, smiling lopsidedly.

Whira swallowed, feeling a weight lifting from her chest. The mission, if she could still call it that, was over. They had drawn far too much attention to themselves. At least there was nothing more she could do.

'Thank you,' she whispered, cradling the device in her free hand and looking up at him. 'I wish you could come in.'

He smiled sadly, then gazed around him at the wintry landscape, which blazed and dimmed beneath shifting cloud shadows. Whira knew it was technically possible, just as he'd passed the two devices through, but the transition would do nothing more than demolish and then rebuild a copy of his constituent atoms from her Myriad, killing him instantly in the process and replacing him with an impermanent clone which would never have known the difference. Teleportation had been mastered for millions of years, but was rarely practised by living beings for just that reason, never mind that his clone would come through in its Real form a few miles long, destroying Gnumph in the blink of an eye.

'I have to go for now,' Tiliph said. 'Sit tight; eat, drink. I'll make sure someone finds you.'

'Will I see you again?' Whira asked, her body suddenly awash with sweat.

'Of course. But not here. The place is under siege. You can call me any time on the tracer—I won't be able to reply in real time, but you'll know I'm listening.'

She glanced down at the device, which possessed a tiny projector eye, then looked up to see him wading off through the snow.

Tiliph waved back at her as he reached his flyer, knowing it was too late. The sky was already tinged with red. The Cheat had found its way here at last.

Oh well. He would've got bored of the game at some point, anyway. And at least now he'd spent his mountain of in-game currency on something worthwhile.

Tiliph logged out, leaving his game character to the mercy of the Cheat, and drew up an urgent message.

The township of Wazting dropped Gnumph off in sight of the local Well station within the day, turning massively and slowly to resume its desert wandering.

Gnumph limped towards the oasis. It was surrounded by a grove of blue trees that were quite clearly not of this planet, judging by what it had seen of the place. A dark lump of a person in a broad sunhat sat in the shade of the trees, listening to a radio set. A shabby tent and some wooden furniture seemed to be the person's only other possessions.

'Want some Falling dust?' asked the person in a cracked, dry voice, speaking through a gap in its all-encompassing cloak. 'Don't need much here.'

'This is the station?' Gnumph asked.

The figure pointed into the trees. 'Just in there.'

'I have no money,' Gnumph said, matter-of-factly. It was in no mood for any more games.

'Doesn't bother me,' said the person. 'Got more than I'll ever need. I'm just the gardener—all these trees floated down as seeds, from the higher realities. Someone's got to keep it nice and tidy.'

Gnumph went and sat in the shade beside the person, drawn to the comforting murmur of the radio.

'Broadcast from Arrahuhl station, three down,' said the unseen person, lifting a dusty, three-toed leather boot and propping it up on the remaining empty chair. 'Here.' It passed Gnumph a flask, revealing its wizened, green-skinned hand.

Gnumph, who hadn't realised how famished it was, thanked the creature and dipped its tongue into the mixture—a cold but not unpleasant soup of roots and weeds. The odious Qaal's tower could just be seen on the horizon, bumbling south. Wazting town had moved sufficiently far away to lose the sense of its huge scale, and as Gnumph watched, a great electronic prong levered down from a mechanism attached to its keel, firing a blaze of energy into the creature's rump. It stretched its neck and roared into the desert wind, its booming voice travelling across the sands and trembling the soup in the flask. The creature shook the town on its back, loosening a cloud of falling roof tiles, and increased its pace, lurching after Qaal.

Gnumph smiled. During its brief stay Wazting had been kind to it; it had only been fair to divulge where Qaal was going.

The uppermost towers of Qaal and Wazting winked to one another in a stuttering series of flashes before the first pulse of fire shot from Wazting's battlements. It rumbled across the desert, missing Qaal by half a mile and blasting a fan of sand into the air. Wazting ignored Qaal's frantic signalling and aimed again, lowering the shot so that it hit the base of Qaal's tower, obliterating its foundations. The entire edifice tipped and fell, collapsing in a trailing plume amongst the lower buildings with a cacophony that rumbled across the wastes. The creature beneath bayed and stamped its massive legs, sloughing the debris into the desert, then resumed its walk.

Gnumph watched impassively, eventually turning its back on the chaos. It thanked the gardener, accepted a little pouch of Falling dust that the person had measured out on a set of scales, and made its way into the shadow of the trees.

Whira was stuck to the table, gazing at the distant ceiling and posting moist chunks of cake into her mouth. Now that she was sated and gaining weight again, she found her mind drifting into unexpected places, old memories, arguments she had won, and lost. Tonight she mused on the formation of existence, the rush of blood sugar firing her imagination.

It was obvious, at least to her: the universe was on its way to developing sentience. It started small, of course, with the blossoming of life across a good scattering of worlds in every galaxy, some of which evolved intelligence over time and built their societies, spreading like a crust of mildew. Civilisations, by now accreted and clumped together and linked across their respective worlds, then reached out to join with others, until over millions of years—as life had witnessed in Yokkun's Depth—a galaxy became inextricably connected by a dense, bundled sprawl of life. The Throlken, the cause of all her misery, were an example of the next step in this process, of an intelligence that had fused with the stars and now turned every sun in the galaxy into a mind, joined and conversant. In the future, no matter how distant that may be, Whira believed the galaxies themselves, each populated with an overarching intelligence so that they could be considered sentient in their own right, would spread their tendrils and link, creating webs that fired together like strands of neurons. The universe would awaken, cluster by cluster, zone by zone, until one day many billions of years hence it would know itself at last.

And what then? What would it do with its newfound gift? Perhaps before the universe's body died, collapsing back upon itself, it would discover a way to avoid its own senescence and extinction. Maybe it would retreat into a dimension of its own making, or learn to upend time, or give birth to progeny that would survive it into the next great expansion, at which point the gradual, gluey accumulation of thought would begin afresh. Whira swallowed another chunk of cake, by now thoroughly bloated, knowing she needed to snap out of it.

She sat up, unsticking herself and leaning on an elbow. During all that navel-gazing she thought she'd felt a rumble through the table's battered surface. Had they hit something?

The vibration travelled through her elbow and up her arm, arriving at the delicate bones of her ears.

Um, sorry about all that, said Gnumph, as if afraid it was going to get a dressing down. *Everyone alright in there?*

THE CURIOUS

I remembered. The day they came for me at last, a pounding attack on the planet's defences waking an entire continent from their sleep.

I hadn't sought conflict. It was my own people who had waged war upon me, in the end.

They were a nocturnal species, at the beginning, before sleep had been done away with for good, and were known amongst the neighbouring systems as the Curious. It was a name so apt for the insatiable, constantly tinkering race that they took it for themselves, climbing over the span of millennia to become the masters of South All.

When Yib'Wor was born the Curious had risen to an unprecedented level of galactic power. They lived luxuriantly, without knowledge of poverty, conflict, hunger or even boredom, absorbed in their own infinitely pleasant existence. The galaxy, then segmented into large, peaceful quarters, watched with fascination to see what they would discover next.

Yib'Wor remembered the moment it all began. When his cousin B'rilim had told him the great secret: that everyone had to die.

But don't worry, Yib, you won't—at least not for a very long time.

When? *he had asked, an unnamed sensation building inside him.*

I don't know. Don't ask silly questions.

But I don't want to die.

Nobody wants to, it's just the law.

The law of what?

The universe, I suppose. Everything will be gone, eventually.

I woke as the stolen tubeship frothed its way through the system and into white, teeming space, drawn to return to its home. I'd spent the days gorging on supplies liberated from the burning homemade's stores (a large hangar stocked with oddities purloined from around the ruined cluster, not to mention the fine ship I'd taken), letting my ravaged body heal as best it could and priming an interpretation bracelet I'd found, saying as many words as I knew until the thing could talk awkwardly back to me.

The majority of the people in the homogenous volume I had left were silkily black-skinned and amphibious, their large silvery eyes perpetually staring, mouths agape. Only one person besides myself had stuck out: a stranger, I had heard. One who'd come seeking answers.

Tall House was a branching conglomeration of ten thousand or more dwellships of every colour hanging fused together in the whiteness, a lush forest of void flora carpeting the city's outer walls, like a weed-coated buoy. It was the largest settlement for many light-years, a magnetic north that drew craft from all across the cluster. I piloted the tubeship—a mottled spear of coral that had evolved crude

180

chemical rocketry all on its own—between the first of Tall House's turret gates, their looming shadows swallowing the ship whole before it emerged again into white light.

The view broadened before my eyes, the glare of stars dazzling. The tubeship seemed to be heading for a port at the top of the structure, and I fidgeted anxiously, excited, knowing precisely what I needed to do.

Someone came here, someone just like me. Someone from before. It was like searching the galaxy for a single particular blade of grass, I knew, but the one small mercy was that this one drew attention to itself, announced its presence. I would find what I needed to know: namely how they had got here from our mutual Surface, and how they had left. The person had stolen some Vanishing crystal, they said, and snapped away before Tall House could muster its defences.

But there was one thing the eyewitnesses had been very clear about.

The perpetrator had travelled not downwards, to an older Phaslair, but *up*.

The tube dropped into shadow, settling vertically with a bump inside a pressurised bay filled with cobbled-together ceramic vessels of every colour.

Nobody waited for me as I descended the ship's spiralling inner stairway to the lower floor: no officials, no bureaucrats checking to see who I was or where I'd come from. I craned my neck for one last look at the curious vessel I'd arrived in; it had served me well, but if all went to plan I would never see it again. I turned and pulled my cape around me, my remaining eye flicking between the creatures I passed—long, thin, stout and crawling, glistening and glimmering with feelers and fangs and multicoloured sequin scales, their various cloudy life supports held suspended in translucent pastel orbs around them, or peering with reflective eyes from brine-filled pressure bubbles of toughened plastic, some sporting cloaks made from nesting, living things. A pungent, churning hub of all the oddments of the region, none of which I'd ever seen before.

I met their indifferent gazes, observing the vaulted, flag-strung ceiling and the colourful comings and goings around me, before strolling through the crowd.

The nameless sensation that B'rilim had introduced him to never left. It ebbed and surged on a tide of nausea. It was as though a hole had formed inside his stomach, a hole through which his mind plummeted to a cold, black place where he felt profoundly alone. Others seemed to go about their blissful lives in the grip of a collective amnesia, as if they were eternal spirits, confident of living forever. Yib'Wor wished he could be like them, longing to forget, just for a minute, that one day it was all going to end, forever and completely. But wishing such things only made the sensation return stronger than ever, fat and gorging like a parasite that clung to his imagination.

He knew its name now, from reading the mythologies. Terror, they had called it. The larger, predatory ancestor of fear, long extinct in Curious society. But within Yib'Wor it thrived, and fed.

He kept his terror secret for as long as he could, all joy and colour leaching from his life until he spent each day as if in a trance. His family extended his schooling, worrying that there might be something wrong with him, and extra years of study took the quiet, unresponsive Yib to areas of Curious philosophy less explored, and into the presence of someone he could talk with at last.

It was Fe'Tril who introduced him to Qocilxilma, *or the* Pretence: *the theory that everything one saw and touched was an illusion painted by some higher, unimaginable power. Fe'Tril held that it was all a game, a test, that all the specks of life in the galaxy were merely sprites of code condemned to run a generated maze. There were ways to test for the presence of the Simulacra, Fe'Tril said, but they were arcane things, not suitable for someone so young.*

Come back when you are ready.

'Vanishing crystal?' asked the white, sleepy-looking head, lolling out of its chrysalis and pouring fleshily through the circular window of the viewing chamber. 'What is this? What crystal vanishes?' The little bracelet computer translated the merchant's sludgy voice into my own.

The merchant listened to the bracelet as it finished its sentence, sliding a mucous-slimy membrane over its four blue eyes as it thought. 'Do you mean Begone, perhaps, or Iliquin?'

I didn't answer, eyeing the huge wooden chrysalis that contained all the merchandise the creature sold, as well as its own body, hidden somewhere inside. The spherical shell sat in a hollow gallery surrounded by transaction windows, rolling itself on wooden casters to speak to whomever had money to buy. Vanishing Crystal. Begone. Whatever it was called, I'd need it soon.

'If that's what you're after, then I'm obliged to bring to your attention the law here: Begone is forbidden in Tall House, illegal even to *ask* for,' continued the head, growing flaccid again as it prepared to shrink back through the window. 'So if there's nothing else—'

The fury, stoked and glowing in my belly, ignited. I hadn't come this far to be denied what I wanted, not now. I wouldn't let it happen. With a flick of a hand I hooked my claws into the folds of the merchant's saggy neck. I hauled, drawing pink, sappy blood, oblivious to the commotion from the other windows.

Its four eyes widened as I unsheathed my knife, the blade flashing in a whirl and sinking into the merchant's throat to slip through rubbery skin until it reached a knot of gristle, which I hacked and sawed my way into while the drum of boots pounded across the balcony. The merchant's head stretched on its last remaining sinew, pulling a bundle of slippery innards after it until the whole lot emerged from the hole in the chrysalis, a spray of thick blood pouring out after it.

I booted the revolting, jerking mass aside, sparing a glance at the arriving sentries as I took a running leap across the gulf of the viewing platform, landing heavily and crawling through the window into the hole in the shell. I slammed the hatch shut behind me, bolting it.

Inside, the spherical cave was lit with lanterns: a library of wooden shelves stacked with commodities, some of it living and imprisoned in cages or tubes, squeaking and whistling at my arrival. The merchant's remains were a still-twitching heap at the bottom, its long hairy limbs stretched out like roots to control the chrysalis's wheels.

'Read,' I said to my bracelet, pulling it off my wrist as I clambered down and directing it at the signs on the cluttered shelves, hoping against hope that the merchant had a secret stash of the illicit substance somewhere. This was as far as my plans went; all that lay beyond was a misted, unknown land. My body, the one I'd found myself inside on that muddy, windswept world, was failing fast, and only Dropping could regenerate me now.

'Dhendell cheese, Mezoon, Lustis spirit,' the bracelet said in my own voice. I raised it to the next shelf. 'Ghizo cartidges, Uhm-Uhms, Molt shells, Phamph pigment—' I moved it on, peering by the light of the lanterns, hearing the commotion growing outside.

'Loophole rifles', said the bracelet, and I stopped, extracting one from its case. I didn't know what a *Loophole* was, but I liked the sound of it. Another shelf housed boxes of simple electric matches, and I grabbed a handful.

They were sawing into the chrysalis by the time I found it, having tapped every rib of the place until I found a hollow. I pried the wooden section open with my knife, discovering a small, matt-black bottle.

It was the first time I'd ever laid eyes on unprocessed stuff, but I was prepared. It was a fine, brilliant blue powder, the individual crystals almost too small to make out with my single eye. I poured it with trembling fingers onto a dish (the merchant must have eaten all his meals in here, and it had taken me some time to find a clean plate), tapping the bottle until every last grain was out. Next I took a handful of water from a jug, squeezing my fist together to make a funnel and dripping it over the crystals. They changed colour at once, the rich blue lightening from mauve to green to yellow. I would only know when I'd used enough water—

Ah, there. The powder turned jet black and softened to a paste. I wiped my hand on my thigh and removed the last of my clothes, the hammering from outside rattling the shelves. I didn't have long. I scooped a handful of the stuff, feeling it fizzing in my palm, and began to smear it carefully all over my body, making sure not to miss a millimetre of exposed skin. Even the socket of my missing eye needed covering, and I bellowed in pain as I applied it, tears streaming.

The pounding stopped. A square of light fell across my body as I worked, a long-nosed head poking in. I shot it with the Loophole weapon, watching with interest as the head imploded and disappeared, a few small flecks of blood spattering the shelves, and returned to the task in hand, rubbing an Iliquin-coated finger over the closed lid of my remaining eye. Was that everywhere? I'd forgotten the soles of my feet.

There. Done. I would need to remember to close my mouth as I fell. I took a box of electric matches and opened it with an unsteady hand, scattering them. I hissed bubbling spit between my remaining teeth, opening another, striking it against the wall and holding the humming white spark at arm's length, then peered out of the hole.

Five Tall House sentries were waiting for me, their round, eyeless faces misted inside coldglobe helmets. I grinned, ducking back inside and aiming the Loophole gun through the hole. Various parts of their anatomy disappeared in quick succession, a moment of silent astonishment followed by groans and squeals. This game was too easy sometimes.

More guards were scurrying in, and it was time to leave. I experienced a shudder of apprehension. I did not want to fall. Not again.

Without allowing myself a moment more to think, I held the electric match to my belly, activating the paste, and vanished.

SHOVELSHIP

It didn't take a genius to work out that someone was after him. He'd been arrested almost immediately on three separate Phaslairs, and Draebol was loath to miss out sections on his atlas. Instead he'd marked each Phaslair off as hostile and Dropped at once, seeing what must have been dismay on the various bizarre faces of his would-be captors as he waved them goodbye. Someone from up above, someone who must have been monitoring his transmissions and payments, knew precisely where to find him and was coordinating with a deeper agent to arrange the pickup. None of this boded well. He'd been away from the Surface for an unknown span—travelling the Phaslairs did that to you, warping and squashing and stretching the apparent passage of time, and Draebol hadn't even been able to count the days off since he'd left, always arriving at some indeterminate hour in a new place, never knowing when one day ended and the next began. At his very best guess he'd been gone in the vicinity of thirteen years, give or take a few either side. Time, he noted as his passage deepened, seemed to pool and coagulate with its own inherent weight, compressing under the accumulated pressure of stacked Phaslairs until Draebol had absolutely no way of quantifying the years at all. What could have happened on the Surface while he was away? Were they hunting Surveyors now? Well, they wouldn't catch him— not unless they managed to seize his Iliquin suit, and he had no intention of allowing that.

Draebol awoke, dazed and irritated, to the squalling of the alarm on his second day inside the shovelship. This new mind—though in essence still his own, as his consciousness moved across the Phaslairs—seemed particularly easily stressed. In the blackness he heard the thump of the rubbish sifters as they made their way down to breakfast, the tin bulkheads rattling around him. The baked, parching air forced him out of the darkness of his tiny cabin, feeling blindly for the little hatchway and squinting at the sudden light.

Draebol stared gloomily around him, shrugging on a dirty waterproof that still contained the previous occupant's possessions in the pockets and ducking through the passageways to get above deck. He opened another hatchway to a blast of stinging, ice-whipped air, climbing out and stooping low into the gale. The rusted refuse vessel was barrelling along above a trench of industrial waste, hoovering everything up as it went. Draebol gazed to the grey horizon, his eyes rolling into his skull as a covering of hard, transparent shell closed over them, looking for any sign of pursuers; he'd paid handsomely for his small cabin, negotiating passage at least to the junkbergs, where he might be able to hide out a little longer and complete his notes on the strata in peace.

Something swept down from the gloom some miles out, a gunmetal haze of rubbish rising under the power of its vacuum, and Draebol heard the crump of compacting debris at the same time as he saw it; either light moved more slowly here on this Phaslair, or sound faster.

Below decks the first shift had begun, the day crew put to work in the bilges sorting through every piece of detritus hoovered up. Metals went into one vault, plastics into another and so on. Any biological waste they dredged up was processed, flash-fried and served during the ship's four daily meals, and it was for one of these that Draebol went and sat, alone, in the mess.

He prodded the flat white steak of compressed protein with his plastic scissor-fork, trying to guess how many different species of rubbish dweller had been mashed into it. The being who'd served him—a blue-scaled, long-snouted thing with glowing eyes much like himself—lurked near the bulk of the meal processor at the far end of the galley, pretending to fix a jammed component while stealing glances at him, possibly wondering how he came into the funds to buy his indolent passage aboard. Draebol went back to his breakfast, sampling a piece of the meat and spitting it straight back out. The piece of unidentifiable flesh was like his own mind after countless transformations: a lingering trace of everything he had ever been. Since his stint as a tree dweller he was no longer afraid of heights, but a phantom smell from some briefly-visited Phaslair seemed always to inhabit his nostrils, even years later. His true identity, whatever it once was, had been scrubbed over so many times that he could no longer tell the difference between what was a recent addition and what was not: an overloaded sink filled with dirty washing-up that Draebol was too lazy to sort through.

The junker's course would take it to system edge, to a place where the dominant species here liked to spew out its rubbish, creating an orbiting shell of waste that shielded the system from intruders. Draebol picked up his flask and gazed into it, removing a hair (complete with bloody follicle) with his claw and flicking it away: he had some sweet, extremely alcoholic blinkberry wine in his bag, but it had come through foul and undrinkable, as though its old molecular makeup weren't feasible here.

He turned back to his writings, scratching out a note about the apparent sluggishness of light here in hieroglyphs he had never seen before, but knew instinctively. The Pattern, translated by a different reality, made every word in a Throlken-inhabited Phaslair readable, so it seemed the gods in their stars watched over this grim world, too. He unfolded an addendum page, opening up a larger map of the local Phaslairs, and jotted a note beside a thin coloured band in the marbled mixture of layers. *Throlkoid*.

At least the fact that he was being tracked answered one question: someone up there was still hearing his transmissions. Unfortunately, short of abandoning his suit, there was nothing he could do to lose them—the armour produced its own unique reverberations. If he threw away his Iliquin and there was no more to be had in the Phaslair then he would be well and truly stuck.

Draebol yawned and rubbed his eyes, pushing away his tray. As he did so a collection of small, vibrantly coloured and keratinous things came skittering along the tabletop to retrieve it. They gibbered to one another excitedly as they saw that there was a full plate of meat left, and stopped to stare at Draebol inquisitively, their beady black eyes waiting. He hesitated and slid the tray over to squeals of delight. The creatures hefted it like a stretcher, opening a hatchway on the table's far end that Draebol hadn't noticed and lowering the tray inside. When the last of them had leapt in after it the door in the table slammed shut, only a thin rectangle of tarnished metal giving away its existence at all. He reached for his plastic mug to find it being carted off in a different direction by another of their kind, and grabbed the handle, clinging on. The beast paused, nonplussed, before shooting him an evil look and tugging as hard as it could.

'No!' Draebol growled, hoisting the squealing thing into the air along with the cup, trying in vain to disentangle its limbs from the handle. 'Not yours!'

It bit him. Draebol screeched and tossed the beast and his mug across the mess, where they clattered against the far wall. The cook cowered behind his food processor.

Draebol folded his arms and watched the creature scuttle away across the mess hall, singing happily to itself as it dragged the empty cup along behind.

It took some days to reach the junkbergs, and when Draebol clambered out of the deck hatch again it was to a view of immense, slowly spinning lumps of colour. Out here the rubbish field was so thick that vacuum flora had taken root in all its crevices, misting the outer ring of the solar system with a heady, breathable atmosphere, almost like the space in his home Surface. It was nevertheless terrifically cold, and he wrapped his waterproofs tightly around himself as he gazed out at the billions of frosted, mountain-sized crags of compacted rubbish rolling lazily across the sky.

One of these belonged to him now, rented for a time from a diseased-looking landlord back on the planet he'd come from. Apparently the last tenant had gone missing, and Draebol could have the place fully furnished at a reduced price. He had no idea what *fully furnished* meant in this Phaslair, but it was presumably better than the alternative.

The shovelship showed no sign of slowing until they were halfway through the great encircling field of debris and had reached a point where the junkbergs were so thickly strewn that they blotted out any trace of the outer stars entirely. Someone rapped on Draebol's door and he hoisted his pack, stooping through the passageways as the nightshift got under way below him spewing their waste into the void.

Outside a flash of sunlight caught his face, warming him against the chill, and he saw the looming, shadowed hulk of his new home some distance below.

Draebol stepped inside, depositing his bag by his feet, breathless from trudging the hundreds of steps up to a large, partially concealed doorway in the crags. The sunlit entrance faded to shadow as the junkberg rolled, and the heavy, scratched metal door thumped shut behind him. He was in darkness until he found the place's single light switch but could just make out that every room had been hewn from the base material of the asteroid, the walls gleaming with a colourful cross-section of polished, compressed rubbish, rather like the way he visualised the arrangement of the Phaslairs. He ran his finger along the dusty surface of a bare shelf, inspecting a heap of oddly-shaped furniture piled in a side chamber and wondering about the landlord's claim that you could catch your own food on the junkberg's perpetually sunlit peaks.

His wheezing breaths inhaled the stale foulness of the air. Something must have died in here, presumably the old tenant. Draebol squatted and rummaged blindly in his bag for a while, used to identifying its contents by touch in favour of tipping everything out all the time, and found his torch. He stuck the little badge to his glove and tapped it twice. The entrance hall was abruptly daubed with light.

Dust balls and the desiccated remains of whatever passed for vermin here littered the corners, their dry droppings crunching underfoot. Draebol wandered the bare rooms and empty hallways in a state of dejected horror. Was this to be his life, hiding in squalor without a drop of wine to keep him company? He'd tried to secure something to drink on the journey over, but this refuse-obsessed empire didn't seem to have invented it.

Night, or the approximation of it, fell at last, after hours spent wandering the nooks and crannies of the place, leaving his possessions at the door. Draebol had kept his heavy suit on, in case of emergencies, and only took it off so that he could have a desultory, dehydrated piss in a shady corner, leaning the thing against a wall.

In the shadows he paused. A ray of light crossed the floor, falling across his clawed boots. Draebol finished his piss and looked around, hunting its source, eventually crouching dangerously near to the puddle on the floor and peering beneath what appeared to be a crack in the wall.

A hidden doorway.

Draebol pressed his ear to the wall, listening for some time. No sound filtered out. He stood back and felt across the wall, his mouth dry, eventually locating the bump of a metal hinge. He worked his way to the opposite side, his finger sliding over a recessed handle.

Pop. The door swung slowly open. The breath caught in his throat.

The previous tenant certainly had been busy. A room larger than any he'd yet found stretched away before him, ringed with steps that led down to a shallow circular depression littered with dirty cushions. At its centre stood a branching, climbing candelabra of sumptuously worked metal, each coiled, antler-spined arm at least ten meters across. Draebol took the steps down into the middle of the chamber, entranced. At the end of every arm a dozen cruel, hooked claws clasped a disk-shaped whirl of what appeared to be thousands of fat, round precious stones of every colour, all bezel-set into a base of filigreed silver. Eight arms, eight cradled galaxies.

It was a model of the Olas, the ancient structure that joined the eight realms, thought to predate Throlken rule by millions, if not billions of years, a structure so elaborate that it was wrongly presumed by many earlier generations of Yokkun's Depth to be a natural formation. Who had built it, when and why remained a mystery.

Draebol walked slowly around the thing, the journey taking some time, his eyes moving from one galaxy to the next, speaking their exotic names under his breath as he recognised each one. *Ehothalong*, *Mostramong*, *Zotulast*, *Lillowuyahl*, *Izadrijjin*, *Yokkunphirelleng*, *Gemit-Galazaph*, *Yokkun's Depth*.

Each was shaped like their real counterpart: three spirals, one elliptical, one barred and three irregulars. One, Salga Izadrijjin, was incomplete, only half the stones applied. Maybe the tenant had run out of cash. But why leave this precious thing here?

Draebol stood beneath Yokkun's Depth, the movement of his torchlight casting a shifting gleam across the jewels of its major clusters. One had fallen from its silver mount and he bent to pick it up, turning the thing in his fingers and peering at the disk of the galaxy above him in an attempt to locate the Almoll it had come from. There was a small gap, a silvery void, like a gum missing its tooth, in the whirl of Tizahn. Draebol examined the stone again, realising firstly that it represented some four or five million stars, and then that it was not a gemstone at all. It was a shiny scrap of bottle green packaging rolled into a ball. He went to the ladder, dragging it across the floor with a hideous squeal that could have woken the dead and climbed until he was at eye level with the galaxy.

It was all made from rubbish.

The maker had even fashioned a webwork of silvery junk at the hole in the galaxy's centre, a miniature model of the obscure, Throlken-built machinery at Yokkun's core that nobody knew the purpose of and all were forbidden from approaching.

Draebol reached across the disk, trying to replace the garbage gem and climbing half off the ladder. He shifted his weight too far over and the ladder wobbled and tipped with a groan, crashing to the ground.

'*Stars!*' he yelled, struggling on the rim of Yokkun's Depth, legs kicking as he slipped, the echoes of the crash and his subsequent scream reverberating through the adjoining chambers.

Draebol levered his leg across the beautifully worked edge, scrabbling for purchase with one boot. His fingers lost their grip, and with a yelp he slid and let go, falling to the floor and winding himself.

He gasped for breath and rolled onto his front, spitting on the floor. Then he heard it.

A clatter, from some adjoining chamber. Something falling and bouncing, then the sharp tinkle of a breakage. A grumble, rich and deep and reverberating. Draebol's movements froze. *The last tenant was still here.*

Shuffling, scraping steps, and a shadow appeared beneath the room's far arch. Draebol moved quickly, scurrying to crouch behind one of the Olas's thick arms.

It—whatever *it* was—paused, just out of sight, for some time.

And then something long and bloated and four times Draebol's size slithered in, propelled by many felt-slippered feet. It wore a threadbare gown over its ten arms, and the two-fingered hands at the end of each arm were gloved. Its wide, saggy face stared into the room, toothless mouth agape. Three deep-set amber eyes flicked around, blinking slowly. It hadn't yet spotted the fallen ladder.

It remained for some time peering into the chamber, before abruptly slithering over the base of the Olas. Draebol inched his way around the arm, keeping his body hidden from view.

The thing had a weapon in one hand, a long chrome spike about half Draebol's length, but he was not unduly alarmed. He should be safe here, on a Throlkoid Phaslair—

unless of course it was a pet, in which case the Throlken's laws took on a degree of plasticity: creatures of below two-point standard intelligence were permitted to kill for sustenance or in self-defence. Draebol dearly hoped it was just a common criminal who'd neglected to pay its rent, and that was only a Drop weapon in its hand.

It grumbled sullenly beneath its breath, and Draebol realised it had seen the ladder. Its head flicked upwards, to the sculpture.

He watched it, crouching behind the limb, seeing how the pupils of the three eyes contracted against the glare of the ceiling light. It studied the sculpture for some minutes, eyes flicking minutely from one place to the next, eventually passing over the section where Draebol hid. He held his breath, the pulse thumping in his neck.

They locked eyes, and then its gaze travelled on. The beast gazed thoughtfully at its weapon for a moment, before trundling out towards the far rim of the chamber, headed for the concealed doorway.

What if it locks me in? The thought shot a bolt of panic through him. He inched his way into the light, staring wildly around for something he could use to create a diversion. He grasped the fallen ladder. As he lifted the thing its top rung caught against the disk of Yokkunphirreleng, tugging it until it came loose, and before Draebol knew what was happening the entire galaxy had crashed to the floor at his feet, a cascade of coloured balls tumbling across the ground. The rest of the huge sculpture came with it, caving in on itself and sending star clusters and chunks of carefully worked silver rubbish everywhere. He stood amongst the fallen ruin, echoes still ringing throughout the space, and heard the rasping of the creature hurriedly dragging itself back into the room.

Draebol sprinted for the dim arch of the creature's living quarters and hid just in time to hear the howl reverberating through the junkberg's rooms. He ran his hands across his scaly scalp, wrinkling his nose at the fetor of the place he'd found himself in, wondering what in all the worlds he was going to do now. The thing's dwelling was littered with torn-open metal canisters—perhaps all that was left of an emergency food supply—and shattered pieces of bone, the marrow sucked dry. Draebol picked up a canister and sniffed it in disgust, seeing from the manufacturer's pattern that the beast had been using the tins for its work. He turned back to the sounds of it shuffling around, and wondered just how long it must have spent down here.

He moved through the hollows of its dwelling, finding no bed or possessions of any kind, just detritus and bones and hard, dried piles of dung. He crept back to the arch and inched his head around the corner.

It had already begun rebuilding over the course of a few short minutes, sorting through the heap of rubbish and setting aside coloured pieces with care. Draebol paced back and forth, wondering how long it would work without a break. He was suddenly ravenous with hunger, and searched in vain for any more food tins.

Nothing. No food, no booze. It would find him, find him and *eat* him. Draebol laid a trembling hand across his brow, thinking.

He peered around the corner again.

The beast had turned its wrinkly back to him, and was hunched over its hobby, sorting meticulously. For a fleeting second Draebol felt a twinge of guilt at ruining so much hard work, but then he saw the weapon lying at the creature's side.

He could have wept. He had to try.

The first step was the hardest. Draebol inched into the light until he was fully exposed, surrounded by empty space. The weapon lay twenty paces away, gleaming in the light.

He crept forward, each footfall a gentle flap of sound. The tenant, absorbed in its work, didn't turn.

Halfway there. It was still impossible to tell what sort of gun it was, if it even was a gun. He would know only when he'd laid hands on it.

Bloody fool, Draebol.

Closer still and he could smell the thing, musty and damp and animal, its breath heaving. Its back shuddered as it cleared its throat, sending a wave of sweat crawling across Draebol's scalp.

The weapon was in reach. He extended a hand, fingers outstretched. *Come on.*

He touched its casing, almost overbalancing as he leant forward, holding his breath. The bulk of the creature brushed his face as it shifted, coiling its tail. Draebol watched, wide-eyed, time slowing as the tail swept across the floor towards his leg, pushing it out from under him.

He fell, the shock immobilising his other limbs so that he dropped flat on his face. The creature turned with a snort of surprise.

Draebol screamed, rolling onto his back as one of the thing's fists came down, missing his head and slamming into the floor. He continued to roll until he was just out of reach.

It heaved its worm-like body around in a slow circle, jabbering in outrage, before remembering the weapon. Draebol seized the chance, climbing to his feet on legs of jelly and bolting for the door.

A sharp *crack* followed him out. Draebol reached the passageway and didn't stop, grabbing his pack by the outer door and dashing into the cold.

He took the winding stair three steps at a time, the low gravity propelling his hopping steps as the door slammed shut behind him. Above him the field of tumbling junkbergs faded into the mist, a hundred million islands just out of reach. He was shivering constantly by the time he reached the berg's landing station, a smooth area of flattened ground amongst the peaks, and waited impatiently for the world to roll back into sunlight again. At last a ray of warmth lanced across the hills, strong and sharp and white, and Dreabol searched the area for any equipment. There was nothing. He needed a station, a dwelling, somewhere able to communicate with the worlds beyond. Or he could just—

He stopped in his tracks, mouth open. *The suit.* He'd left it in the doorway of the hidden chamber, the front door key in its pocket.

'*Idiot!*' Draebol screamed, collapsing onto his knees and clawing at his face. He pounded his skull with a clenched fist. 'Imbecile!'

'That's it then!' he cried to the desolate hills, arms raised. 'That's it, gone forever! You *moron*!' He curled into a ball on the cold ground, groaning, shocked at how relieved he felt. It was over.

He tramped back up the hillside, slipping occasionally in icy pockets of shadow that never saw the sun, cursing with every breath. At the top of a peak, trying to absorb as much heat as he could before the world turned into shadow again, Draebol gazed out at the surrounding junkbergs. He'd heard collisions were common in such a densely packed area of space, but he could see none that were particularly close.

Quite a few must have been inhabited, and glowed with stippled light as they rotated into shadow. Others were home to a solitary flashing beacon or trail of winking lights: floating ship docks, perhaps. Draebol waited an hour for another full revolution of the berg, watching the heavens, and settled on what he thought was the nearest of the worlds—an asymmetric spike of crimson rubbish.

A tower had been built at its gnarled tip, and as the berg spun lazily back into the light Draebol could make out a settlement on its ridge, but it was impossible to guess the scale, or how far away it might be.

He waited a few more rotations, his throat scratchy with thirst, deciding that the berg was indeed drifting slowly in his direction. He could wait five years until the worlds collided, or he could try to get across there now.

Draebol searched the side of the peak, scrabbling down the slope until he came upon stands of flora. He pulled up a weed, digging into the cold soil until he hit metal. The roots were thin and stringy, but might be enough.

He pulled up as many armfuls as he could, piling them in the sun and sitting cross-legged to weave them together. Nothing to lose now.

He took the sour wine from his pack and pulled out the stopper with his teeth, tipping the entirety of it down his throat and grimacing as it heated his insides. Might as well have one last buzz, if this was really it.

He went to work.

Half a day later Draebol was done, weighting the end with a chunk of rubbish and tying the whole knotted length of weeds to a rusted pole. The patch of sunlight had shifted until his rump was raw from scraping across metal to chase it, and the wine had worn off. Now or never.

He climbed until he could see the neighbouring berg once more, and threw out the line. He steeled himself as it unravelled across the distance, and then jumped with it.

Draebol sensed the weak grip of the junkberg releasing him until he was weightless and sailing, beginning to spin. The other berg drifted closer, growing in size, and soon he could make out the details of its rugged peaks, the dwellings nestled in their shadows.

Slow down. How do I slow down?

The junkberg was vast, expanding in his field of view. For another minute Draebol was weightless, and then he felt its drag, drawing him ever more swiftly on until he was almost upon it. The thing swelled until he could make out the colourful marbling of its surfaces, the tower he'd seen earlier zipping by below, his tiny shadow flashing across hills and crags.

Slow down! Draebol opened his mouth to the cold and let out a yell. A mountain reared before him and he passed an inch or two above its sharp peak, the anchor snagging. Before his brain could process what had happened the force had travelled along the line, sending his body into a jarring spiral back to the peak and whipping him hard against its slope.

He felt his face crunch against icy metal as the vine rope snapped, and he fell.

Draebol gasped, opening his eyes. On any larger world the fall would have killed him instantly, but he must have bounced in the low gravity. He'd ended up in a valley of hard, frozen trash boulders, the cold numbing his skin and scales. Draebol waited for the freezing air to refill in his lungs, checking himself cautiously for any major injuries; aside from a shallow cut on his lip and a few missing teeth, he seemed intact. He clambered to his feet, hoisted his bag, and hobbled off in what he hoped was the direction of the settlement, glancing up occasionally at the drifting specks of junkbergs above, unable now to tell which he'd come from.

Draebol rapped on the small wooden door. It was set flush against the hillside, apparently perpetually in shade. He hopped from foot to foot, freezing. After a few minutes he heard voices, dull behind the thick planks of the door, and a circular letterbox opened at waist height. Draebol peered inside, seeing only darkness within. A high, breathless voice drifted out.

'Yes?'

'Do you have a terminal or something I could use?'

The darkness hesitated. 'Go around the side.'

Draebol stared at the hatch as it closed, then stumbled along the edge of the hillside, unable to see what they were directing him towards. He rounded a crag to find a door standing open to the cold.

'Quickly,' hissed a new voice.

He crept in, into warm darkness so complete it was as if his eyes had been removed. The door clunked shut behind him, latching and locking as an invisible hand scrabbled with a jangling set of keys.

A small, hairy paw explored his cheek, making him flinch. 'Donation?'

'Oh, er,' Draebol rummaged blind in his pockets, pulling out the last of his local currency. 'Here.' The ceramic counters were scooped out of his palm by clammy fingers, and then the voice was somewhere up ahead.

'Follow my sound.'

He did so, walking upon what felt like rough carpet. A frenzy of muttering drifted from further in, accompanied by the sharp, synthetic odour of some unknown manufacturing.

'What do you do here?' he asked, unsure if the voice had left him already and he was just talking to himself, part of some elaborate practical joke. He felt no fear, which surprised him, only an intense curiosity coupled with the relief that he didn't have to run anymore. It was warm enough in here to feel the ice crystals in his lungs melting and evaporating as the feeling returned to his hands.

'We're a scripture house,' said an entirely different voice at his side, almost whispering in his ear. 'We compose messages to Greater and Lesser Minuscule, notably the Ambient Svesh.'

'What's that?' he asked, angling his head away from the person's breath.

'You don't know the Svesh? They are the friends and translators of the Zilble.'

'Oh, alright.' Draebol didn't care much for religion, having encountered so many, but even he had heard of the Zilble.

'And do the Svesh ever respond?' asked Draebol, partly to break the dark silence.

'Not as yet,' answered another new voice, so close in front of him that Draebol stopped in his tracks. 'But we are getting very close. We can write our letters in M-Scale now, using new machines. It can't be long before we get a reply. Then we shall no longer be strangers to them, and we can ask them to speak to the Zilble on our behalf.'

Draebol smiled as he processed this, trying to feel ahead of him for any sign of the speaker, but it was gone again. 'How do you write, though, without light?'

'The M-Scale devices let us write at normal size,' said a voice Draebol recognised as the first he'd spoken to, this time from behind him. 'They translate it into Minuscule.'

'But the darkness—?'

'It allows us to focus on the quality of our prose. The Svesh are petitioned from all over the galaxy—they will choose to answer the best correspondence first.'

He nodded, unsure whether they could even see him or his gestures, and they continued their slow walk in silence, the gentle, stinking breaths of an unknown number of unseen beings guiding him forwards without stepping on anyone's feet. If they *had* feet.

What a waste of time, he thought in the darkness. In all his 182 years Draebol had heard only one creation myth he'd liked: that the present universe and all its iterations had begun as a single block of exotic stone about eleven and a half billion years ago, and the creator was merely the breath of wind that carved channels and shapes in its surface. Worlds and creatures and people, they were all of them just the negative shapes left over by the passage of that wind, all formed from the same block of base material that had existed since the dawn of time. He liked that image, especially with a bottle of something nice in his hand. Well, whatever the differences in their beliefs, Draebol understood they were all of them hardwired to mine reality for its truths, digging and digging until they found the answer, little pieces of the universe working to discover its own nature, as though it didn't really know itself.

He came to what he guessed was a smaller space, and a sticky hand guided him to the smooth, warm metal of a terminal station. Draebol let his finger be manoeuvred into position over some dials and a circular red screen lit up, dazzling his eyes. He blinked and peered through his fingers at it, scanning the basic text before it occurred to him to take a look behind him. The red-lit room was empty.

Draebol turned uneasily back to the terminal, punching one of the system's emergency numbers. He would meet these agents, whoever they were, and see what they wanted.

After some time spent in a dark cell, quite unable to see the meal they'd given him or to find the toilet, Draebol had been given a room aboard another junker heading out of the system. The ship, crewed by more of Draebol's blue-scaled adopted species, accelerated out between the drifting bergs to the edge of the garbage ring, slowing only after a day's travel above a spinning-top shape of compacted junk. A flotilla of hundreds of shovelships were docked in orbit around it, and they descended through the maze of hanging craft to rendezvous with the only new-looking ship. Draebol watched from the window as they coupled, wondering how high up this business went, and who was on that vessel waiting for him.

He went through to the other ship, stepping into a softly lit corridor that seemed cleaner than anything he'd yet encountered on this Phaslair and proceeding to a viewing gallery that looked out over the Junkworld and its flotilla. Draebol stood at the window for some time, his anticipation forgotten as he marvelled at the millions of slowly spinning worlds, knowing he would never be able to relocate the bergs he'd found, even if he spent his life searching. His suit of Iliquin was lost, he supposed, forever.

A reflection appeared behind him, Draebol's eyes focussing on his visitor.

It was a Lazziar, from his home surface. He hadn't seen one in years.

'Good evening,' said the diminutive female, sitting in a bowl-shaped chair and beckoning for Draebol to do the same.

He sat, stunned. 'How are you able to—?'

'Myriad projection of our Surface image. Would you like one?'

He gulped, nodded. The Lazziar whispered, and he felt a soft breeze caress him. She seemed satisfied, though he didn't feel any different. He turned and looked at his reflection in the sloping gallery window. A stocky male Lazziar gazed back from black-rimmed eyes—his old face again. He ran a hand along the hollow yellow horns that grew upwards from the bony protrusion at the nape of his neck, shorter and thicker than the female's. They were both of them dressed in fine Myriad-woven clothes, tight around the neck and cuffs in what had been the fashion when he'd last seen home.

'You've been avoiding us,' she said, 'all the agencies we sent to bring you in. What changed your mind?'

'Curiosity.'

'There's a lot of that around at the moment. I suppose I'm a little curious about this place,' she said, gazing out at the windows. 'Why so much rubbish?'

'Oh'—he gestured impatiently behind him—'ancients, long gone. Left all the raw materials lying around, so this lot didn't have to put in the work when they came of age. They squandered it all as fast as they could, only worked out recently how to recycle.'

She nodded, apparently satisfied, still staring past him at the view of drifting bergs.

'So?' Draebol asked. 'Why drop seventeen thousand Phaslairs to find me? What have I done this time?'

She gestured to his old knapsack, sitting on the floor between them.

He blew out his cheeks, his *real* cheeks, still getting to grips with this shock from the past. 'Right, of course. Well, I'll save you time now; my atlas isn't for sale.'

'That's fine,' she replied, her blank gaze drifting back to the windows. 'I don't want to buy it.'

'Alright,' he said cautiously, dragging the knapsack over and propping it between his legs. 'What, then?'

She opened her mouth a degree, hesitating, exposing a row of those sharp little Lazziar peg teeth he'd almost forgotten about. Draebol could tell already that asking for favours didn't come naturally to her. 'All the reliable Phaslair charts that haven't been lost or destroyed are under lock and key, horded by various Alms who aren't inclined to share, even with their counterparts. I represent Thelgald, who would make use of some of the information you've collected over the years.'

'What information?'

The Lazziar gazed steadily at him, as if weighing his character, and he found the sudden full glare of her eye contact uncomfortable. After so much time spent with alien faces, he could barely look at one of his own.

'We would like,' she said finally, 'to set a trap.'

A WAY THROUGH

Yib'Wor finished his education and travelled, taking his time to see as much of the All as he could. And it was wondrous: a vision of kaleidoscopic colour almost rich enough to distract him, to subdue the Terror. But in the quiet moments it always returned, and he thought again of Fe'Tril's teaching. Come back when you are ready.

Yib'Wor took one last grand looping course of the galaxy to visit the realms of the Dreamers, a species renowned for their clairvoyance.

What will I become? *he asked the beings in a clumsy approximation of their language.* Show me.

The Dreamers showed him only one thing. A roaring purple furnace of energy that baked his skin and shrivelled his eyes.

What does it mean?

We don't know, *they said.* But you will, when the time comes.

Yib'Wor returned from his travels much changed, and his family and few friends saw the difference at once. He had hardened, somehow, and when he looked at others he looked through them with an empty gaze, as though they weren't quite real. Embracing his mother after an absence of more than three years, he felt nothing.

He went to see Fe'Tril, now ensconced in his own work, but the tutor had nothing left to teach him.

The places where they tested for the Pretence have been closed down, Yib. They won't allow it anymore.

The world fell away beneath him. All that he had hoped for seemed dashed in an instant and he was trapped, trapped inside a dream until death came for him. He might live for thousands of years, perpetually extending his tenure, but it would come all the same, eventually, when the false galaxies dissolved and the suns burnt out.

And that he could not countenance.

In a fury he killed his old friend, throttling the life from him. When it was done Yib raided the Teachery for Fe'Tril's work, taking it all before burning the place to the ground.

He wandered, changing his name to something common and forgettable, suspecting this was only the first of such changes, and the future would prove him right. What to do with himself now? There had been only one goal, before— to learn how to rip down the Pretence and win the game, to show himself worthy to the creators and be elevated beyond the status of a mere pixel. To live forever.

He found a burrow at the edges of society, and began at once to study the workings of wild artificial minds, trapping them and dissecting their brains as Fe'Tril had done, in the hope that they might yield some clues. But they were not enough, and soon the hermit that had once been Yib'Wor progressed to organic beings. He invited his last friend to visit, pleading that he come alone, and when Xig'fis arrived Yib murdered him without a second thought. It was all of it just a game, after all, and none of them were real.

But I will be, *he thought.* In the end.

Darkness, my head pounding. The air seemed too thick to inhale. Fe'Tril's face appeared before me, disgusted, and I batted it away with a growl.

I scrambled, blind, feeling carefully in the nothingness. The walls were a pitted sponge of holes, their razor edges slicing into my palms.

Ah. I lit one of my electric matches, squinting from the flare.

It was a warren of caves, their walls glittering with fused minerals.

Could this be—

A deformed reality. A solid realm, where matter had multiplied unchecked.

I had heard of these places, but never encountered one.

I wandered for some time, intrigued. If I'd Dropped with a ship the thing would have dashed itself to pieces, never finding a way through. It was pure luck that I had fallen naked, small enough to fit through the cracks.

This wouldn't do on the way back up, especially if I was to avoid the seemingly well-travelled byway of the Hole.

What I needed was a map. A chart of the reefs and rocks that littered the eternal ocean of stacked realities. Something that would show me the way.

TOGETHER

Her ship was docked in one of the loading bays. Draebol hadn't been sure what to expect—some grandiose spike of colourful crystal, most likely, considering the operation was being funded by both Salqar and Lihreat—but certainly not this.

He accompanied Whirazomar down to the junk-stacked concourse of the bay, ignoring the stares of the blue-scaled workers milling around the ship. If that was what you could call it.

'Draebol,' said Whirazomar, stopping at the gaping mouth of the thing, 'meet Gnumph of Ingaal, our transportation for the foreseeable future.'

Draebol nodded to the creature uncertainly, meeting one of its bulbous silver eyes.

'It's not feeling itself at the moment,' she said, patting the thing's smooth white flank. 'Came through much larger here than usual, but will still do the job. Come on.' She stepped up onto what he thought might be a tongue and walked inside the thing's mouth.

Draebol cast a glance backwards, noting the hundreds of glowing red eyes watching him keenly, and followed her inside.

He felt at once that something wasn't right. The tunnel

of the creature's throat seemed to stretch for a hundred meters, spiralling at a gentle angle until Draebol was quite sure they were now walking upside down.

'I don't feel so well,' he began, looking with a surge of nausea back at a strangely shrunken view of the loading bay. It was all inverted.

'It's quite normal,' said Whirazomar briskly.

Ahead of them was the suggestion of light. Draebol could see the view magnifying unnaturally as he walked, making out a vast interior living space teeming with multicoloured beings that floated and paddled through the air, swarms of smaller beasts flitting amongst them. He gazed back one last time, and the bay was the right way up again, but appeared to be over half a mile away.

So, a transmission from the fabled Well, she had said. Some ancient warning sifted from the trillions of useless messages still filtering up through that crack in the realities, and here Draebol was, trembling from withdrawal and stepping into the mouth of an animal that claimed to be a ship, on his way to risk his life's work.

They floated down into the huge interior space.

'Surface conditions in here,' said Whirazomar, drifting over to a large, battered table. 'You won't need the Myriad anymore to look like your real self.'

He floated clumsily after her, picking up speed and missing the table entirely.

'Stick pads,' she called after him, throwing a string bag of the things in his direction. Draebol twisted in mid-air, missing the catch, and watched the bag sail off into the distance. He turned to find every passenger watching him.

A Phrailish Igmus arrived, smiling an unsettling, puckered-lips smile.

'Go with Nodo,' said Whirazomar. 'He'll make up a room for you.'

Draebol did as commanded, bumping off the wall.

He hadn't much hope for his quarters after seeing the communal area, and wished he'd got round to seeding a subdimension in his bag, so that he'd always have a place to sleep.

Are you Whirazomar's replacement? asked a floating Qathis as he and Nodo arrived outside the door to his room. Draebol could feel the chill rising from the translucent globe that surrounded its body.

Has she gone? asked another. *At last.*

He didn't quite know how to respond, and left them with the barest of nods to watch Nodo making up a sagging cot. Another, piled high with semi-weightless possessions, occupied the room.

'You're sharing with Lemuu,' said Nodo, once he'd tucked in the sticksheets. Draebol picked his way amongst the debris, tossed his bag on the bed—where it tried at once to float away again—and sat down beside it.

Nodo hovered at the doorway for a moment longer than seemed polite, gazing with avid pink eyes at the new arrival. Draebol stared back at him, waiting, until the silence seemed to thicken. The Igmus cleared his throat and smiled again, ducking out into the corridor.

Draebol took a deep breath as the door swung shut, staring around the grim, stinking little space, and shook his head.

Gnumph yawned with a subvocal rumble, stretching its claws and pushing off from the bay floor. Outside the bay it encountered vacuum and puffed itself out further, engorging as it passed through the network of junk ships drifting in and out of the hangar and powering out amongst the system's debris shell in a matter of seconds, a rate of acceleration thousands of times faster than anything the junker civilisation had ever known.

'So, anything happen while I've been away?' Draebol asked Whira, savouring the melodious, warbling chorus of his Surface dialect, a blend he hadn't heard since he'd left home. The string of sounds, unbroken by needless pauses for breath, stirred up old memories as perfectly as a scent. He had floated down clumsily from the second floor, missing the table and landing in the allotment, a dozen passengers applauding his descent.

'How long do you think you've been away for?' she asked, offering him some leftover dinner.

Draebol considered this as he wrangled his soup, which kept trying to make a break for it out of the hardlight bowl. 'Thirteen years, by my count.'

The vague look of disgust with which she'd been watching him trying to slurp up his soup disappeared. It was replaced, Draebol thought, with something worryingly like pity.

'What?' he asked. 'Give or take, of course. Could be fourteen, I suppose.'

'Sit down.'

He sat, feeling the pads on the chair sucking him in place. 'Fifteen?'

'Look, Draebol.' Whira sat beside him, a cluster of passengers listening keenly around them. 'We only caught up with you by shooting straight down the Well with a massive payload of Iliquin—'

He held up a finger, glancing desperately about for something to drink. 'How long have I been down here, Whirazomar?'

She scowled at the interruption, fiddling with a chunky ring on one finger. 'Well—' Her eyes flicked to meet his. 'As far as we can tell... just over two and a half thousand years.'

Draebol sat very still, his surroundings forgotten.

'I can't be any more precise than that, now that I'm below the Surface, too. Years might have passed since I left Salqar—there's no way of knowing down here.'

Draebol nodded absently, placing the bowl on top of some odd scratches on the table's surface—as if someone had marked off the days—and watched as it floated up with stately languor, slowly turning until its contents drifted across the room. A tiny dart of electric blue swooped from a higher floor, hoovering up as many morsels as it could.

He thought of his parents, back in Eldra, and his sister. He hadn't expected ever to see them again, of course, and had been so drunk when he'd said his goodbyes that their looks of disappointment and sadness still haunted him in his dreams. He had assumed that the slowing down and final cessation of their messages to him had reflected nothing but a lack of anything more to say, that perhaps they had just moved on with their lives, but it had never in all his dangerous travels occurred to him that he might outlive them, not so soon. Two *thousand* years. Now all of them, assuming they hadn't applied for an Extension, were gone.

Gone forever, unless what that Throlken had told him was true.

He picked up the bag and removed his bulging book of charts, cradling it in his hands before passing it over. Whira took it carefully, removing the clasps on the spool and unfurling it across the table.

Draebol cleared his throat, rising shakily to his feet. 'I've been mapping the pattern of the Phaslair seams. I think I can predict the strata as I go, now.'

'I know,' Whira said, her eyes not rising from the atlas. 'That's why we chose you.'

He kneaded his trembling hands, spotting a bottle of something at last and gesturing for it.

'They compress like rock,' he said, in between swigs. 'In regular layers. We're on the edge of a dense knot of mutated Phaslairs, I think.' He drained the bottle.

Whira said nothing while she unspooled the reams of the atlas to its end. Years of carefully transcribed notes flowed through her fingers, Draebol's scratchy writing appearing again in the Throlken alphabet—jagged, overlapping spirals of lettering he hadn't seen since he'd left the Surface.

Draebol looked at the scribbles he'd spent so long bent over, afraid for the first time that he might have wasted his life. He had lost his family, and for what? He was glad to hand the wretched thing over, to be rid of it.

They'll come from far and wide for this, Whira thought, forgetting Draebol's presence entirely as she gazed upon the thing she'd come so far to find. *And Thelgald and Phrail will fight amongst themselves for it, by the end. But will it come? This ancient creature? We must sow the seeds, lure it closer, so that it cannot help but take a peek.* She wondered not for the first time if it wasn't all just some ruse, if this wandering being existed at all. She imagined giving up on the whole mission, taking the atlas and selling it in the next place they came to, retiring nicely on the proceeds and forgetting about the whole thing. They would hunt her, she presumed, the Alms sending agent after agent until they found her at last; Phaslair membranes were no barrier, no matter how deep she hid.

She excused herself from the table, pressing with the pads of her feet and kicking up towards Gnumph's arched ceiling. She floated through a mid-air game of *Nonsense*, the three players grumbling and clutching at their drifting game pieces, and twisted in the direction of an unmarked doorway on the second floor. She reached out a hand to grab the railings, swinging herself onto the landing and whispering a command. At once a translucent mist of coagulating particles thickened around her, hardening into a clear Myriad environment suit.

Whira rapped smartly on the door, peering through a spyhole to make sure the airlock was engaged, and entered.

The chamber inside was another volume of unguessably vast space, a sealed subdimension imbued with a mighty, crushing pressure that would have flattened Whira to a frozen puddle of gore had the Myriad not conjured her up this armour. It was the home of something she had never seen properly—a pressure dweller named Gonce-Zo who only ever came out for meals wearing a bulbous plastic garment that resembled a house tottering around on five squat legs.

She stepped into Gonce's domain, comfortable that it would be sleeping at this time of day. The frozen ground crunched beneath her feet. A dim figure strolled at the corner of her vision: the peculiar fog in the room, sucked from a baby gas giant, sometimes made you see things. Whira ignored the mirror image of herself walking alongside. Another apparition, this time with its back to her, strolled ahead. Whira gazed at the back of her own head for a moment, admiring her painted horns until she came to the entrance of one of the tunnels set into the chamber floor.

Gnumph used this chamber for the storage of high-pressure goods—exotic foods and passengers, gas-giant technology and caches of watermoon pearls, as well as the bodies of all those who had died on the journey, swaddled against the pressure. In amongst this grisly cargo Whira had hidden something particularly special, and as she stepped down into the cavern's mouth she whispered to the translucent fingers of her Myriad suit so that billions of microscopic generators fired into life, conjuring a torch.

She opened her palm, casting a disk of light into the icy darkness. The weight of the atmosphere seemed more oppressive down here, squeezing and constricting her shoulders. It was all in her head—the Myriad, when locked together, were capable of hardening into one of the strongest substances known in Yokkun's Depth—but still she wanted to be gone from here as soon as possible. It was a bad place, and it held bad things.

She made her way through the passages of the cave, passing egg-shaped pressure cases of goods stacked haphazardly in sunken shelves. Motes of ice-dust, pressed together into lumps of grit by the motion of her passing, tinkled as they hit the ground. It was like wading through a settled avalanche of transparent snow.

Whira arrived at a whisperlocked case, its obsidian sides stamped with the portrait of Thelgald, and pressed her hand to the bolt, speaking her full name. It snapped open, and she levered off the lid.

Good. It hadn't shifted at all in transit, as far as she could tell. Whira bent and reached inside, unscrewing the elaborate black shell as carefully as she could and inspecting the contents. It slept soundly, perfectly contained by a planet's worth of pressure and trapped in its own weight. Indeed that was precisely where they built and stored them, she'd been told—on an installation inside the core of a giant planet at the very edge of Yokkun's Depth, a long-range Drop cannon permanently tracking its motions across the heavens should anything go wrong. The Throlken, in their ungraspable wisdom, seemed to allow such things, though Whira couldn't fathom why. Perhaps it amused them to see how far their subjects would try to bend their rules. Perhaps it was all a game to them. The mind boggled at what fantastically deadly weaponry the star gods themselves must have concocted over their three-hundred-million-year reign—technology they kept from the galaxy, even from the Alms themselves. Deathless teleportation, perpetual motion, time travel; the conspiracy theories abounded.

She sat down on one of the boxes, hands trembling slightly as she reattached the bomb's casing. It was safe. The warhead could sleep here for eternity, until the galaxy whirled itself to wisps and the universe collapsed upon itself once more; she needn't fear it. But still it terrified her more than anything she'd ever laid eyes on. She hesitated for a while before placing a finger on the cold, ice-slick surface of the casing, the imagined sensation of ungraspable power rising through the Myriad coating around her fingertip, and pulled her hand away.

DAZOR

Dazor: a coal black ice moon hiding a layer of ocean beneath its dirty shell, a society sealed away inside.

Through a forest of hanging weed I flew, slipping with quick jet thrusts into cold pockets of shadow. The siege was still ongoing, and the ice-formed daggers of hostile craft were everywhere amongst the weeds. I could hear them, through the green-tinted thickness of the water, zipping blips of sound pulsing into my cramped little cockpit. They sounded like whining, wheedling voices. I hated them already.

I lifted a three-fingered hand to twiddle a dial, shifting from my hunched position. I had opened my eyes here as a flabby, bone-white beast possessed of a single large spiralling horn, in a civilisation paralysed by four hundred and sixty years of constant war and siege. The aggressors, so they said, came from the darkness beneath the weed woods, and, after millennia of pillaging, the undercities had unified to make a stand.

Somewhere ahead lay a castle. What the enemy ships wanted with it I had no idea. Didn't care. All I knew, having interrogated my fair share of habitat libraries and their respective indignant—but eventually cooperative—librarians, was that it housed a person, a refugee from another land known as the Keeper of the Ways; a grandiose title for someone or something who might be able to point me in the right direction. The stranger from my homeland, also seeking the same, had come this way before me, foolishly signposting their trip. All I had to do was follow.

The sprouting stalactite of castle appeared between the weed forests at last, secreted inside a natural concavity on the inside of the moon's shell so that it could see for miles around it into the darkness of the ocean. I gazed at the immensity of it—a tiered, inverted encrustation of age-polished ice that glowed with an internal light, the guns of its battlements firing bright flashes into the murk. Some parts of the great structure were not shielded by ice, but by something more impregnable. For generations the life here had worked with their own brand of nuclear fission, and the castle wore an invisible cloak of directed radiation, deadly to anyone who came near without thick lead protection—something I happened to know could not be found here, where metals could only be mined in the crushing depths.

But *I* had some. And I would get what I wanted.

A gust of pressure across the distance, and I saw the first of the retreating armada streaming my way. It was now or never.

I banked my rubberised ship, expelling a burst of air and a huge silvery bubble, slipping out of the oncoming stream of a hundred or more retreating fighters, and shot straight for the glowing fortress.

The turret fire intensified, zipping through the bubble-streamered darkness. I kept to my course, sighting on a newer section of the castle so heavily shielded with radiation that its walls lay open, like a cross section, the frenzied movement and activity visible now inside. The turrets targeted me, one after the other, pounding flickers of light into the depths, but I twisted and spun, avoiding everything they hurled.

At last, as the stronghold reared before my eyes, I felt it. The radiation struck me like a hot, stinging slap across the head and chest, scalding my exposed skin. My vision doubled, tripled, diluting the lights of the place into glowing orbs. My fishy last meal came swimming up my gullet, stomach heaving. Not far now. With a handful of Vanishing Crystal none of this would matter.

The force of it grew, like hot branding irons stamped into my skin, clasping my skull, pressing into my eye sockets. I began to groan, to howl, to scream.

I limped between pillars as clear as cut glass, my body throbbing with pain. None of the occupants had dared to try and stop me, presumably because I was emitting so much radiation; they huddled at the rim of the hall, distorted apparitions glimpsed through clear columns of ice.

I raised my harpoon rifle weakly, but the soft folk who lived in the castle's hall had anticipated already what I wanted, and had brought it for me.

The Keeper of the Ways squirmed in the grip of the very people it had trusted to keep it safe. It was some sort of wriggling pupa, its skin spotted with livid red and yellow rings. At my approach its lips peeled apart with a hiss, exposing three serrated, venomous fangs.

'Do you bite?' I asked, my rasping voice echoing somewhere in the ice-carved ceiling of the hall. I snatched the thing out of its carer's hands, blocking its closing fangs with the barrel of the harpoon. 'I don't mind.'

I nodded to the residents of the castle and made my retreat, careful not to turn my back on any of them, the

Keeper struggling in my arms. As an afterthought I looked up to where my echoes had lingered, perhaps meeting the eyes of Those Who Watched. I had progressed on the board, I felt sure of it.

THE CRAVER

The Craver dwelt in the tunnels of the wooden mountain, spending its long life climbing blind through vertical darkness, where it preyed exclusively on a sentient species of fungus. It sired only one pup every two hundred and fifty years, fertilising itself without need of a mate when its belly was sufficiently full, and carried its young in a dangling, nut-like pouch beneath its long-legged body for up to a decade, feeding it solely with the regurgitated remains of its meals. It had no language, no personality, no social skills (never having come into contact with another of its kind), and when the time came for the mute child to leave it simply gnawed its way out of its mother's pouch, plopping into the cold, smooth tunnels and scampering away to a life of blind, black solitude.

It was not a good life, by any stretch of the imagination, and what was more unfortunate still was that in the Great Long Ago some extremely adventurous traveller had discovered that the regurgitated remnants of the Craver's fungal dinner presented a singularly delicious (if acquired) taste, and over the years a clandestine banqueting club had been set up, unbeknownst to the Craver, in its pouch. The weight of the dozen or so patrons (not to mention their luggage, porters, servants and plus-ones) more than equalled that of a gestating pup, and so the blind Craver carried them without complaint, fooled into believing it was with child and content to mindlessly and perpetually wander the tunnels for century after century, regurgitating its load of pre-mashed fungus into its pouch for the benefit of parasitic gluttons and gourmands from all across the cluster.

Inside the pouch, in a hollow precisely moulded by the imprint of the foetus the first diners had killed and tossed away, a kitchen of cooks worked the fungus mash into hundreds of varied and colourful delicacies, so that a never-ending dinner party raged always in the dark beneath the mountain, supplied by the duped and continually feeding Craver.

Luphro Dhahiel Zelt Taador of Alas, within Deephrull (Surface) had followed the scent this far. He was quite sure there were other agents of other Alms on the same trail, but as a Deep Eye, commissioned to lie in wait in the deepest Phaslairs within transmission range of the Surface, he had been one of the first activated in response to whatever unknown threat seemed to be making its way upwards, towards home.

And now here he was, having braved the war between the ice moons and journeyed to their parent planet of Ostrus, down into the polished tunnels of the wooden mountain and into the lair of the fearsome Craver (which still believed it was carrying its pup, and was therefore twice as dangerous to encounter in the black, claustrophobic tunnels). In a past life, Luphro had been a forty-mile-long titan of a male Om-Vorl, his wings more brightly patterned than any mating rival. Here he was a pale, wiry runt of a thing with an ungainly coiled horn growing out of his snout, one of the many related species that had evolved on one moon or another and multiplied across the whole system, conquering ice and water and desert moons and finally the single colossal planet of Ostrus, at the centre of it all, which, coincidentally, was where he now sat.

The table, set beneath an ornate, swaying candelabra, was a hammock of knotted rope containing twenty or more starter bowls at a time, in a state of constant flux between being delivered and taken away. The Ostroid natives of half a dozen moons reclined on cushions around the ever-changing feast, some clad in spectacular pressure and water suits, reaching across one another to hook or spoon what took their fancy, all gabbling away in a variety of local languages Luphro was only just getting the hang of. Everything here was frightfully expensive, but, since Luphro's Deep Eye contract gave him cart-blanche to spend whatever he needed, he ordered and ate as he pleased, just about catching the gist of the conversation around the hammock.

Talk predictably returned to the war—known as the War of a Hundred Pressures—beneath the ice-shelled moon of Dazor, which was only now coming to an uneasy end. Luphro had travelled here under the guise of a journalist—a front he'd employed many times throughout his travels—and now the person who had really drawn his interest sat right beside him.

He was a large, battle-scarred specimen. His skin had been burned a livid red and hung in loose, painful-looking rolls around his face. His single tooth was stained and crusted, and when he reached for food his hands shook with palsy. Luphro could scarcely believe what he'd found. *This was what they were afraid of? After all that?* Was that appalling scream he'd heard, pumped up through the rent in the Phaslairs at the cost of an empire's worth of energy, really to warn the peoples of the future about this pitiful thing? What in all the worlds could it do to harm anyone,

227

let alone a galaxy? He wished he could have come through in his one true form, tearing down through the sky towards this rotten mountain and obliterating it in one blow. All their problems could be over, just like that.

But such thinking was pointless. Nobody had any idea yet what type of creature the ancient thing had been when it was sent down; Luphro ought to be thankful they were the same here—a meeting on the Surface was a game of chance he could, conceivably, lose.

What if it's the size of a moon? he thought, watching the thing eat from the corner of his eye. *Or a star? Perhaps in its true form it's a deadly pathogen? Or a sea monster?* If there was one thing the gargantuan Vorl of Deephrull hated, it was the sea.

He took care, under the pretence of writing a piece about the Craver's dining club, not to speak too much to any one creature there, but tried to engage the being beside him in conversation all the same.

'So you have come from the war, mirhu?' he asked, using the polite term of address for one from the Dazor moon.

The battle-ruined thing nodded, shovelling more food into its mouth without meeting his glance, fingers and lips smeared. Luphro was acutely aware that he was perhaps the first Sovereign agent ever to meet with it.

'You must have a few stories.'

For this he was rewarded with a sharp glance. He gazed into yellow, cataract-clouded eyes that looked almost dead, like a mask.

The pouch shifted violently, creaking like a wooden vessel in a gale, which Luphro knew meant a fresh arrival was dealing with the Craver. Some muted shouts drifted in from outside, the rumble of the beast's challenge vibrating in reply. They would be waving flaming torches at it, trying to get it to rear up so they could reach the rope ladder dangling underneath.

The noises stilled, replaced with a muffled grunting, and finally a curse. Mowllish porters heaved in baggage and furniture. Then came their master, a Durgoh, from the desert moon, thickly robed in red. His long white nose twitched as he scented the banquet and exchanged greetings with the dining club in a variant of the dialect that Luphro hadn't yet learnt. When the Durgoh merchant's eyes met those of Luphro's table companion something seemed to pass between them, and the sunburned creature rose at once and made for its room, the Durgoh following soon after.

Luphro eyed the closed door, unprepared, and did the only thing he could think of: he twisted the cap from the vial hung around his neck and released its invisible contents into the air.

The Microscopia, his partners in crime and the only things that could have escaped detection by the complex scanners that had searched him at Ostrus Junction, ascended without a word. Luphro screwed the cap shut again and excused himself.

The view from the balcony was nothing but hot, stinking blackness, a sense of movement as the pouch swayed, and the sound of the Craver's feet padding across ancient layers of deposited wood buffed smooth by its eternal wanderings, occasionally taking long, huffing sniffs of the air.

He felt them returning, whispering past his ears and settling in his hair.

They spoke of a spoiled Phaslair, the microscopic things said to him, *and a Worldtrain loaded with all the treasures of the galaxy. There's something there it wants, a picture of something. The merchant said he would lead our target to the Worldtrain, for a considerable sum. More than this they would not say, as if they sensed us, then.*

Luphro nodded imperceptibly, opening the vial for them

to re-enter. That was that then: his target was confirmed, and perhaps the answer the Alms sought.

How to travel upwards.

He dared to smile in the darkness. He would be rich, after all. He took a handful of Ostrus money from his pocket and inspected it by the light of his glowing ring. Rough, woody red stones, like fruit pips, with holes bored carefully into their surface.

And now for the matter of the assassination, once they had led him to the prize. Poisoning, with the Microscopia's help, seemed the most poetic answer. They knew nothing of the microscopic creatures here, since the Throlken did not exist on any of these Phaslairs. The seething had minds of their own and seemed perfectly content to travel and commit murder with him, and though they sometimes came through giant-sized or incomprehensible, they were never less than helpful.

He turned in the blackness, ready to go in, his spirits buoyed like never before, and sensed only then that he was not alone.

The tooth sawed through his throat with a series of strong, tugging rips that Luphro felt the force of rather than any pain. It was only when his head peeled back and dangled from his neck that he understood something was majorly wrong, and by the time it had dropped to strike the floor of the tunnel he was barely capable of understanding anything at all.

The Microscopia watched it all as if in slow motion. They could have stopped the target from killing their master, they supposed, but enough of their number agreed in silent whispers that it was the way of the universe, and they could be free now to see what this entity would do with its newfound abilities.

Before they dispersed into the tunnels of the mountain they had time to witness the Craver scoop up Luphro's head, crunch thoughtfully on it, and drool the remaining soup into its pouch for the diners to enjoy.

TALES

It was his first real hangover since leaving home.

Draebol awoke beneath the commons table, suspended globules of vomit hovering around his face. He blinked, screwing his eyes shut again. Breakfast was going on above, and nobody seemed to have noticed him under their feet.

He recalled raiding the cupboards, downing everything he could find; arguments and shouting and broken jugs, a late night feast of stolen supplies, crumbs everywhere.

Draebol moaned softly, rolling and opening his eyes. They had shrivelled in their sockets, his vision blurry. Every pore on his skin was purging, leaking white sweat, and his tongue had enlarged to twice its size. His crotch felt clammy; he probed down there with a trembling hand. He'd pissed himself.

Normally, if you were good to them, Microscopia cleaned that sort of thing up for you, using whatever they found for their own mysterious purposes. But not Draebol, who had slighted them somehow in the dim and distant past—he could not recall when or how. He inched his way out from under the table, not caring what the breakfasters thought of him. What else was there to do when you discovered that everyone you knew and loved was most likely dead and gone? Draebol floated into the air, not looking back, the hubbub pausing a moment behind him before resuming.

Screw them. This was a sporeship, after all, with tickets as cheap as blummy cakes: they'd seen worse.

Draebol navigated his way delicately to the toilet, ducking inside the chamber. Thanks to the Myriad's general fastidiousness of late, it was sparklingly clean, but an aura of untold horrors still hung around the pan-species room. All manner of illicit things must have happened in here, Draebol imagined, selecting one of the gravity troughs and vomiting in sobbing, self-pitying heaves. When he was done he gazed through tear-rimmed eyes at the ruined walls, every centimetre decorated with names and dates and scraped lettering from a hundred thousand systems, all of which he could read.

Four hundred and six and one quarter days aboard, read one of the scratched notes, singled out amongst the constellations of thoughts. *Forgotten where I'm going now.*

Draebol cradled his head for a while, then picked up a stained toothstick from the floor and scraped tentatively at the wall himself, working over the top of some crudely drawn Luppsark genitalia. *Draebol of Eldra lost everything here.*

'Ever used that locket around your neck?' he asked, tipping a shovel of synthetic sticky-dust into the allotment and patting it down, still feeling delicate despite a restorative breakfast. Whira was floating cross-legged on the floor above, spooling through a Myriad datastream of his very own Phaslair charts. The swirling layers coiled together like mixing paint.

'It's an antique,' she muttered, half-absorbed in the conjured curve of imagery in front of her. 'Probably too dangerous to use.' She took a sip from her steaming cup and glanced down at where Draebol was gardening with Lemuu and Nurtil. 'My Myriad could probably magic me up something better, couldn't you darlings?'

He cocked his head, listening keenly to the silence that fell after her question. If the Myriad replied, only Whira could hear them.

'But it's a crystal Sovereignty pendant, isn't it?' Draebol asked. 'Worth a lot of money.'

She sniffed, not meeting his gaze, the conversation apparently at an end. He recognised his own charts, rendered into three dimensions, and marvelled at the change that had come over him; for the first time in millennia he found himself in the presence of a female of his own species, and yet he felt nothing—no urge to show off, to impress. He felt empty.

'Mmm, well, it must be nice for you to have the Myriad's ear,' Draebol muttered, getting back to the planting. 'I don't think they like me.'

'I'm sure it's nothing personal,' Whira said with a small smile, still absorbed in her charts. 'They don't like anyone.'

'How did you manage to win them over?' he asked. 'Or is it a secret?'

'Even I'd like to know the answer to that one,' she replied. 'They just came to me. Perhaps they'll leave again one day—they won't say.'

To command the Myriad to any extent was a rare talent indeed, manifested in only a fraction of a percent of the galaxy's inhabitants. Say the right thing and they might decide to help you in any number of ways, from assembling into computronium substrates, shields or items in the blink of an eye, interfering with complex security systems or revealing an enemy's every secret. But they could be mischievous, and were known to play havoc with the lives and fortunes of those they didn't respect: just imagining what they might be capable of in a Lawless Phaslair, where they could meddle unobserved by the Throlken, made Draebol profoundly uneasy. But, to a blessed few—those deemed more witty or noble or fascinating than most, known colloquially as *the Polite*—the Myriad were a source of great and wonderful powers; to others (particularly the rude) they were a curse, especially if you wanted something complicated done, in which case you had to pay for access to slaved volumes of considerably less ingenious Microscopia or buy into a subdimension. Academies dedicated to learning how to win the Myriad's favour had been founded across the galaxy, all without success; it was as though the swarm of sentient viruses, machines and particles knew precisely who was trying to butter them up, and acted accordingly.

Draebol planted his shovel in the soil, leaning on it. 'So? Show us some tricks, then.'

Whira yawned, cracking her knuckles as she stretched, the Myriad dissolving the maps in front of her without a word passing between them. 'Must I?'

Draebol shrugged. Nurtil and Lemuu tied their floating baskets down and gazed up at her, expectant. They were both upper atmosphere dwellers from the same world, their bodies and faces hidden entirely by folds of their own rubbery flesh, which had been grown out to form clothing.

The Myriad took it upon themselves without Whira having to say a word, surrounding Draebol with a gust of air. His voice filled the space, accompanied after a moment by more than a dozen three-dimensional images of himself floating amongst them and promenading on the upper floors. Draebol heard a great, tide-like overlapping of his own words, some of them spoken many years before, and recognised himself at different ages. He broke out in a sweat. *Recordings.* The Myriad had recorded him.

There he was, being knocked back by that local girl in Omuzz; swearing as he accidentally speared himself through the leg during a ceremonial duel (it had had to be cancelled after that, he recalled); falling off his mount in Farovar and ruining the trip for everyone; standing up too early to receive his academy prize and lingering, crippled with embarrassment, at the front of the hall while other names were called out. Draebol winced as he watched the last, tucking his head into his shoulders.

'Alright!' he called, gesturing to the invisible mass of Myriad. 'I get it. Thank you very much. And thank you for invading my privacy.'

'*My* Myriad didn't,' replied Whira as the spectral Draebols vanished, 'but they move as one; each speck holds the memories of them all.'

That made sense, Draebol supposed. He'd never wondered precisely how the Myriad did what they did. He cocked his head. 'How about they show us some of the more interesting moments in my life, then? My encounter with the fearsome—'

'Got to get back to work,' interjected Whira, summoning up the Phaslair seams once more. 'Apologies.'

Draebol cleared his throat and went back to his gardening, refilling the hole he'd just dug.

'You forgot to put the seed in—' mumbled Nurtil. Draebol glared at her and handed the shovel over, dusting off his hands.

That wasn't very kind, Whirazomar, rumbled Gnumph through the walls when Draebol had gone.

'He'll be fine,' she said, turning back to her charts. 'I've got us at nineteen thousand Phaslairs down, the second vein.'

Thereabouts.

Whira brought up the relevant pages, scrolling through simulated bands of Phaslairs written into existence by the

Myriad that morning after they'd studied Draebol's chart. 'Are we in Lawless territory yet?'

Yes. They all are down here.

The Myriad had been sifting the rising signals for days, collating everything in the hope of finding a suitable place. Uncountable Phaslairs below Whira's quarry rose to greet them, passing through a frontier of realities that had never known the Throlken's rule. But where to stop? It was guesswork: dropping deep enough that the scent of their bait could drift and entice, without falling too far and missing their target entirely. The transmissions of a handful of Deep Eye Sovereignty agents acted as a regular compass reading, advising on the suitability of Phaslairs where illicit trade still existed, their signals a distant light in the dark. Every once in a while Gnumph would fall silent, and Whira knew they were passing through realms in which—from the outside—she and the other passengers in its stomach did not exist. With each loss of contact she felt her guts constrict, remembering that unbearable month confined to this place, and was instantly soothed with thoughts of Tiliph, wherever he was, watching out for her.

Whira thought she knew everything. She treated the other passengers like filth, like a herd of brainless livestock whose natural place in the universe was several rungs below hers. She didn't know them. Even one day and night into his voyage, Draebol understood more about the creatures he shared this place with than she ever had. The realities the two of them occupied simply weren't the same.

She didn't know a thing.

He curled up in bed, a few of the baby Yiths wriggling under the covers to share his warmth; they seemed to never tire of chattering to one another, even in the middle of the night. Luckily for them, Draebol hated silence. In every moment of silence he heard the Throlken's words, spoken with an empty, formless voice in what had felt like the core of his brain.

He closed his eyes, recalling the landscape of rolling, liquid flame, the currents of heat that parted before them. The Irraith had taken him within a section of its globe, and dropped swiftly through the dazzling, gaseous lands of its people to an ocean of flattened fire. Draebol recalled the darkness of that fire as they'd sunk below it to the star's convection zone, a baking, black heat that flickered with scales of rusty flame.

He'd had no idea what he would see. The rumours of the Throlkens' appearance all contradicted one another. Fear had paralysed him.

They'd travelled under a heavier darkness. Silence filled his ears, enclosed inside the scorching mass of the star.

Nothing. No voice had spoken, no light appeared. Even the Irraith seemed to have vanished. Draebol had wondered if he might have died, perhaps on the way down, the globe failing somehow, and this was what it was like.

You often wonder what it will be like, he'd thought, and then done the mental equivalent of a double take. That thought had not been his own.

His hearts could have given out. All the highfalutin ceremony of his practised greetings had evaporated at once.

What is *it like?* asked the thought that wasn't his. *What is it like to die?*

It's like this.

And then he'd known.

THE COLLECTORS

Ahawoph had fished the holy river since he'd been a sproutling, traipsing the weedy banks with his wire nets and baskets, catching all manner of curiosities that came up from the unknown. He knew from what he'd been told that the bottomless river went right through the world and out into space, leaking into other places that he could never comprehend. Whatever. It was a good living, and he'd lost any sense of wonder as he sat by the bank, listening for the bells that jangled periodically from his nets.

He squatted and pissed into the dark water, mind far away. Old Aphral was burning something on the meadow, he could smell it. The crescent moon Higroth floated in the dull, muggy sky, while a small red sun skirted the horizon, sinking only once a lifetime.

It was mostly cheap stuff that came up along this part of the river: wild things that didn't know they'd Dropped, or bits of rubbish and wrecked ships. The best places to fish were upstream, at the Pond, but he couldn't afford a spot. You caught a traveller almost every day up there, following some invisible road they all knew. But occasionally some missed the mark and bubbled up in Ahawoph's patch, and he and his children could break their fast.

Ahawoph's long ears twitched at the jingle of a bell. He

ambled over to check the nets, pulling out some thrashing, hissing gobbler sprats and tossing them back in further downstream, waiting. What *was* Aphral burning over there? Smelled like—

A surge of water turned his head. The surface of the river erupted as a huge water beast tore its way through a net and flopped into the weeds on the bank, gasping. It retched violently, coughing up a slimy assortment of beings that wore mismatching spacewear and helmets. A few of them began exclaiming loudly in a language Ahawoph had never heard and wiping themselves down. The thing coughed again, vomiting up some furniture and equipment, followed by a haze of sooty air that swept up into the sky.

Ahawoph watched, grinning, as they collected themselves.

Whira, having checked with the Myriad that the air was suitable, opened her helmet to look at her reflection in the water's edge, frightened of what she might see. She took a deep breath, relieved beyond measure; Gnumph's belly had carried her here unchanged.

Gnumph itself, however, had come through as something else entirely. Its scaly, iridescent body lay panting on the bank.

'Head count,' she shouted, calling names. Most of the larger passengers had made it out. 'For everyone wishing to get off,' she said, 'this is it. Last stop. I repeat: *last stop.*'

One of the locals was observing them from over by some broken nets: a long-eared bipedal being with ebony skin and a pair of gangly, multiply jointed arms twice the length of its legs. One small crimson eye, its pupil all white, gazed back at her from a chinless face, and it seemed to smile, revealing tangled rows of pale, hooked thorns that must have been teeth. The thing wore a jumble sale of tatty clothing and equipment, and approached them carrying a small clear bottle. Whira hesitated, watching as it went to work bottling the air around them, carefully screwing on the lid and packing it away inside a fur-lined case.

'*Iyeba ahar, gyobmyetts*,' the person said in a voice so high that it hurt her ears, examining them all from head to toe as if he or she were measuring them for a set of clothes.

Whira cast her gaze around the sticky debris pile for Draebol's plastic translator. The ring was in one of the table's drawers, and she took it out while the local gabbled on, setting it with three sharp taps to voice mode.

'*Bragseg al vol dyetma sum*—GET SOME OF YOUR HAIR.' They glanced at the ring, which was on full volume by accident. How on earth it could work so quickly and from such a short sample she had no idea. Whira could only assume it had met a similar language structure before and was recycling what it knew, employing some heavy-duty guesswork while it tuned itself up. She searched the dull sky for the Myriad, but they were nowhere to be seen.

'What was that about hair?' asked Nodo.

The local answered his question for him, taking some hooked shears out of its pocket and snipping a clump of Whira's ear tuft before she could react. It dropped the hairs into a little packet, sealing it.

'VALUABLE,' the ring translated. 'BECAUSE YOU FROM ABOVE PHASLAIR. WORTH MANY CONDIMENTS.'

Whira rubbed her eyebrow, assuming the device still wasn't working at full speed.

The red sun cried less shrilly here than on most worlds of Whira's Surface, perhaps because there was less detritus between the star and its planets. It was still just audible over the cacophony of animal life in the meadow as a thin, plaintive roar. Amongst their feet an array of ground-dwelling species extended brightly coloured feelers and tongues into the air like flower stalks, apparently lapping at nothing but the daylight. As each creature collected a tongueful of light they left a scratch of pure, matt darkness behind, like a shadow on the surface of space. Draebol flinched as one of the tongues stretched up to lick his hand, leaving a scar of blackness. He stared in horror at the patch of shadow, passing his hand in front and behind, watching as it slowly filled with light again.

The creature led the way, holding tightly onto Whira's hand, while most of the other passengers were employed in hauling their furniture and possessions. Shumholl, Draebol and Nurtil carried Gnumph on their shoulders, while the Zabbas slithered along behind, a procession of the slower, smaller passengers bringing up the rear.

Soon she spied the destination: a tumbledown heap of a dwelling rising from the meadow, smoke coiling from three bent chimneys in its thatched roof. A crowd of smaller, no less hunched and shabbily dressed individuals stood in the vegetable patch, awaiting their arrival.

'MY CHILDREN,' said their guide through the translator.

The children surrounded Draebol first, wheeling over a complicated, battered-looking machine that must have been their equivalent of a camera and filming him very close up. He turned his head away from the probing nozzle of the device, batting it to one side when he'd had enough. They seemed particularly interested in the horns that grew from the back of his skull, reaching to caress them.

'Don't these people give their guests a drink first?' he growled, miming an imaginary bottle for their host's benefit and bringing it to his lips. 'Drink?'

'AH, WATER, YES.'

'No,' Draebol countered, clearly alarmed. 'Not water.' He glanced at the other passengers desperately. 'Something, er—' He crossed his eyes and staggered about, miming extreme drunkenness. The children giggled; a wince-inducing noise like sheets of metal scraping together.

Their host gazed at him with its single unblinking eye. 'NO WATER?'

'By the Irraith.' He snatched the translator ring out of Whira's hand and pushed it onto his finger. 'Alcohol! Ring, say *alcohol*.'

'DOYISAVATMAHARYUMNETOGOBAFLOTSIMIN-EATOCROBAVASULE—'

Their host cocked its head at the ring, which was still reeling off a chain of phonemes. Whira tapped it and it fell silent. 'They don't *have* any, Draebol.'

'Something else, then,' said Draebol, visibly sweating. 'Anything. What have you got that cleans things—'

'*Stop it*,' hissed Whira, grabbing his finger and pulling off the ring. She turned to their host. 'Water, thank you.'

It shuffled off, sending its children on various errands around the cluttered house. A few remained, gaping at the visitors, their attention drawn to Gnumph, who lay with a dejected expression in the middle of the floor.

Whira smiled awkwardly at them and went to the thick glass of the window. The place was like a gloomy junk shop of interdimensional trinkets. 'What have you got for me?'

The Myriad whispered back, having surrounded the house in a swirling, invisible swarm. Riders were on their way, they told her, alerted by a radio call. And there was more. Travellers Dropping to this world's equivalent of the Well Station—a round, scummy lake about three miles upriver—were being detained in a small town.

'What do you mean, detained?'

Whira listened. She turned to the others, some of whom were trying to make bumbling conversation with the children, to little effect. The creatures just watched and smiled.

'Show me the riders.'

A circle appeared in the air before her, showing three elaborately dressed beings riding shaggy, six-legged mounts through the meadow flowers. At the sight of the Myriad's projection the children gasped, gabbling to one another and fleeing the room.

'Do they have weapons?' Whira asked.

The Myriad magnified, zooming in on bulges in the riders' gear. The image turned x-ray, detailing the mechanisms of a variety of interesting guns.

'Alright. Keep them occupied.'

The Collectors caught sight of Ahawoph's house. A tumultuous reddish cloud had settled over the roof, and was now descending to meet them. It flattened and opened, its softness hardening until a high, smooth wall surrounded the party. They twisted in their saddles, the Trowzels baying, seeing that they were trapped, and opened fire upon the wall.

It absorbed everything they threw at it, sucking up every bolt of light.

The rider at the head of the column folded his arms, unprepared for such clever Abovers. He rummaged in his saddlebags for the radio.

'So we can't leave here,' said the Zabbas. 'Is that what you're saying?'

'Be my guest,' said Whira tersely, 'if you want to be eaten.'

'Scrapher was right,' the Zabbas moaned. 'You've taken us down here against our will, to our doom—'

Whira turned away and blanked out the beast's irritating voice, listening to more whispers.

'There's an aircraft on its way,' Whira said, crouching beside Draebol.

Draebol was searching the cupboards for anything he could drink or snort, and had to replay what she'd just said. 'A *what*?'

A group of passengers turned to look at them, mouths open.

The wall of Myriad grew a slim tower, stretching until it rose a few hundred feet over the meadow. It sighted the approaching craft at once, a twinkle of weak sunlight some way off, and fired a narrow beam of itself across the land.

The pilot fell fast asleep inside his cockpit, the controls working without him. The Myriad brought the four-winged bomber down for a soft landing on one of the meadow lanes, dismantling it as it rolled to a stop and stacking every component in order of size, fluffing the seat padding into a pillow for the dozing pilot.

Whira and the passengers watched from an upstairs window. The Myriad wall stood like an amphitheatre of smoke between them and the river, the glimmer of shots occasionally lighting its interior. The house's inhabitants, aware at last that things weren't going to plan, had left quickly by the backdoor. Whira went to a south-facing window and waved them goodbye.

Out in the walled vegetable garden, surrounded on all sides by stinking orange buds, they went through everything coming out of Gnumph's belly. The poor creature had been carried gently over to a patch of soil, and was busy vomiting up chairs, crockery, bags and cases. Lucky came waddling out of Gnumph's mouth, slick with saliva and hurriedly refocussing his eyes. Whira watched anxiously as the passengers swarmed the leavings, looking for their personal possessions. A fight had broken out between Shumholl and Zees over a set of goblets, but she paid it no heed.

Drebol came to stand beside her. 'Looking for something?'

'What?' she stared at him a moment, then back at the throng. 'No.'

Draebol patted the dirty old knapsack slung over one shoulder. In his hand he had a clear flask of something viscous. 'Got my stuff.'

Gnumph's mouth distended as it brought up something large. The fighting stopped for a second as people stood back to watch. An angular, wheeled vehicle came tumbling out sideways, shiny with slobber.

'Amphibious landing craft,' said Gnumph in between swallows and gasps for air. Its singsong voice was high-pitched but resonant. 'I've had it in the hold for sixty years. Was supposed to deliver it, but nobody came to collect. Some of my passengers on that trip got bored, assembled it.'

There were a lot of *oohs* and *aahs* as people crowded around the thing, tipping it the right way up and pushing it over to the far side of the garden for a test run.

'Might come in useful,' said Draebol.

'Mmm.' Whira barely heard him. She stalked up to Gnumph. 'That everything?'

He looked apologetic. 'I believe so. Barring the still incarcerated Scrapher, of course, the contents of rooms six and nine, the environment spheres and the pressure chambers—'

'Good,' she interjected. 'We should make ready to leave.' A thought slowed her step, and she turned. 'You alright?'

Gnumph smiled. 'Yes, thank you. Keen to be myself again.'

'Hmm, well. Let's get on with it.'

At Whira's command the Myriad prison dissolved, drifting across the meadow like bonfire smoke. The Collectors kicked their dozing mounts to their feet and climbed

248

into their saddles, sighting their weapons on the party of strangers.

Whira sat atop the garden wall, her Drop rifle steady. She squeezed off a shot as the Myriad's cloud shadow darkened the field. A rider vanished, spooking its mount and sending it bolting away towards the river. She panned the scope, catching another in its saddle and disappearing its head and left arm. Whira breathed in sharply, the sight wobbling. If she wasn't mistaken, she had just killed someone for the very first time in her life. Her skin prickled, despite the knowledge that there were no Throlken here to see.

No time. Get the job done, think about it later.

They were galloping faster now, and she wasn't confident she could hit another before the glimmering light bolts found her position.

A portion of the Myriad turned in the air, forming into flickering obelisks of solid matter that jumped in and out of existence to intercept each bolt of light. Whira slowed her breathing and steadied her aim, firing another Iliquin bullet and vanishing a galloping beast's front legs so that its rider tumbled into the flowers.

The passengers were crowded behind her in a nervous group, Gnumph already loaded along with the rest of the furniture, food and belongings onto the racks on the amphibious vehicle's roof. A storm of Myriad dropped over the meadow like ragged mist, enveloping them just as Whira sighted her rifle once more.

The transformation was a sight to behold. A hull glowed into being around them, bathing the passengers in a waft of hot air as translucent armour fused from binding Myriad, bursting apart the garden walls. The interior grew a succession of nested partitions as they rose above the meadow, a web of components hardening into a Dzull drive and flickering into life as the Myriad formed a vacuum chamber and introduced their swiftly manufactured load of antimatter. Whira found herself in a clear-nosed observation deck, still in a crouch. The writhing, manifold complexity around her grew a splendid white carapace of translucent moulding, followed by a carpeting of upholstered material that blossomed out of the interior shell like a fine fungal growth, soft as the densest fur.

Whira sat back in her supremely comfortable chair, her Drop rifle hovering and stowing itself inside a recessed armoury in the bulkhead, while yelps of delight filtered from other chambers in the ship. The process had taken a matter of moments, and they were already above the clouds and soaring into the black-tinged blue, ready to tear away.

'That went surprisingly well,' said Draebol, joining her and settling into a hastily formed seat. The stars hardened into fine strobing lines of light beyond the curve of the clear hull, their positions trembling as the drive warmed up.

'Well done,' Whira whispered to her Myriad, patting the soft wall. It vibrated beneath her palm in recognition. Their journey beyond the atmosphere and out of the world's gravity well was otherwise silent and without any sensation of movement, as though everything she saw outside was nothing but a projection.

The silence lingered, and then Draebol spoke.

'It's on a timer, isn't it?' he said, almost too softly to hear. She didn't look at him.

'It must be very powerful, if you have to keep it pressurised.'

Whira took a deep breath, sensing the weight of the silver pistol on her hip. 'It's called an immersion warhead. It's a small one.'

'Oh well, that's alright then,' scoffed Draebol. 'What's it going to do, tickle everyone to death—'

'*It expands in low pressure*,' Whira growled, raising her voice over him. 'It fills up empty space and freezes solid. A few solar systems, at most.'

Draebol blinked. 'A few *systems*? I don't know how insane the Alms have gone since I left, but I'd call that overkill, wouldn't you?'

'We don't know what we're dealing with. We don't know what it *wants*. We have to be sure we've neutralised the threat.'

Draebol shook his head, studying his hands. When he spoke at last he sounded sad. 'I suppose Gnumph doesn't know? You're just going to let it off inside it, without so much as a goodbye? And what about all these other folk, stuck in the wrong reality?'

She rounded on him, every hair on her body bristling. 'Those were my *orders*. I gave that useless lot every chance to disembark. If you've got a better idea—' She sniffed, glancing away. 'If you don't like it I can leave you here, too.'

Draebol's voice was soft. 'You must tell them, Whira.'

She opened her mouth and promptly closed it again, shaking her head.

OUBLISH

Winter approached with a flurry of storms, the berries maturing swiftly in their caverns. Tiliph sang gently to them while he bustled about, admiring their burnished glow as the weather worsened beyond the caves, roaring across the land of Oublish.

The day had come to travel to market, there to provide his buyer with a sample of this year's crop. Tiliph dug his travelling gear out from storage, humming contentedly in the dim cavelight as he packed his bags and hefted a selection of the largest berries into a sling hamper, buckling the whole assemblage to his back while he draped the bags from his outstretched wings.

Satisfied that the remaining berry crops were warm and cosy, he dropped from his inverted home to the distant floor of the cave, opening his eight wings and gliding over the swathes of his neighbours' plantations, headed for the cave mouth's pinprick of light.

He heard the wind before he felt it, a plaintive wail that cried from the white circle of the open cave. Tiliph braced himself against the blast, hovering to say his goodbyes to the Om-Vorl at the gate, and flapped out into the storm.

The snow, driven screaming through the chasm, coated him at once. He descended through the tearing wind, his extremities frozen numb already, until he was beneath the cloud layer. The snow melted to sleet, then to drizzle. He felt his muscles warming as he pumped his wings, and soon the world below was revealed through the cloud.

The seventy-mile-wide channel of Slunopapat Gorge had not been dug or eroded, but clawed out. It had happened sometime before Tiliph's species ever existed: some unidentified visitor from the dim and distant large enough to grasp the planet Zingost with one claw as it passed, tearing a gouge across its surface and hurling it briefly out of the orbit of its parent star. As such the planet sailed on an extremely irregular ellipse that took it far from its sun for many years at a time, resulting in long winters of hibernation. Unfortunately for Tiliph, transistor berries only ripened in the coldest season, keeping him underground for the summer years and out peddling his crop around greater Oublish and Vounel in winter. He could easily have found himself a new profession, he was sure, but his was a family business many generations old, and he would be ashamed to let it go to someone who didn't love the berries as he did.

He glided through the drizzle into the lower levels of the gorge, passing the worked arches of sunken dwellings and halls, his wings carrying him two miles with every beat. The walls of the chasm were plated with Hizzidion shell, and spangled radiant, sickly green reflections that lit up the lower world beneath the bruised bluster of the storm. Larger Vorls passed in the dimness of the gorge: streamlined shapes sailing by with a great gust of turbulence that rattled the teeth in his jaw and sent smaller flying creatures and the flitting ships of other, tinier species dancing like feathers in a breeze. As he rounded a curve, a flotilla of minuscule swellships passed him by, their lights blazing in the gloom, followed by the gnarled white dagger of a crystal Sovereignty vessel that swept beneath him, its course quite unperturbed by the downthrust of his wings.

*　　*　　*

After a few days' flight Tiliph stopped for a meal, hovering in the smog of the lowest layer while he bellowed his business to the owner of a feasting hall until the surly cook ushered him inside. He stalked into the dim warmth of the cavern, depositing his bags and crop.

Finally, warm and dry and perching upside down, Tiliph opened his portal. He usually read the gaming news while he ate, but today he searched the channels, hoping to hear her voice again.

There she was. He snarled an upside down grin, happy beyond words to hear she was safe. *Whira*. She had sent him some footage of their voyage, showing some of the other passengers, but he only had eyes for her. It pained him each selling season to know that he wouldn't be able to get out into the infrasphere so much, but this winter he'd stopped caring about such things. He finished his food and settled up, composing a lengthy reply and sending her some images of himself, bashful at the thought of how he would appear.

I apologise for my face, he wrote, wondering for the tenth time whether he ought to delete the pictures. *It must look monstrous to you. But I assure you that—*

He paused, trying to phrase his thoughts.

—that I see nothing but beauty in yours.

WORLDTRAIN

Years passed in obscurity, but he couldn't escape his crimes forever. Yib'Wor was chased from his ramshackle home and hounded into the wilderness of South All, to become a hermit in the Worlds of Little Governance. The deaths he had left in his passing taught him only one thing: that this was not the game board—it existed elsewhere. He must have access to the machinery *that Fe'Tril had spoken of, the machinery that could break reality open.*

The place where most of the experiments were conducted was in a region of South All known as the Inescapable Hole, *an ancient crevice in the membranes. The equipment surrounding it had fallen silent and still, on the orders of* every *Quarter of the All. The Curious had dug too far, they believed, weakening the structure of reality, and it was ruled that their efforts be thwarted before existence literally caved in around them.*

There was only one way to restart the research against the All's wishes, but for that he needed power. *Extraordinary* power.

He would have to focus his energies on a single task: influence. To become emperor of South All required the sacrifice of a lifetime of devoted selflessness. Most who fancied themselves for the job could barely manage a hundred years before giving up, settling into respectably lofty careers in the echelons below. But Yib'Wor knew he would stay the course, for there was no other alternative.

He began by applying for a stewardship on one of the forgotten planets, perfectly placed to begin the task of helping the lesser creatures of the All. He gained no satisfaction from the work—an endless drudgery of serving petitions and answering complaints, cooking and cleaning and caring: the route to power was a staircase of interstellar dimensions, each step taking a year's hard graft to climb, but with each step he exalted, knowing he was one year closer. He was on the board at last, playing the game, and everyone he met was a piece to be taken, consumed, shunted aside.

Years passed, and the selfless life he constructed drew a modicum of attention at long last. The name Yib'Wor had by now been forgotten, and the rulers of South All saw nothing but a fresh new face toiling in obscurity. Here was an example of true goodness, they said—a creature worthy of higher office.

He affected baffled humility, accepting their honour, he said, only from a continued desire to help, all the while accruing friends and influence, finessing his plans and advancing slowly across the great board that nobody else could see.

They had made their drawings on the sandy seabed of their world, retracing each line with the careful reverence of ritual. The cosmography of images extended from pole to pole; a geoglyph of unprecedented proportions carved only with the gentle sweep of a fin. Individuals spent their entire lives drifting in a single square mile of featureless territory, only seeing the small portion of the line they worked on, never wondering where it led, what it became or how it all might look as a whole. They never breached the surface, or saw it from the air. Someone observing the water moon from orbit would have seen the design in all its glory—a web of connected hieroglyphs representing creatures and worlds their makers had no knowledge of—engraved in angled geometry beneath the shallows. But nobody did. Life in the Lawless Phaslair was sparse and chaotic, and the bright green moon, known by its inhabitants only as *This Place*, remained undiscovered for an age.

Time passed, and the system's sun engorged, baking its small collection of planets. The moon's ocean evaporated, leaving a biscuit-dry surface etched with elaborate lines. Only then was the life's work of an entire species seen by anyone other than themselves.

In my dreams I walked for months upon that fossil crust, spread out across a colossal hangar floor. Someone—sometimes the Mowllish trader, sometimes the wooden-shelled merchant, the Keeper of the Ways or even Fe'Tril himself—guided me, beckoning, to the place where the dead species had drawn the thing I wanted. But in my dreams I never quite made it, always waking before I got there.

I awoke now on the muddy red roadside, a stolen sonic rifle propped between my three emaciated new legs. My coat was soaked and torn, my belly empty. But the dream was sustenance enough.

They had promised me that the fossil seabed was there, kept safe in the treasure vault of a Worldtrain fleeing a ruined galaxy. That it showed the way to ascend the realities, if you knew where to look.

I was very close now.

* * *

I doubted they understood the true worth of what they had; it was just one of a thousand hoarded treasures being spirited into the unknown. The Geoglyph of Yow, named after the dead sun responsible for its exposure. I wanted it more than any object I have ever known, and yet the only way to possess it at all was to look upon its secrets, and remember them.

I lay lengthways, watching the heavens part before me in the needle creature *Apocalypse Outpaced* as it dashed through the cloudy void, racing to catch up with the treasure before it left the galaxy forever. Here I was a gangly, jaundiced twig of a being four meters tall, with limbs like jointed branches equipped with only one finger each. I hoped that this would be the last of my changing forms, for a while, at least.

They'd said I would be able to see it soon, but my eyes were already near-blinded by the expanse of snowy white, as if I were staring into sunlit cloud. Was that something? A miniscule dash of colour. The systems of this Phaslair had been subjected to a crippling Omnivirus that had changed its form to destroy in every conceivable way. But those with the means had done what they could, and I glimpsed their refuge at last.

It was called a Worldtrain: a string of planets driven through space, all that remained of the manicured, wealthy systems that had survived the war. Extending like a bayonet from the delicate apparatus that held the planets in place was a radiation shield, a spear of pale light that sheltered the worlds it shaded. Trailing the final planet in the chain lay the moon-sized engine: the motor, hurled by repulsion, could never stop, for if it did every world in the chain would be shunted off into the whiteness of space and lost forever.

My eyes drank in the sight of the train as it drew closer, a string of precious trading beads propelled away from danger, the keys to my ultimate escape hidden somewhere amongst them. I often wondered how much time had passed since they had tossed me into the Hole; it felt like only a year or two, but the experts of my day had said that time moved differently in the realities below. They might all be gone now, my people. But that didn't matter a jot where I was going—the universe would know I'd made it back, even if my old adversaries did not.

My rotted mind snagged once again on something heard in the last reality. I'd spent only a day there, preparing for the Drop, listening to the comings and goings of simple folk around me. The lords of that place must have been powerful indeed, from the hushed, fearful manner in which the locals mentioned their name. *Throlken*. Whatever that meant. I would make sure to avoid that place on the way back up.

The Worldtrain twisted, the *Apocalypse* descending. We were heading for the final planet in the chain, falling past a vast, grubby ceramic wing lit with strings of artificial suns. Passage aboard *Apocalypse* had been outrageously expensive, but in this age of mud—where everything seemed to be built from porcelain or clay—my haul of metal had served me well.

The planet expanded beneath me: a curve of smoked crimson and blue, wreathed in sunlit spires of cloud. We fell through atmosphere, the cushioning gel of my cradle inflating around my body, until the vista of the new world sprawled beneath me, warmth pouring through the clear blister of my pod.

That *other* had been here, too—whomever they had sent after me when they'd realised their mistake. When they'd realised that I would not fall forever.

* * *

A world of fuchsia woodlands dwelt beneath the cloud tops, a river's coils sparkling under artificial sun. What I sought lay in one of the deep grey pools that pocked the landscape: the entrance to the repository.

I took the steps, walking on weak, unused legs into startlingly cold water and descending to an airlock. Inside it was dry again, the air spiced. Here they looked after themselves well. Lumbering, golden-scaled giants stalked the high white passageways, and it was a challenge to avoid their feet. I passed the crushed remnants of those who'd failed until I found the lane designated for smaller inhabitants.

I took rooms in the undercity, looking out upon a view of soft, grey underwater light. Gifts of fruits and delicacies arrived at my door, brought in by slaved beings I was permitted to keep, should any take my fancy. And they did, all of them. I locked the door behind the wretched, panicked creatures, savouring the scent of their fear, and crouched very close, gazing into their eyes, searching for the tell-tale signs of unreality, for the Pretence. For all my life the fleshy pleasures had eluded me; I knew little of lust. Perhaps it was why I'd progressed so far, freed from such distractions. I told my slaves this much, hoping to calm them, but they only seemed to grow more agitated by the minute.

'Shhh' I hissed, drawing the smallest of them towards me. 'You aren't real, and neither is your pain—our makers put it there.' I saw the terror that I knew so well darken its face, and for a moment I wondered. But no, that doubt was just another clever trick in the tapestry of the Pretence.

Centuries of planning paid off, and with a cosmic sense of anticlimax the last few pieces of his scheme fell into place, locking tight. It was done: he had accrued seven hundred and four years of service and catapulted himself into one of the four thrones, forced by the laws of millennia to share his power with three others. He could stomach that, for now.

Freshly crowned, he sat in the circle of the four emperors, the stars of South All now under his direct control.

Yib'Wor wasted no time, embezzling what he needed and restarting the machines at the Inescapable Hole. He knew he would have to work fast; he had reached the end of the board, where it was most dangerous, and nothing short of a swift strike would succeed.

It was the emperor Ny'ime who first noticed his deception, for they had never liked one another. But Yib'Wor had used his time wisely. He framed his fellow emperor for misappropriation, unveiling a detailed history of theft stretching back more than eighty years, and used his political weight to erode all confidence in Ny'ime's character until it took little more than a breath of air to topple him.

Yib'Wor exercised no mercy, casting Ny'ime at once into the Inescapable Hole. It was a punishment that had not been used since antiquity. Now it was a warning.

The remaining two emperors were no fools. They had been slow in seeing his plan unfold, but were now beginning to mobilise. Yib'Wor unleashed the full strength of South All's fleet (held in reserve for precisely this eventuality) against their hurriedly cobbled-together forces, and drove them from the empire.

A war was not something his plans expressly required, but it would serve to buy him time.

'This, as far as we are aware, is the only known likeness of the philosopher Sile Sunoyum made in her lifetime.'

I walked past the mounted etching, leaving the tour group behind and heading for the window that overlooked the hangar.

'And here we have the Waemish sword—'

'What is this, below?' I asked, turning to the guide.

The guide glanced, irritated, in my direction, the attention of the group moving to me.

'The Yow Geoglyph,' he said. 'We'll get to that—'

I leant on the window ledge and gazed out, Fe'Tril standing by my side.

There it was.

The vista of baked brown stone beneath me had taken generations to lift, piece by careful piece, from the surface of the dead moon. The slabs of rock, some no thicker than a sheaf of dense paper, had then collected dust in a library complex for hundreds of years before an ambitious eschatologist had decided to try their hand at reassembling the jigsaw, piecing it together over the course of a whole career devoted to little else. I silently congratulated the long dead being on their work. If only they had known what wonders they'd unleash.

The floating gantry we stood on began to move, pivoting silently out across the bay. Patterns in the stone moved beneath my feet. The Mowllish trader had mentioned a particular motif, surrounded by a constellation. I was lucky, very lucky, for here, in this layer of existence, the stars did not drift with quite the exuberance that they did back home, and the map could still be used.

All I had to do now was find the right section.

I walked across the gantry as it shifted slowly above the bay, passing the guide and standing to look out at the surface of the geoglyph. The angular patterns were just recognisable as creatures and locations: great five-headed beings that slithered across the stars, winged monstrosities with tongues for eyes. For a blissful few seconds I forgot it all. I was just a tourist, enjoying the view.

I might have stayed that way for some time longer had not the crowd begun to murmur to themselves, pointing to a thoroughfare that divided the vast squares of the geoglyph. I moved to one of the gantry's scopes to look for myself, spying people down there. They were waving frantically at our viewing platform, and I instinctively knew. My trail had been picked up.

I went to one of the panels the guide had shown us at the start, tapping a button. The platform I stood on unstuck from the others and began to float away. As I drifted I removed from my pocket a scrawl of directions.

Look for the spear thrower. Follow the pointing finger.

Spear thrower? I saw no spear thrower. The guide called after me, but I didn't look back. I found out how to accelerate the platform's motor and sped away across the hangar, peering intently over the railing. Constellations drifted by below, but nothing resembling a—

Unless *that* was what they meant.

I stopped the platform, spinning it, glancing quickly over my shoulder to see another of the floating walkways floating in my direction. There. I had been the wrong way up.

The crude figure stretched across the scene below me, a bipedal creature in the act of hurling its weapon. Its other hand was pointed straight upwards, and I followed the finger.

Directly above the spear thrower was a jumble of etched stars in the shape of a hexagon. At the centre of the hexagon lay my prize. The creature of my dreams.

My eyes dilated as I gazed upon it: a six-legged, feathered animal rearing on its hind paws, a single fang jutting from its lower jaw.

I wasn't about to let anyone stop me now. I descended as fast as the platform would allow. My pursuers kept up their pace, dropping with me. I pushed with all my weight on the throttle and ducked below the railing as the geoglyph rushed to meet me, hoping I wasn't mistaken about the thickness of the stone. With a monumental boom of shattered rock and grinding metal what remained of my platform burst through the geoglyph's surface and into the dark level below, where the heat from the artificial star bled through the porcelain. The shattered craft wobbled and spun, tipping me into the air.

I fell in darkness, once again, but this time I struck a hard, unyielding floor. I lay, looking up at the hole I'd made, watching as the underside of the geoglyph began to crumble inwards, drawn by the gravity of the star beneath. I crawled, then limped, as the devastation rained down from above.

I scudded out of the Worldtrain's jurisdiction in a stolen tugship, watching from a distance as the string of planets faltered, unbalanced by the weight of material that had fallen into its second starboard fin. The pilots overcompensated, banking, and I looked on in wonder as the first of the planets drifted slowly from its cradle of forces, separating from the train. Its gravity dragged another with it, then another, until all five worlds were moving away from the spinning craft in opposing directions.

It was just a game, but I was beginning to play it *beautifully*.

It was no small task restructuring South All to serve his every need, but hurling enough enemies into the Hole soon produced the desired effect. The machines began their monolithic crunching into the fabric of reality, and a heady daze of elation settled over Yib'Wor. This was it; he was poised to win. Eternity would be his for the taking.

On the same day, the tide of the war turned against him. He'd known it would, of course, but had counted on being further along by the time the rest of the galaxy had mobilised to the outcast emperors' cause.

He wasn't finished. The job was taking longer than anticipated, even with the resources of an empire channelled into building more and more of the breaking machines. Twenty-nine of them now surrounded the hole, reaching into its depths. And it was working: the membranes were thinning, but not nearly fast enough.

He felt the dream slipping beneath him, just as he had the day Fe'Tril had summoned him to his house. In the days when he went by his real name. Before he had changed. Before he had killed.

He took to stalking the same stretch of floor, muttering and weeping, crying out to the gods of the Pretence that he had done enough, he had passed the test, even as the battlefronts shrank back towards South All, pressing from all directions into his dominion.

He lost interest in his war the moment they broke through, obliterating the weakened defences and streaming into the empire. Ten days and it would all be over. Ten days spent brooding in his chambers, refusing all callers. He could flee, try again somewhere in another patch of the galaxy, perhaps even another galaxy, if such a journey were possible. It would take centuries more, but it could be done. Yes. He would win the game from another board. He would survive the beating pulse of the universe and wake in a better world. A place where death did not exist.

He resolved not to let them take him, fleeing the capital just as the system's outer defences were pummelled into submission by the combined fleets of the All.

But, as with every plan that was ever hatched, something went wrong. In all his years Yib'Wor had never bothered to learn about the dispensable people that surrounded him, *unable to identify with the hordes of simplistic mannequins designed to look and sound alive.*

Yib'Wor's people turned against him.

When they caught him, he was riding at the head of a private army, headed for the coast. He sacrificed his troops, ordering that they fight to the death while he made one last frantic dash for his waiting ship, but to no avail. Another misunderstanding of living beings. They surrendered at once, joining the force that pursued him. Warships began pouring into the atmosphere above the sea, and it was then that Yib'Wor knew he was caught.

The trial was brief, and without defence. It was decreed that Yib'Wor the Sorcerer, murderer and disgrace to the All, would be subjected to the same torment he had inflicted upon so many others: to fall forever.

FANG

I knew every scream in the jungle by now; I had names for them all. A Cacklejoy whooped in the canopies, its braying hysteria dissolving into a gurgling mutter that echoed through the trees. The cries of a pod of Weeplings rose in response, their shrill, demented wailing drifting from the undergrowth. Then tittering from above, the plop-plop-plop of a Squelcher, grunting a mating invitation that carried for miles around.

I squatted, loose-limbed, drinking in the sounds. My gangly body was perfect for climbing through the never-ending forest, or snaring things that wandered too close. I had caught and sampled them all, trying to match the taste to the sound. Some were quite toxic, inducing fevers and hallucinations that lasted for days, and in those dark times Fe'Tril stooped over me, screaming into my sweating face.

I unfolded myself, crawling back along the branch to my poor excuse for a hut: a ball of bundled red leaves hanging suspended from the canopy. Something—an animal that shrunk rapidly in size to attract its prey—had managed to eat my ship, but it didn't matter. If all went to plan I wouldn't need one again.

The years slipped by, unnoticed. I might have died and been reborn, for all I knew. Fe'Tril had once speculated that you were nothing but a still, frozen image, and that time was motion, spinning the still frames of your being into life. With each new frame you perished and were remade, the memories carrying on. If that were true then I had died enough already, and ought not to fear the end.

Nevertheless, here I was, on the one planet where they were said to live, chasing a rumour that might never appear. Their migrations lasted years, the geoglyph had said.

And so I waited.

He was held down, writhing and snarling while his skin was painted all over with a black layer of the mystical powder. Then the representatives of the New South All carried him to the bare patch of industrial wasteland that had been the epicentre of his crimes, the towering machines that had occupied that land now dismantled and scrapped, and threw him to the ground. A marksman stepped forward, aiming swiftly and firing a brief, flickering burst of voltage at the doomed figure of their defrocked emperor.

And with that he was gone.

He fell, the Phaslairs flashing by so swiftly that they were nothing but a blur of dully glowing crimson. His body changed just as quickly, snapping through the permutations of a million worlds so that it became a dash of shapeless grey, his ever-changing screams pouring together like the formless roar of a waterfall.

His mind moved from snapshot to snapshot as it plummeted, his personality drained through a sieve of fresh chemicals every microsecond as he awoke within a new brain, a flickering zoetrope of frozen states spun to create incongruous, maddening movement. It was a unique and perfect torture, regenerating, unending, and a great span of screaming through a host of different and freshly formed larynxes must have elapsed before he recognised that he had got his wish.

He would fall practically forever, the baby Phaslairs budding as fast as he dropped, a fresh body waiting for him in each. He would never age, never spoil. He would die only when the ultraverse collapsed upon itself in the silence before the beat.

He had got his wish, and with that revelation he screamed with more ferocity than he'd ever screamed before.

Aeons upon aeons. A weight of time no mind, however often it regenerated, could endure.

But something broke his fall.

The imperfect Iliquin of the ancients had a half-life, after all.

The planet had no name—it was not known except as a numeral, part of the hexagonal star cluster, a memory mistranslated again and again. Life drifted in colourful streamers before my eyes, darting and floating and settling, a cacophony of sound and smell that spoke to me, now that I knew the words. Eleven visible moons hung in the sky glimpsed beyond the canopy, painted in all the colours of the world around me, as though the seeds of life here had hopped the short distance some time ago.

They were coming soon, I felt it. I had found their lairs, hollowed into the root systems of the trees. I had crumbled and sniffed their droppings, touched the tips of shed feathers to my tongue. Fe'Tril walked with me, lunging every now and then with an imaginary blade, but I'd learnt to ignore him.

It is the only verified example of an inter-Phaslair ecosystem, the travelling Durgoh had told me, *in which creatures from a lower reality migrate up and down to feed, in apparent contradiction of the universe's laws.*

Their prey evolved to escape their reach, and they, in turn, evolved to follow.

I glanced into the twilight branches, aware at last that I had been sitting still for days, cross-legged and vacant, my limbs numb.

I had been wondering what I would see, when the time came. What lived at Phaslairs' end? Would there be a creator? Or just a door? The terror that had driven me to this place and time resurfaced, and once more I was afraid.

I would rip it down regardless. I would win the game.

It had been a day like any other, a day spent staring into the middle distance, contemplating. And then, with the twitch of an ear, I looked up.

The creatures had returned.

They popped into existence in the branches of the trees with great hooting bellows, one after the other. They perched for a moment before scrabbling down to climb into their burrows and sleep off the feast.

The large fang that adorns their chins must have evolved for burrowing, but it came to be used for something much, much more.

I stood, watching their arrival, the things I'd been searching for all this time, time in which years or centuries or even millennia might have passed.

They were six meters or so in wingspan, tufted in shades of violet and lugging bulging stomachs. They were eyeless, it seemed, their prominent jawbones crowned by what I'd come for: a silvery, spoon-shaped incisor tipped with an asymmetric, serrated barb.

Its form is said to be unique, the only shape in existence that can tear the membrane of an older reality. When they reach their destination in the Phaslair above they gorge themselves on their prey—seasonal migrations of fat-rich swarmers—before gliding hundreds of miles to the mouth of a broad river and crunching down its Iliquin-rich stones. When enough of the element has suffused their blood, they Drop effortlessly back to their homes, there to sleep away the season.

I knew their habits now, and that they would stay bundled up in their burrows for years, comatose in digestive slumbers. I took my time, selecting one of the dozen or so knives I'd fashioned during my wait.

The calls were subsiding into soft, growling grumbles that reverberated through the darkness of the caverns: snores and grunts and gurgling stomachs, the scrabbling of claws as they settled into their dwellings. Smaller feeder creatures had already set to work cleaning their mouths and feathers, and I was accepted as one of them. I didn't need to light my way—I had explored these places and knew them perfectly, and my eyes drank in the shadow as if it were sunlight, marking every glint and flash of the large serrated fang up ahead.

They had no natural predators, and if they smelled me they showed no fear. I drew the blade.

AUCTION

Perhaps it was why he binged; it wouldn't have surprised him. Knowing something like that was coming.

Maybe he wanted to overdose. Maybe he should.

Draebol thought every day on what the Throlken had told him. About the moment of death.

The planetary ring was an orphan, abandoned. They were heading straight for it on the plane of its orbit, keeping—under strict instructions—to the confines of the shipping lane.

Draebol sat alone in the luxuriant lounge of the Myriad-generated ship, shivering. His body was in withdrawal, his thoughts spiralling beyond his control. He found the darkness outside profoundly unsettling, whilst simultaneously wishing he could escape into it and leave all this—Whira, her dreaded plans, all of it—behind forever. The Myriad had taken some small measure of pity on him and concocted a sedative, but the pill had remained folded in his closed hand. He opened his palm and stared at it for a long while, before popping it into his mouth.

A spare few million Myriad had formed together into a moving map inside the observation deck, showing their own ship, a smooth cone blistered with unusual bulges, rushing through the blackness. The hazy implication of the ring existed somewhere up ahead; its exact location was kept hidden on star maps as well as in real space by means of some sort of cloak.

And then without ceremony they were right on top of it, flying side-on to the vast range of fused, stationary rocks, a landscape of stained marble outcrops sweeping beneath their left flank. Voices swarmed around them, translated badly by the ring on Whira's finger and then more tidily by the Myriad, and Whira went to work relaying her codes of introduction—provided a few days ago by a Sovereignty Deep Eye—and the details of their cargo.

Hundreds of alabaster castles speckled the ring, sprouting from the summits of the rocks. Beyond, at ring's eye, lay a great emptiness: once the home of a planet. Whira wasn't at all surprised—this being another Lawless Phaslair—to hear that it had been stolen. Its rings had then been artificially stabilised by their wealthy inhabitants to drift on, intact.

The blips of other vessels began to register, a few glimmering convoys dashing beneath, and they followed a luminescent blue diamond of a ship as it descended towards one of the mountain docks.

The Myriad ship dropped, smoothly reconfiguring its shape and perching without a tremor. In case of an eventful journey it had grown an array of nondescript, violently effective weaponry beneath the skin of its hull, and these it kept primed, watching.

The passengers clustered to a rapidly expanding clear section of hull, gazing out at the marble concourse. Castles rose in the distance, towers reaching into blackness. Unlike most civilised places, the atmosphere here had been bottled under angular domes, and the Myriad ship extended a proboscis-like transit tube to connect with a portal in the wall of the nearest, completing its dock.

'They won't tell me which castle it is until they've seen the goods,' Whira said to Draebol, unpacking a set of trill-petal attire from her bag and letting the Myriad that weren't already part of her thin flight suit dress her. She turned full circle as they applied the soft petal-wear, buttoning her at the collar. 'This place is *high* security, covered by anti-Drop and Bubble technology. Ships aren't allowed anywhere near it.' A haze like mist seeped from her sleeve, vanishing in the air. 'No Myriad either.'

Draebol shrugged, slouching in his chair. The sedative had kicked in instantly, and none of what she said seemed to matter in the slightest.

Whira looked at him. 'Are you coming? Seeing as it's your map—'

Of course, the chart. 'Do I get to keep the money?' Draebol blurted.

'You'll be compensated handsomely by Thelgald, like I said.'

'How much do you think they'll pay—' Draebol frowned, trying to find the words. 'You know, what will they list it for?'

'No idea,' Whira said, buckling the atlas inside a case and offering it to Draebol. 'But they sounded very excited.'

Draebol stared gormlessly at the case in her outstretched hand. The interior of the ship smelt funny, like burning. He had forgotten the words for *thank you*.

Whira withdrew her hand, clutching the case to her. 'I'd better hold onto this, for now.'

In the ship's main bay—rapidly expanded upon landing—sat the amphibious vehicle, which Lemuu had tinkered with over the two-day voyage. Other passengers were milling around, enjoying delicacies cooked up by the Myriad from a selection of flora and fauna grabbed in the vegetable patch before their departure. Gnumph splashed and frolicked inside a vat of cloudy green water, also conjured from Myriad. Whira went and stuck her hand in the water, patting Gnumph on the nose.

'Are we safe here?' asked Shumholl, licking one of his transparent eyes.

'Perfectly,' said Whira, drying her hand and walking over to the vehicle. She set the case on the backseat, followed by two old but solid environment suits Draebol had lent her from his things. She turned to Shumholl. 'There's nowhere safer than this ship for a thousand million miles. Stay here. Do not leave. Do everything the Myriad tell you.'

Shumholl held her eye. 'And when you're done? What happens then? When can we go back to the Surface? You promised us you'd be able to get us back.'

'I promised, yes. Let me do my job.' Whira took Draebol by the elbow, guiding him into the backseat to sit alongside their prized possession, and climbed behind the wheel. She fiddled with a ratchet and reversed the vehicle slowly towards the transit tube, not sparing the passengers another glance.

They waited at a circular door while an inbuilt nostril in the wall sampled the air, along with any pathogens and possessions they were bringing with them. The nostril took a long, thoughtful breath, thousands of small spikes quivering inside it, and relaxed. The door rolled sideways into a translucent, rather dirty hallway, allowing them a vague view of the jungly interior of the dome.

A couple of officials, each standing waist-high to Whira and dressed in bright patterned robes, were waiting. One was a nacreous, glossy-skinned creature that studied them with a dappling of jewel-like eyes arranged along the sides of its beak; the other was a rather less impressive specimen with fewer eyes and a pelt of downy, balding white fur.

'I think this is them,' said the many-eyed one, its squeaking voice picked up and decoded by the ring on Whira's finger. Their words, unlike those of the Pattern, were separated by pauses for breath, stringing their sentences out to an infuriating length. Whira waited and drummed her fingers while the creature turned out its pockets, searching for something and scattering what might have been sweets across the floor, eventually producing a small, hand-painted sign.

XIRAZOMAH & DRIBLE.

Whira discovered a few minutes into the journey that Lemuu hadn't assembled the vehicle properly. The thing rattled as though it were about to fall apart at any moment, reaching a crescendo when they encountered any sort of ramp or rise, the bolts wobbling in their sockets. Draebol—after much pleading—was allowed to drive, unaware that the vehicle had an autopilot system in the likely event of him falling deeper under the sedative's spell. He sat crammed in the front with his knees pushed up to his chin, while Whira and the two small auctioneers—the younger specimen with his full complement of eyes was named Uco, the other Mirzuela—sat together in the back, perusing the atlas.

Uco and Mirzuela were clearly entranced, and whispered reverentially to one another with each unspooled new page. Though they wore soft black gloves, their hovering fingers never quite touched it, as if afraid that the book might fall apart at the lightest pressure.

They travelled beneath inverted forests that clung to the underside of the domes. The gravity was light enough to make steering and handling quite easy, and Draebol's mind rode the bumps smoothly; whatever the Myriad had given him had soothed him into a state of calm deliberation. He felt certain there was something he ought to be concerned about just over the horizon—something he had been told, perhaps by Whira—but when he turned a corner there was never anything there.

Soon they were out under the open stars, the interior of the vehicle growing chilly all at once. Draebol turned the heating on after a few minutes spent searching for the correct dial, and followed Uco's directions, taking a smooth marble road blasted into the rock. Towers loomed above them, dazzling white against the black, their turrets and windows streaked with sooty stains.

'Are we close?' he asked with a voice he hardly recognised, interrupting a squeaking exchange between the auctioneers. There were more squeaks and squeals as the plastic computer around Whira's finger translated his words for them.

'Not far,' said Mirzuela. 'We use this minor road for deliveries.'

They rounded a corner, driving beneath a precarious outcrop of bone white rock, and the walls of the castle of Lusque filled the view.

Draebol decelerated to take in the sight. The place towered over them, a forest of connected spires and cupolas all carved from that same dazzling alabaster, as if it had grown out of the rock. This castle was somewhat cleaner than the others he'd seen, its hundreds of speckled windows glittering with warm light.

The road led them into a brightly lit underground chasm that echoed with the grumble of their arrival. A hinged section of floor rose behind them, sealing the space, while jets of warm air blasted down from the ceiling, matching the atmosphere further inside.

Draebol's door was still stuck firm with frost when he tried to open it, and with a composure he hardly recognised he leant his weight against the thing until it popped open,

280

scattering bolts and falling off the chassis with a bang. The others made no move to get out, and he walked calmly around to the back door, opening it for them. This was good stuff, whatever it was; he would have to get some more.

Whira stepped out, catching sight of a portion of the ceiling lighting up ahead of them. She put out a hand, and Draebol stopped at her side.

'It's alright,' said Uco. 'We must all be scanned before we can go in. Just step underneath.'

Uco went first by way of demonstration, walking beneath the band of light.

'*Ucoyani Merchantgraduate with high honours,*' croaked the sentient ceiling. '*Regular clearance. Proceed.*'

Mirzuela received a similarly impersonal statement as he passed through. Both turned to look at Whira and Draebol.

Whira stepped across the line.

'*Unidentified species, provisional clearance. Silver chain and locket, seventy-nine point seven one percent purity, crystalloid mass. Assorted rings: plastoid foambrain, crystalloid mineral various, silver eighty-one point three four percent purity, iron various, unidentified material: presumed bone—composition clear of mechanical function at atomic level. Outer suit of flexible synthetic, mechanisms checked at atomic level, low chance of ulterior function. Inner fabrics of synthetic make. Bone (presumed) buttons times three. Gold leaf. Shoes: ceramic heel, plastoids, synthetic. Gloves: unidentified cured flesh, hair lining. Item, held in left hand: scrollwork, cleared for ulterior function. No Microscopia detected. Internals: low fat density, multiple unrecognised organs with no clear ulterior functions. Cleared. Internal genitalia (assumed) of unidentifiable nature, sex unknown. Stomach (assumed) contents: pan-brine, proteinaceous synthetics, sucralose composite—clear. Bone density and composition checked* for ulterior functions, materials unknown. Circulatory fluid analysed at atomic level, compositions unknown.' The ceiling mulled things over, falling silent. 'High chance clear.'

Whira thanked it and walked on. Draebol followed, stretching his hand experimentally under whatever invisible beam it was projecting.

'Pass beneath at regular pace.'

'Alright.'

'Species now recognised, provisional clearance. Silkoid fabrics, iron buttons times seven. Outer suit of flexible synthetic, mechanisms checked at atomic level, low chance of ulterior function. Ring: gold fifty-two point nine nine percent purity. Shoes—'

Draebol listened until the thing delved into his innards, sorting and classifying. It stopped abruptly. He glanced calmly up at the light.

'Significant scarring indicating attrition and possible loss of function. Assorted organs operating at sub-optimal level (assumed). High fat density, congestion of vascular network. Cognitive function altered (assumed) by presence of unknown compounds.'

The ceiling carried on in a similar vein, revealing the presence of a variety of Phaslair-hopping parasites that had hitched a ride inside him over the years and finally clearing him with a dubious provisional. Draebol walked on, nodding to himself. He'd expected as much.

They ascended into what must have been the visible body of the castle. Every wall and ceiling inside the place had been painted in a luminescent blue coating called echopaint, the auctioneers explained, hurrying their guests along: a coating of varnish that trapped sound. Draebol pressed his two left ears to the wall, making out the faint mumbling of a crowded room—all the people that must have passed through these chambers over the centuries.

'Echo!' he shouted, and listened. The sound of his cry repeated around him, copied into the walls.

Uco and Mirzuela stopped in their tracks, their beaks open. 'Why did you do that?' Uco shrieked. 'That's stuck there now!'

Uco stopped himself, blushing furious technicolour. Now his words were imprinted too, like a footprint in wet cement.

Whira clasped the handle of the case tightly in her fist with a rising impatience, feeling everything hanging by a thread, a millimetre from disaster. She grasped Draebol by the arm and ushered him down the hall, the auctioneers scuttling after them.

'It's set to be the best turnout in a good long while,' said Mirzuela as they settled themselves down to watch the first arrivals. A floating platter of drinks and canapes hovered across the balcony to where they sat alone in marble seats, high above the auditorium. Whira waved it away; she hadn't eaten in more than a day, but her stomach had knotted into a ball as soon as they'd arrived, and food was the last thing on her mind. Draebol helped himself, rubbing his hands together and offloading as many things from the tray as he could before it moved on.

The cavernous auditorium lay inside the castle's uppermost cupola, and the segmented dome that reached overhead was patterned with a mosaic of moving, dappled colour that Whira thought at first was formed of mere tiles. She squinted upwards, trying to make it out, and then she saw: they were thousands of individual faces, looking down into the chamber.

Mirzuela followed her gaze. 'Plenty of people tuning in, too,' he said. Whira couldn't help but feel sorry for the unsuspecting fellow, but there was no backing out now.

Draebol, slouched on the far side of the auctioneers with a half-finished drink in his hand and a scattering of crumbs around his mouth, was gazing with empty eyes into the amphitheatre beneath their balcony, where fourteen conical marble platforms tipped with large bowl-shaped indentations stood, waiting. A few early guests had begun to arrive, and were mingling near the entrance.

Whira nudged Uco. 'I want the names of everyone turning up. If you don't recognise someone, point them out to me.'

Uco searched his pockets for a pair of spectacles, fitting them over his beak and peering avidly down to the chamber floor. The spectacles branched into six pale green stalks, one for each of Uco's eyes.

Mirzuela handed Whira and Draebol a set each, and Whira squinted through them at the growing crowd below. Draebol fitted his on upside down and gazed at the ceiling, spilling the last of his drink as the sea of watching faces jumped into focus.

'Lots of familiar dealers,' Uco said, his eyestalks elongating until they reached over the edge of the balcony. 'Antiquities, for the most part.' He pointed down to a large, pink quadrupedal beast sporting a clear bubble in its thorax, from which something hazy peered out. It was talking with a floating ribbon of a creature encrusted with silver equipment at either tip. 'That four-legged fellow is Opthal of Sulge, fossil collector. And that's Riquis Czat he's talking to, a well-known artist from in-system.'

Whira looked to see where he pointed. Her Deep Eyes had been putting the word out for some time, making sure it got tracked around as many Phaslairs as possible, reaching every sensory organ it could. Perhaps the one she sought still wouldn't come, sensing a trap; perhaps she had missed it entirely, Dropping too deep. It was too late to worry about that now. She had selected her bridgehead and the charge was set, as per the Alms' orders, no matter whether their quarry appeared or not.

A stooped humanoid robed in dark, velvety layers strolled in, the auction programme gripped in one taloned hand. 'And there's Dzimunzing, from—'

'I know that face,' interrupted Whira. 'He's a Throlken legislator, from our Surface.' The legislators travelled the galaxy and its Phaslairs noting down any new instances of Throlken retribution in great compendia, which, when combined, formed the basis of Throlken law. She turned to Uco. 'You're projecting a Surface field in here?'

Uco looked affronted, and removed the spectacles from his beak. 'It's a basic security measure. We don't want any old riffraff coming along in disguise.'

Whira sat forward, scanning the swelling crowd with a new intensity in her eyes. Everyone here had no choice but to take their Surface form. 'Keep going.'

Uco and Mirzuela peeped over the balcony again at the coloured specks of the crowd. 'That's Yor-Zaldo Zohlm just arrived,' said Mirzuela, nodding to a floating mass of translucent crystal ten metres long. Its surface was chiselled with fabulous and intricate carvings that Whira could barely make out. As the chunk of crystal hovered into the middle of the chamber, she saw that Yor-Zaldo itself was actually a small, prickly being floating inside. It communicated with the others through cerulean holograms that danced from the surface of its crystal enclosure. 'Yor always wins something, she does; very good with the mazes.'

Uco tapped excitedly on the balcony, drawing Whira's attention. 'Quite a few I haven't seen before coming in now.'

She looked down, confident that she was well hidden in the wings. At least fifteen new guests had poured in and now swirled amongst the others, some chattering away to those they recognised, others taking seats amongst the concentric rings of the steep-sided auditorium. Uco and

Mirzuela were conferring frantically, trying to sort out who was who.

Whira counted a few bipedal symmetrics, a polypform housed inside a hollow sphere and a group of angular, crimson-winged things that kept to themselves, perching as far from the others as possible. A huge one-legged creature cowled in a sparkling gown loped towards the central platforms and tipped its wrinkled neck up to the ceiling. Whira thought she caught its multifaceted eye.

'Could be any of them,' she whispered to Draebol, still slouching to her left. He seemed to be lost in his own little world. She studied the faces of the crowd as a general hush fell, and another of Uco and Mirzuela's colleagues walked out into the centre of the auditorium to showcase the lots.

He did so in complete silence, owing to the difficulty of mass-translation in this reality, gesturing to four plinths that rose on either side. Floating bubblescreens winked into existence, magnifying the treasures.

'Lurdaal will save the best for last,' said Mirzuela, tapping his beak with a clawed finger.

Whira had already leafed through the brochure, and knew what was on offer besides Draebol's life's work. An iron ingot from a planet's core, hammered into a medallion, sat on one of the plinths. It in itself was worth almost nothing, but it represented the private planet it had come from, there for the taking. The collected works of some millennia-dead poet bound inside a giant nutshell came next, followed by the mummified head of someone apparently quite famous: it looked to Whira like an old black shoe that had been dropped down the stairs one too many times. And then the star attraction, unrolled carefully by Lurdaal for the benefit of the magnifying screens. Draebol sat up a little as his work sprang into focus, but Whira only had eyes for the crowd.

The winged creatures shuffled together in a whisper of papery skin. One craned its neck up to the dome's multitude

286

of faces, revealing four fang-studded mouths. Whira's gaze moved on to the humanoids. The creature sitting closest to them wore a cream dress suit and was around her own height, with small red eyes that glittered from a charcoal-hued, earless head. Wiry white hair spilled from the nape of its neck, like a mane. Her eyes flicked on, to the smaller bipedal slouching in the red-eyed person's shadow. Its head was set deep into its black-and-white-banded sternum, a pair of Y-shaped arms folded under its chin. It tapped a booted foot impatiently. Her attention moved to the next seat, examining a blue-faced humanoid a head taller than the others. Beneath a long black beard and even longer neck it wore an exquisite suit of golden studs, a cape of matching blue spilling across the steps and pooling around its feet.

Where are you?

Her concentration was broken by the groaning of a wide set of doors behind the plinths. A deep, gurgling growl drifted from the opening doors, followed by the thump of plodding footsteps.

'You'll like our Qhozeons,' said Uco. 'Fattened them up specially for tonight.'

The two beasts padded into the light, their glimmering rolls of blubber swaying with each step. They scented the crowd with pink, bulbous noses and flicked their scaly tails, turning their eyeless heads to the tiny auctioneer at their feet. Lurdaal had produced a wooden broom, and led the first by a chained collar to one of the platforms while the other rose massively onto its haunches, scratching its furred chest with a paw.

Whira wasn't prepared for what happened next. The auctioneer raised the broom in both hands and scrubbed the Qhozeon vigorously under its belly, as though trying to scour away a thick layer of dirt. Its mouth opened and it began to shudder, rolls of fat rippling as it squatted over the first platform and raised its tail to eject a slimy ball of black stone, which rolled heavily into the bowl. Lurdaal cooed, patting it softly on the flank, and led the drooling creature to the next, inducing six more stones. He repeated the trick with the other Qhozeon, to much applause from the crowd, and they were sent back down to their underground lair.

'I don't think I was briefed for this,' Whira whispered to Uco. 'What's—?'

'Shh,' he hissed, adjusting his spectacles. 'It's starting.'

Lurdaal took a handful of eyeball-sized silver bearings from his pocket and balanced one at the top of each stone ball, which Whira could now see were inscribed with a tracery of channels, like a maze. When he was done he stood back, admiring his handiwork.

At some signal from Lurdaal a transparent globe rose from each of the bowls, enclosing the stone balls. Each ball tilted and rolled inside, rearranging itself until the bearing had dropped into a channel on the surface.

'Calcified excretia,' said Uco, his breath heavy with the stench of his drink. 'The channels are carved by the Qhozeon's gut lining, creating a different pattern every time—no maze is the same.'

Draebol wasn't watching. Whatever the Myriad had given him seemed to be interacting badly with the drinks. The vast chamber ebbed and pulsed, the colours dimming, then brightening. Sounds from below boomed like an incoming tide, whispering as they fell away. His thoughts had travelled back to the Throlken's baking home, to the things it had told him in his own voice, soundless inside his head.

The contestants had made their way up to the platforms. The one-footed creature went first, extending its hands to touch the surface of the globe. A timer appeared on the magnification screen, the large revolving numerals counting down as everyone took their places. Whira watched as they clustered around the plinths like members of a jostling, worshipful cult, and the timer wound to zero.

The ship was already accelerating hard out of the system by the time any passengers noticed they were no longer at the dock, its Dzull drive finessed as the swarm of Myriad perfected their new trade. The cloak descended over the rings as the ship passed beyond the last outcrop and left them far behind.

'Well that's that,' muttered the Zabbas, lighting his pipe. The Myriad snuffed it out before he could put it in his mouth. 'Good riddance to her, I say.' He tipped his translucent head up to the ceiling. 'Where to now, ship?'

The Myriad gave no answer. Gnumph, still wallowing in its vat, was looking out through the transparent bulkhead of the mainbay, watching the stars. A swarm of craft was stationed at the edge of the rings' influence, and the Myriad ship passed swiftly amongst them, receiving the occasional blip of a greeting.

'Farewell Whirazomar,' said Shumholl, taking in the mass of floating ships.

'But we're not stuck here?' asked Immonod, glancing between the other passengers. 'It knows how to take us home, yes?'

Silent faces, ghastly under the clean white light, looked back.

Lurdaal watched the timer, all eyes on him. Whira could tell he relished his role. At zero he held an arm in the air, surveying the crowd. A silence fell.

Lurdaal dropped his arm.

The globes unfroze. The contestants began to spin them experimentally, the bearings rolling in their channels amidst a hush of concentration. Some sort of whispered commentary drifted down from the dome's watching faces.

Draebol burped, swallowed the acidic taste in his mouth and glanced around. He felt a sudden energy as his mind cleared all at once, knocking a memory loose. His eyes widened in their sockets.

There was a bomb.

He leaned forward, gazing past the auctioneers to where Whira sat. She had muttered something aboard the Myriad ship about 'Dropping out with plenty of time,' but what about Gnumph, and the others? His gaze travelled to the crystal pendant around her neck. It seemed to grow a face as he looked at it, smiling at him.

Something at the edge of the auditorium caught his eye. A figure was striding across the floor, making its way up to the platforms.

Whira focussed her spectacles: a new arrival. She magnified.

Charcoal grey skin, a pale mane of hair sprouting from its neck. When it glanced up at the domed ceiling she glimpsed a flash of crimson eyes.

It approached the other of its kind, still working on the maze. The timer pulsed.

Whira stood from her chair, hands clasping the marble balcony. A few other contestants had paused in their work to watch what looked like a private dispute, but Whira knew better.

Her briefing had covered a range of possible outcomes, all of them dreamt up by some savant behind the scenes, all of which she had been required to read. A small codicil had concerned the possibility of a second entity, sent through the Phaslairs to apprehend the other. She had dismissed it at the time.

Now she turned the magnification of her glasses to maximum.

The blow landed before the other contestant could react, knocking it to the ground. It lay for a moment, stunned, and then a hiss of what Whira could only describe as pure fury reached them on the balcony. It stood, hunching its shoulders and hurling itself at its attacker. The two of them fell, rolling, and Whira witnessed a flash of white as the contestant bared its teeth, sinking them into the new arrival's neck.

Uco and Mirzuela rose to their feet beside Whira, beaks open.

Lurdaal ducked behind a plinth as the blue-faced contestant stepped forward, perhaps meaning to break up the fight. He reached out, and was slashed across the throat with a clawed hand.

'Cut the feed!' squeaked Mirzuela to Uco, and the elder auctioneer whispered frantically into a patch on his sleeve. The dome went blank.

The two auctioneers excused themselves hurriedly, picking up their skirts and making their way unsteadily along the balcony.

Draebol turned his full attention to the auditorium, leaning forward in his seat. The blue-faced contestant was kneeling now, his hands clasped around his neck. He put out an arm to steady himself and collapsed, the studs of his golden outfit ringing as they struck the floor. Of the two who had fought, only one remained: the contestant in the cream suit. He climbed to his feet, his teeth smeared with blood. The auditorium watched in silence.

'Is this what I think it is?' asked Draebol, fidgeting with his spectacles.

Whira clasped the Arqot ring on her index finger and a

Bubble sprang into existence above it, a range of weaponry revealed as if out of thin air. She took out her Drop pistol and placed it on the arm of her chair.

He stared at her. 'I thought this place didn't allow Bubbles and Drops.'

'I've just turned off the field,' she muttered, distracted, selecting a slender rifle from the Bubble and checking it over quickly.

Draebol's eyes were drawn to the weapon. A real weapon. 'How did you do that? We weren't allowed to bring anything in—'

Something tumbled from above, and they glanced up. The object was followed swiftly by another, and soon a steady rain of weapons were falling into the auditorium.

'Stars, they've worked it out already.'

The first gun landed and was scooped up by Dzimunzing the lawmaker. He checked the settings and pressed the muzzle to his head, concealed by a puff of vapourised Iliquin that flashed with a sudden charge, Dropping him at once. The shower of weaponry followed, many bouncing and shattering, discharging with flashes and flickers. Riquis caught a pistol and aimed it at those closest to the plinths, firing an invisible light round that curved in the air, seeking the most likely target. The laser bolt sailed straight through the large one-legged creature, slamming into the far wall and drilling a scorched hole through the marble.

Whira's breath caught in her throat. The one-legged being straightened to its full height and dissolved before their eyes, collapsing into a haze of evaporating red dust. The contestants, crouching for cover behind platforms and plinths, glanced at one another. Something that looked like a large black egg lay on the ground where the creature had disappeared.

'Oh,' Draebol moaned. 'You didn't.'

The Immersion warhead's casing snapped open, a stuttering of white light appearing from inside.

Draebol snatched the Drop pistol from the arm of the chair before Whira could intercept his hand. He dodged her lunge, aimed and sprayed electrified bolts of Iliquin down into the auditorium. Drop fire sizzled across the marble around the bomb, snapping away slivers of the flagstones.

Whira threw herself at him, shoving him to the floor. The pistol tipped and fired into the air, vanishing a portion of the dome and a smoothly sliced chunk of Whira's horn. She gasped, feeling behind her head, and punched him squarely in the mouth.

Draebol had been slapped with such regularity by a variety of muscular species that he absorbed the blow with ease, flexing his neck. He aimed the Drop pistol again and fired.

The warhead disappeared from the floor of the auditorium in a blink of blue flame, detonating as it winked in and out of existence across a seam of Phaslairs. At least a hundred thousand individuals in fourteen separate realities witnessed a column of pale cloud erupting and expanding across their skies.

The spent casing, its charge exhausted, tumbled with a dash of surf into a lifeless sea, sinking into darkness. It left behind fourteen pillars of rapidly solidifying matter like a frozen explosion the width of a hurricane's eye.

The Myriad ship reconfigured its AM thrust in a sliver of a second, padding its internals with a globular field and powering in the opposite direction, sweeping back towards the invisible ring. It looked ahead, compensating for the slight light lag by firing a stream of Myriad ahead of it so that a chain of faster-than-light information linked the ship to the ring. The Lusque auditorium was already descending into the castle, which had sprouted defensive turrets and a swarm of attack ships from its outer towers.

'What the hell are you doing *now*?' cried the Zabbas, who'd only just managed to light his pipe again. 'Don't take us back there!' A stream of invisible Myriad grabbed the pipe out of his hand and snapped it in half.

'I feel sick,' whined Immonod from inside his floating globe.

A moment of stunned silence followed the vanishing of the warhead. Time enough for Draebol to reach out and grasp Whira's pendant. She turned her incredulous gaze on him, and he flicked the sliver casing to one side, exposing the crystal.

'*No!*' she managed, before a growth of jagged pink and white shards expanded fractally around her, shoving Draebol backwards into his seat. The crystal Sovereignty ship grew like an erupting timelapse of a snowflake, elongating into a blade and tipping. The balcony cracked beneath its weight.

Draebol climbed out of his seat as the slab of marble beneath them gave way, spilling the ship out above the auditorium and the firefight far below.

The crystal ship struck the floor with an echoing boom, fanning a web of cracks across the flagstones and rolling. Far above, Draebol gripped the edge of the balcony, his sweat-slick fingers slipping. The dome crumpled inwards with an ear-popping blast and the black arrow of the Myriad ship emerged in a storm of tumbling stone, unfurling into the auditorium.

* * *

Gnumph steadied itself in the still, untroubled water of its vat as they obliterated the dome, the screams of the passengers vibrating in its ears. The ship's hull grew instantly thin.

The Myriad poured across the chamber like smog, enveloping the dais where Lurdaal had stood. They fortified it quickly against any further attack and deposited the melting kernel containing the passengers, crushing the plinths and their complement of treasures. Sections of the fortification's walls unstuck and marched stiffly out into the firefight, sculpting themselves into dark, angular figures spined all over with sprouting weaponry. The swarm that had once made up the one-legged contestant swept down to join them, blossoming into a floating shield that repulsed every incoming bolt of light.

The passengers, huddling together inside a tornado of soft Myriad smoke, heard only muffled detonations and distant cries. Lucky, who had tuned his eyes to the present for once, found himself sitting on something hard, and reached down to find an iron nugget that must have fallen from one of the plinths. He turned it in his furred hands for a while, oblivious once more to the commotion around him, and stuffed it into a pocket of his rags.

Draebol's fingers were losing their grip on the stone, slipping free one by one.

It is time *that you take for granted, Draebol,* said the silent voice from the darkness of the star.

But time is nothing.

To stop a thought stops time.

He imagined it, night after night. That moment of death.

The mechanism in your brain that generates time will fail first.

Then you are left at the mercy of the one true *reality: the Background.*

He imagined it as a blaze of white noise. A scream that never died. A twisted blur of paused colour feeding into eyes that could never blink again.

There you will remain for the span of eternity, locked inside your final moment.

Make sure it is a pleasant one.

He was falling before he realised what was happening, a moment's weightlessness rising in his stomach.

The tumbling body dropped eighty meters to the ruined auditorium floor and struck the ground. There was no pain. Only the crisp slap as he broke against marble informed him that he had landed at all.

A figure stepped across his dimming sight, looking down at him as it passed. Draebol gazed into the inverted, blood-smeared face, meeting the ruby eyes of the dark-skinned being. His eyes dropped, noticing his atlas clutched in one of its hands. He fixed his gaze on the spool of precious charts, seeing how the binding had torn.

And the moment seemed to last forever.

Whira's glistening crystal vessel completed its final roll, scattering the flock of crimson-winged creatures into the updrafts of the ruined dome. The chamber continued its rumbling descent into the castle, and a dark covering slid overhead at last.

Whira opened her eyes to find herself enveloped inside a crystal throne spoked with nodes of glassy apparatus, a multifaceted view of the auditorium projected into her mind. She found she could see several viewpoints at once: a cubist accumulation of angles that revealed every corner of the great chamber to her. She thought of rising and the jagged, dagger-shaped ship rose, spinning slowly upright as it hovered over the auditorium.

'I'll have those,' she said, her voice booming over what remained of the crowd. Their weapons flew out of their hands, drawn swiftly through the air and melted by an invisible field surrounding the ship.

'You weren't supposed to come back,' she said to the wall of Myriad. Its cadaverous soldiers were striding through the debris and up to the platforms, ready to be reabsorbed. 'I told you to get as far away as you could.'

It's leaving, said the Myriad with a voice like the wailing of the wind.

Whira turned the ship with nothing but her thoughts, rising above the ruins of the chamber and examining its every remaining occupant seemingly at once. 'Where—?'

Her gaze fell across what remained of Draebol.

His eyes were open, staring sadly from his fractured body at something that was no longer there.

Oh, Draebol. Whira felt a welling of tears that ought to have blurred her vision, and yet it remained sharp and clear.

She swallowed, using her newly gifted mind's eye to search the corridors and chambers of the castle. There: a lone figure, hurrying through the echoing blue hallways, the atlas in its hand. *Let's not have done this for nothing, then.*

'Too late,' someone chuckled, and she flicked her attention momentarily back into the auditorium. The contestant, Yor-Zaldo Zohlm, was peering at her from her protective shell. She pointed upwards.

The dome's covering glowed briefly white, flooding the auditorium with a surge of light, before raining down in molten drops. A storm of craft descended through the hole.

The Myriad ballooned, sucking the passengers and the remains of the plinths inside and slimming to a needle in a fragment of a second to shoot upwards. The sonic boom detonated inside the auditorium.

Whira imagined where she wanted to go and the ship rose, looping untouched through the vortex of plummeting ships and shooting into the high hallway that led away from the auditorium. She leant forward in her crystal seat, the ship accelerating hard.

The Myriad exploded out of the ruined castle, rising through the cloud of battling ships and extending tendrils of itself like a vast, branching weed. It snared four thousand, three hundred and twenty-nine separate craft, pulling them out of the skies of the Ring as it zipped high overhead, deactivating every system on the ships before hurling them far out into the blackness to tumble, powerless but unharmed.

A quarter of a second after lifting off, Whira had him in her sights.

The person turned, time slowing to a crawl as the ship concentrated every facet of its vision on the view ahead.

His face appeared, enhanced and huge before her eyes, as though they stood no more than a foot apart.

I see you now, she thought.

Small red eyes, containing no pupil, set deep into creased pouches of flesh. Pale grey upper lip beginning to curl into a smile, revealing jagged teeth still bloodstained in their gaps. The rising breeze of her approach stirred the first hair in his coarse white mane.

He could not escape. He had no Iliqin, no ship. Only the atlas in one hand. He had nothing.

But then something happened. He looked calmly down to his left, and the air there began to blaze.

What are you doing?

A spoon-shaped blade crowned with a serrated spike appeared through the burning rip, held out by a gloved, disembodied hand. He took the sword's hilt, grasping the heavy thing in one fist, and the rip closed. Whira felt the stirring of a cackle rise in her throat, her ship decelerating.

He swung, as if imagining he could defend himself against *her,* a vessel belonging to the most powerful Almoll in any Phaslair of the galaxy.

The blade slid a micrometre through the air.

The air flashed, burning at its touch.

Whira's thoughts, sped up somehow by the ship so that they travelled as fast as it did, only began to comprehend.

The scorched air re-opened, splitting as his blade scythed through it, a glimpse of colour peeping through.

Whira's laughter morphed into an embryonic scream of rage. With the beginning of an impulse she loosed a volley of invisible beam weaponry across the narrowing distance, accelerating hard.

But he had already passed through the rip, and was gone.

She burst through the space he had occupied a shade of second before, firing through the wall and soaring into the blackness above the castle, her scream echoing across the void.

A morning meeting, for once, and Phrail was not taking it well.

The Alm of Salqar was dozing off almost before he'd sat down. Thelgald waited, the Orrery floating vast and unnoticed. When Phrail still didn't stir she opened her mouth for the benefit of the Microscopia, exposing her small, sharp teeth.

''Ave I 'ot 'omethin' 'uck i' 'ere?'

She felt a breath of air across her tongue, and a *pop* as something was teased out. A chunk of breakfast, dissolved before her eyes as her seething repurposed its atoms.

When she glanced back, Phrail was being prodded awake by a steward, who scurried quickly out of shot. He grunted and sat up stiffly on his throne, gazing at the Orrery as if deep in thought.

'News has come up of an unsanctioned detonation in the deep Phaslairs,' she said slowly, attempting to gauge Phrail's mood. 'Involving materials stolen from the Djarimus Pressure Installation.'

Phrail didn't seem to have heard her, at first. He steepled his fingers. 'How terribly unfortunate.' He glanced at her. 'There must be an inquiry.'

She bowed her head. 'An inquiry will take time. I have suggested that in its stead we close down operations on the Djarimus Installation for the foreseeable future and offer reparations to the Phaslairs involved, in the hope that such a... calamity can never be repeated, and, in the absence of any guilty parties taking responsibility, as a show of goodwill.'

Phrail nodded his acceptance at once, putting an end to the matter. Thelgald took a breath, hoping their wooden acting would satisfy those who watched.

'I must inform you, however, that a Lazziar dissident named Whirazomar Swulis Zelt Ghenge of Thilean has implicated our two Almolls in this crime, and that must be refuted at all costs.'

Phrail went very still, eyeing her. This part he hadn't been privy to. 'A subject of yours?'

'Yes. She has been stripped of her titles and property, but remains at large in the Deep Phaslairs.'

Phrail rubbed his brow sleepily. 'Well then let her stay down there, without recourse to our help or civilisation. Show her the price of disloyalty.'

'She expresses no wish to return.'

'Good.'

Thelgald smiled. It had come at a cost, but the fang, examined in all its glorious detail by the eyes of the crystal Sovereignty ship and relayed back to the Surface, had been worth it after all. They had its measurements and compositions now, replicable ad infinitum, the very first copy gifted to Whirazomar should she wish to return. And since nobody on a Throlkoid Phaslair had directly suffered any loss of life due to their actions, it seemed the Throlken were prepared to allow them to keep their treasure. The upper Phaslairs and all the delights therein were open to Thelgald's Surface now; she had accomplished something during her reign at long last.

The question of whoever had been using it to travel in the first place remained unsolved. A smattering of reports from the auctioneers at Lusque confirmed the brief appearance of something bipedal symmetric, but whatever it was had now gone, perhaps for good. Her agents guessed that it had attempted a *Long Ascent*, shooting for the eldest Phaslairs. If that were the case then all was well and they would never hear from it again; anyone versed in strata physics understood such a passage (hypothetical, until now) could take two or three billion years at least. Let the Throlken, should they still be around in that unimaginable future, deal with the problem themselves. Thelgald very much suspected they could already go wherever they pleased in space and time, anyway, perhaps without even leaving home.

A heap of breakfast had arrived in front of Phrail, who pored over it with evident delight, apparently forgetting Thelgald's presence entirely. He speared a piece of stewed fruit and tucked in, sucking toothlessly.

'You know,' he said with his mouth full, 'if we are being so good as to close the Installation, then the Alm Ningemus ought to follow suit and disband his experiments in Trilm, don't you thin—' He broke off, spluttering, as something wedged in his gullet. The same steward appeared from out of the frame once more and slapped him on the back. Phrail raised an impatient hand and deposited whatever it was into a fold of his sleeve, blinking away tears.

Thelgald rolled her eyes. 'Are you alright?'

'I'm *fine*.' He was already lifting another morsel to his mouth, seemingly recovered.

'I'll leave you to it,' she muttered, waving away the mirage so that she was alone.

Thelgald dropped her head into her hands, exhaling long and deep, a tremor running through the small muscles of her neck. She stiffened, lowering her hands and raising her eyes furtively to the ceiling. *Imbecile. You will never be alone again.*

Gnumph touched down on the world of Obaneo's Daughter three hundred days later than anticipated, disgorging its dazed cache of passengers with barely a word of goodbye. Scrapher went freely, his charges dropped, disappearing into the bustling port before Gnumph could change its mind.

The spore deflated with a delicious, drawn-out sigh, until finally it was no larger than anyone else in the crowded place, and wandered on scrawny legs into the crowd.

In the depths of its belly the banked embers of the fire still glowed in the grate, coating the dimness in an aromatic pall of smoke. A soft chime woke the Zabbas, who had been coiled, fast asleep, around the fireplace. He yawned in the dark, gazing around for a sign of anyone else in the huge interior space, and checked his messages.

Most esteemed Elazihing, Zabbas of Thite.
Thank you very much for sending your latest work, The Voyage of the Seedpod, *which we read with interest.*
Unfortunately, we felt that it did not quite meet the rigorous standards we strive at all times to

uphold, and have regretfully decided not to publish it at this time.

Today she chose her own body, spending an hour or more sculpting her face as she saw it, the missing section of her horn left unfixed, in memory. He had wanted to come through the way they'd first met, yellow and bearded and bald, but humanoid, at least.

No, Whira told him. *I want to see you as you are.*

She waited for him beneath a copse of sighing trees, in a Sphere quite different from the one she knew. This place had been painted in a level of detail her mind couldn't fathom. It was as if she stood in a real place, on a solid planet, and they were meeting physically for the first time.

But that would be impossible, if she wished to stay hidden from the Alms. Tiliph's involvement in her journey had been discovered, and he couldn't leave Oublish, let alone his Phaslair, without fear of being tailed.

Whira stood in the dappled shade, looking out across a view of gently rolling hills. Bland, she supposed, but she quite liked bland right now. Somewhere, in a world beyond this one, her hearts raced at the thought of seeing him again, touching him, even if at a great remove. The thought of their previous meeting, as she lay starving and scrawny at the entrance of room nine, danced fluttering circles around her belly. She hoped he liked what he saw, now.

'Oh, come on,' she breathed, impatient and trembling. She considered leaving, postponing for another day. This was ridiculous; they hardly knew a thing about one another. She turned full circle, looking out across the blue smudge of hills for any figures striding across the grass, never considering that he might not be walking.

'Whira,' came a pleasant voice from above, and she

303

looked to see a blot of darkness hovering overhead. The one concession he had made was to shrink himself down, and as he landed in front of her she clasped her hands tightly together.

They looked at one another, his eight-winged form blurred by tears. Tiliph reached out a hand, taking her fingertips in his, and the great gulf of Phaslairs drifted away.

The planet swelled out of the green, a gleaming crescent hanging moonless and alone. Sensing the arrival of a ship, the planet's encircling, Sovereignty-grade shield orb reached out, probing. The ship relayed its introductory message, offering the stamped metal ingot of the planet's own core as proof of ownership.

Recognising the only part of itself that had ever escaped, the orb faded, strengthening again once the speck of the ship had entered the world's atmosphere, a silent, transparent sentry that would guard the unnamed planet for the rest of its life.

The sentient ship descended through a stipple of cloud and into the warm currents of air above a circular atoll, landing on a broad swathe of volcanic beach lapped by mint green waves.

Lucky stepped into the sunlight, dropping the ingot into the sand. To his eyes the world was still inhabited, and he waved to ghostly figures that strolled along the beach, shuffling out from beneath the shadow of his ship to cross the baking sand. He did not know that the planet had been sealed for millennia, and was now home only to a swarm of delicate white service automata who sculpted and pruned the trees, swept the ground and filtered the lakes, scrubbing every scuff. They watched his approach with curiosity: the world's first master in recent times, come to claim his property and examine his new home.

Lucky stripped to his stained, tatty underwear, tossing the remainder of his rags aside, eyes dilating at the beauty of the place and its long-dead inhabitants. He stumbled heavily to the water's edge, approaching a sorting mech that was busy sifting pebbles and crushing it underfoot.

He waved once more at the empty beach, knowing he would never be lonely again.

THE FIRST
NINETY-THIRD ERA OF THE THROLKEN

I used my map to plot an oblique course up the fissure, then slept for the ascent; a sleep of eras, my dreams cascading from mind to mind as the tooth pierced each successive reality like a blade dragged through a bolt of cloth. Sometimes I forgot who I was or what I was doing; my dagger and I had become a blur of possibility, soft as soot, all colours spun to a tawny grey.

I believe then that I entered a state of hibernation, my thoughts lost to the winds. With each regenerated mind my consciousness sparked afresh, pulsing with a beat of energy before it was replaced. I became a lone thought, a single frame, motionless.

But I was still alive, in some sense of the word, and—though I had ceased to perceive it—I still moved across the landscape of the Phaslairs.

And then, without warning, the moment unfroze. My single experience, my thought, drifted in my head for some time before I noticed that it continued, unbroken. I opened my eyes.

I had stopped. All around me was a rumbling purple forest of flame.

I looked at my body. I was made from the same currents of fire, marbled with gaseous indigo. Beyond, great shapes drifted in the flames, darker patches of fire that circled me.

Why had I stopped? What had gone wrong? The memories poured back.

Had I reached my destination?

I swung the flaming blade experimentally, chopping the air.

Nothing. Even Fe'Tril was gone.

I tried to clamber to my feet, crawling and floundering in the flames, which felt no firmer than water. I had forgotten how to walk. My body possessed limbs, but of fire. Had I come through in my true form, translated?

I could not stand. Instead I bobbed, buffeted by the inferno. I felt no heat, no cold. The sounds of the place were like blood pulsing in my ears. I looked at the shapes in the haze, and they seemed to look back at me.

I found my voice, unused except to scream. When I spoke only a tongue of magenta flame left my mouth, drifting and coiling smoke. Their language, perhaps.

Is this it? Have I reached the first place?

The shadows in the flame looked back, expressionless.

Have I passed the test?

For all I knew they were not beings at all, but patterns in the fire. I swam towards them, hoping to see better, sensing more presences looming beneath my feet.

I've passed! I did it! There's nothing else!

Their forms did not resolve, no matter how hard I swam, and I felt my elation melting away. Treacherous thoughts, birthed in fire, began to whisper that perhaps there really was no game, after all.

Tell me! Tell me what it means!

The terror returned, recalled like a scent from my youth, as if no time had passed at all.

Please.

I bobbed in the ocean of flickering violet, waiting, while the forms began to shift and move on. At length I raised my blade, its tip pouring smog.

I used it as a paddle, keeping the shadows in sight as I rolled on the waves. Was this the centre of the explosion? The spark that burst the Phaslairs into existence? I would get my answers. They would see.

A form in the distance had lingered, and watched me through the haze.

Tell me! I screamed, dragging the tooth above my head and pointing its smoking tip in the shadow's direction. It suddenly seemed very close, as if it were bobbing just in front of me, the fin of something greater below the surface.

Tell me if it was all for nothing! You owe me that!

Below the waves the shadow lengthened, a limb stretching out towards me. I recoiled, trying to swim away through the flames, but felt its fire join with mine.

You've come very far, haven't you? The voice made itself known as a thought, birthed in my own mind.

I'll take you back.

Time is snipped. A length of ages has been cut, tossed away, the ribbons reattached with barely a seam. And I am home.

I am young.

My eyes were already open, and they contract now in the afternoon sun. The forested hills rise in shadow beyond, and all about me people—my people—stroll and chatter, their language of quick, monosyllabic words bristling the hairs on my fresh, unwrinkled skin.

Even my thoughts seem freshened, unclouded and clear and crisp as the day, which is cold in the shade. Tears spring, smeared by a rapid blinking of my lashes so that all I see is a wash of dappled colour. I was ill, before; that wasn't me. I am better now.

But how?

I turn to look for who must have brought me here. Behind me a market—a market I recognise—is closing for the day, but someone, tall and angular and somehow androgynous, lingers. They—it—watches me for a moment more, its face a blur as I wipe my eyes, and when I've blinked away the last of the tears it is to a view of the person leaving, its gown billowing with every step.

'What are you?' I ask, rushing to grasp the person's sleeve. 'Who can command time?'

By way of an answer, the material slips slickly out of my fingers, as if it isn't really material at all.

'Am I not to be punished, for the things I've done?' A few people glance at me then, a wariness in their crimson eyes, as though I were talking to myself.

I let the figure walk away, contemplating what I have been given. Another chance, a new life. The waft of something roasting turns my head, more delicious than anything I have ever smelled. My parents must still be alive, only a few miles down the road. Why did I do the things I did, when I had all *this*, an enchanted life?

Because you were afraid. My own thoughts this time, answering from wherever the madness had crawled off to.

The Pretence.

Was I being punished already, for getting too close?

The person, taller by at least a head than anyone else, is about to disappear into the crowd.

'What are you?' I scream, following. A pace away and I reach out and shove the figure's back, feeling nothing but that same oily slick material beneath my hands.

Its pace slows, and I hesitate, all eyes upon me. At once I am young and diffident again, at sea in a mature world where I never felt I belonged, hobbled by my fears.

I will not be afraid. It has faded like a nightmare now, endured many years ago, but I was *there*; I made it to the *end*. Or the beginning. Somewhere I was not supposed to go.

I will not be afraid again.

To my left I spy a rusty hook, still bloody from the butcher's stall and lying on a bench. I snatch it up. No more fear.

The person begins to turn. I know, somehow, that theirs is a face I do not want to see, that just a glimpse will stop my heart.

So I swing.

And the moment seems to last forever.

THE END

AFTERWORD

This is a story of another era, of a generation of stars long gone. I was, regrettably, not there, but all that you have read is a faithful translation of the story of someone who was.

Together we have begun the unenviable task of taking the collective minutes of nine hundred billion years of history, and I hope you'll join me again on my leisurely trip across this immeasurable heaven, for there are many more tales to tell.

CAST OF CHARACTERS

Draebol Naeglis Zelt Thurn of Eldra, within Lihreat: Licensed surveyor of the Phaslairs under the Alm Thelgald.

Whirazomar Swulis Zelt Ghenge of Thilean, within Lihreat: Lazziar agent to Thelgald, tasked with reaching the fabled Well before the Throlken can stop her.

Gnumph, Sporangium of Ingaal: A megaspore employed as a transport service across the galaxy.

Yib'Wor the Sorcerer: Once the tyrannical ruler of South-All, a portion of the galaxy that would come to be known as Yokkun's Depth, now consigned to the Inescapable Hole.

Scrapher Qeret Zelt Mlaarm of Hwathithein, within Youl: Unpleasant Speckled Larl, traveller on board Gnumph.

Nodo Steck Zelt Ong of Queat, within Salqar: Igmus traveller onboard Gnumph, subject of Phrail.

Drethenor Tiliph Zelt Friest of Oublish, within Deephrull: A player in the infrasphere, originally from Deephrull.

Luphro Dhahiel Zelt Taador of Alas, within Deephrull: Deep Eye agent of Izzogath, Alm of Deephrull.

The Irraith: The Helium Folk, natural gaseous inhabitants of most stars who have lived and watched the galaxy's development over the aeons.

The Throlken: The collective term for the billions of postbiological Intelligences spread across the galaxy of Yokkun's Depth, each claiming a star for itself and living (recomposed as helium) within it, amongst the Irraith. They are considered by the Alms and their subjects as living gods, the progenitors of the synthetic bloodline and the inventors of the Pattern language spoken by all in Yokkun's Depth.

The Myriad: A vast swarm of microscopic creatures, machines and tamed, ancient virus and microbe strains who inhabit nearly all the breathable air in Yokkun's Depth. They act like a living substrate, turning the galaxy into one huge computer, and instantly fix, update or correct every piece of data or machinery they find to be broken, wrong or inaccurate—even if it is handwritten, hand-made or hand-drawn—swarming together to form pen styluses, tools and machinery. Some Alms have attempted to clear their kingdoms of the tiny beasts, without success. They are found everywhere except the Forbidden Almoll.

The Jhahzang: Another distant relative of the Throlken, part of the complex AI family tree.

The Ambient Svesh: A school of sentient particles said to live amongst the Myriad.

The Zilble: A hypothetical entity smaller than a single atom, believed to have existed in 57 separate universes.

WORLD, SHIPS, WEAPONS AND TECHNOLOGY

Homemades: Ships of all kinds cobbled together from anything the occupants can find, usually built from wood and plastoids and cannibalised synthetic materials, coated with a layer of metal or ceramic to survive takeoff and re-entry.

Tubes: Naturally occurring cylindrical structures, similar to gigantic coral polyps, that leap away from predators using primitive chemical rocketry. They have been farmed and used as simple star ships for millions of years.

Crystal vessels: Almost indestructible crystalline spears, fitted with Zurmis Mode-Nines and the most advanced Sovereign technology imaginable.

Worldcraft: Colossal vessels housing habitats and even planets, sometimes also dragging them along behind in *Worldtrains* that can be many hundreds of planets long.

Spores: Sentient megaspores of the Ingaal tree, found throughout the galaxy on migrations that can last thousands of years. Some make a little money on the side transporting cargo or passengers, even occasionally operating as spies.

Jewelcraft: A type of crystal vessel set into a ring or necklace, capable of growing into an entire ship at a single command.

Infrasphere: Large virtual realities, housed in subdimensions, that host billions of players from across the galaxy.

Mode-Nine: A potent FTL technology based upon the principle of stellar convection and gifted long ago to the Alms by the Throlken. It was found that spacetime works quite differently in the still and silent cores of all stars, a volume only a metre or so across in which even the Throlken cannot survive (although it has long been suspected that they use the empty cores as wormholes, teleporting between the stars). The bizarre physics of stellar cores became the basis for the drives, which tear the universe's laws apart when they are activated.

Iliquin: A synthetic element capable of increasing rapidly in mass until it is heavier than the densest neutron star. Used to Drop through the membranes between Phaslairs.

Arqot: A sister element of Iliquin, often shielded and embedded in keepsakes. When exposed to surface dimensions, Arqot instantly begins to decay, releasing rays of exotic particles that strip away the onion-like outer layers of a Phaslair to expose Bubbles, or subdimensions. Arqot is found in the stomach linings of megaspores like Gnumph, and secreted in their waste.

Bubble suit/hole: A bubble of exposed subdimension that encloses the wearer of a piece of Arqot, making the safest possible space suit or storage area, impregnable by anything existing in the Surface.

Drop weaponry: Iliqin-based weapons capable of vanishing anything they target into a younger Phaslair.

Dzull drive: Antimatter-based engines operating in Lawless Phaslairs. They work on the principle of repulsion and attraction to matter: activate near any star cluster and you are drawn to the mass of matter faster than light ought to allow. Shielding the antimatter then allows the ship to sail on at colossal speeds, using stars as a slingshot. Deceleration is brought about by opening specific shields around the antimatter, reintroducing drag by attracting it to stars already left behind.

Junkberg: An inhabited lump of accreted rubbish, often the size of a large mountain, floating in space around the Ghomi system.

Salga Ehothalong: Nearest galaxy to Yokkun's Depth, *Salga* being the Throlken word for galaxy. The other seven housed in the cluster of the Olas are Salgas Zotulast, Izadrijjin, Mostramong, Yokkunphirelleng, Lillowuyahl, Gemit-Galazaph, and Yokkun's Depth, where this tale takes place.

Gigaverses: The earliest known (and exceedingly patchy) histories of the galaxy, composed before the Throlken's rule.

TIMELINE

500 million years BPD (before present day)**:** Downfall of Yib'Wor, ruler of South-All, cast into the Inescapable Hole.

340 million years BPD: Estimated inception of the Throlken, from a line of AI progenitors, in a galaxy of mostly biological life.

320 million years BPD: Estimated accession of the Throlken to the stars. Creation of the Throlken Pattern. The last great war of the biological. Installation of the Alms as stewards of the galaxy's sixty-seven realms.

210 million years BPD: 85% of all life in Yokkun's Depth is now interbred with AI—unification.

14.7 million years BPD: Rediscovery of the Inescapable Hole, rechristened *the Well*.

7,909 years BPD: Budding of Gnumph, in a flower of the Ingaal tree, Thron.

2,500 BPD: Birth of Draebol, in the Eldra cluster, Lihreat.

36 BPD: Birth of Whirazomar, in the Thilean cluster, Lihreat.

One era of the Throlken: Thirty million years.

DICTIONARY OF THE THROLKEN PATTERN

The agglutinative nature of the synthetic language means that any word can be made by sticking other combinations of words together into strings of meaning and speaking without a pause. A slow, ten-legged land ship built on the planet of Muwl, in Plitipek, for example, would be called a *Sarailiemqhalirzekchilzaruo'Muwluo'Plitipek.*

The identification of species throughout Yokkun's Depth is made firstly from the number of digits, eyes and limbs (if applicable), followed by the dimensions of sensory organs according to a universal scale and the galactic jurisdiction they can usually be found within, capped by the species' own chosen name and any interesting footnotes on their distribution, average mental capacity, whether they are extant or extinct etc. tacked on thereafter. It is a vague, ill-regulated system, and many billions of species are 'discovered' dozens, hundreds and even thousands of times over before anyone notices their mistake. Attempting to classify large ecosystems in Yokkun's Depth is generally pointless anyway, because by the time you'd finished cataloguing everything, entire star clusters would have gone nova, birthed new generations of suns, formed fresh worlds and repopulated the galaxy with other variants of life, and you'd have to start all over again. Add another Phaslair into the equation, let alone the millions born each day, and the work becomes something only a Throlken could begin to attempt. As another example of the stickiness of the Throlken Pattern, Whira's taxonomic description (noting that she is a fourteen-fingered, two-eyed, four-limbed, small-headed female bipedal symmetric from the Almoll of Lihreat known as the Lazziar, one of a large, still extant and self-aware population) would be as follows: *Drozealldhinazarthoqhalignennumnrithuulluo'Lihreatlazz iar-ulzathrathamod*

AI/god: **crileth/throlk**

alone: **oril**

also: **bhe**

anger: **salphe**

animal: **thael**

at: **vrin**

bad: **threl**

because: **igead**

big: **saegaill**

book: **mahrill**

clever: **thamod**

close: **av**

clothing: **rill**

dangerous: **ehrar**

day(s): **bir(z)**

down: **ell**

drink: **ihmol**

enemy: **thissoth**

eternity: **aelton**

evil: **zilgor**

eye: **ezar**

far: **chulph**

fast: **imae**

few: **bhe**

finger: **zeall**

food: **shemph**

fool: **dhen**

friend: **chaith**

future: **vrer**

galaxy: **salga**

gas: **drind**

good: **phulien**

guest: **thone**

happy: **alzai**

he: **ghun**

head: **numn**

hunger: **shemphdruuhl**

I: **phes**

it: **irs**

jealousy: **salphulg**

kind: **ohn**

king/emperor: **zahm/alm**

kingdom: **almoll**

knowledge: **shaess**

land: **irzek**

life/existence: **esloh**

limb: **qhal**

liquid: **inkri**

lust: **phulg**

many: **ulza**

map: **saangal**
mineral: **lahn**
money/currency: **bhoqe**
of: **uo'/ol**
past: **straa**
planet: **bhahm**
present: **thra**
rude: **zelvir**
sad: **druuhl**
she: **rith**
ship/vessel: **stral/chilzar**
slow: **sarail**
small: **ignen**
solid: **sheel**
space: **leere**
species/race: **naelle/leigad**
star: **zorzaed**
tail: **usal**
technology: **scruule**
that: **cret**
the: **dral**
they: **craan**
this: **strohl**
time: **eqa**
together: **suldil**
travel: **veir**
uniform: **uull**
up: **vold**
us/we: **ads**
vegetable: **aeso**
what: **hengor**
when: **zamall**
where: **alno**
who: **phelluh**
why: **neessor**
wise: **steerl**

wish: **nuriel**
with: **thrat**
wonder: **gei**
year(s): **helmah(z)**
you: **vilk**

1: **nen**
2: **dhin**
3: **garu**
4: **tho**
5: **do**
6: **phal**
7: **ye**
8: **draa**
9: **qhies**
10: **iem**
11: **ieph**
12: **thei**
13: **sosl**
14: **dro**
15: **phi**

ACKNOWLEDGEMENTS

My huge thanks to Ed Wilson and David Moore for their belief in this book, and to everyone who was so encouraging along the way, including Jon and Jim Wallace, Olivia Hofer, Steve Andrews, and Stark Holborn. Also lots of love to Bob and Janet Toner, Tony Pemberton, Rita Rita (I *still* have your laptop, sorry), and the Bloody Billies.

ABOUT THE AUTHOR

Caspar Geon has lived many lives in many different dimensions, and published books in all of them. *The Immeasurable Heaven* is his first book set in the infinite realities of the Phaslairs.

🌐 caspargeon.com

FIND US ONLINE!

www.rebellionpublishing.com

/solarisbooks   /solarisbks

/solarisbooks   /solarisbooks.
bsky.social

SIGN UP TO OUR NEWSLETTER!

rebellionpublishing.com/newsletter

YOUR REVIEWS MATTER!

Enjoy this book? Got something to say?

Leave a review on Amazon, GoodReads or with your
favourite bookseller and let the world know!

DEREK KÜNSKEN

"An audacious con job,
scintillating future technology,
and meditations on the nature of
fractured humanity."
Yoon Ha Lee

THE QUANTUM
MAGICIAN

BOOK ONE OF THE QUANTUM EVOLUTION

"LEAVES THE AUDIENCE GASPING" – The Times
MICKEY
7
SOON TO BE A MOTION PICTURE
EDWARD ASHTON

UNDER FORTUNATE STARS

Two ships. One chance to save the future.

REN HUTCHINGS